BROOKLYN NOIR 3

BROOKLYN NOIR 3

NOTHING BUT THE TRUTH

EDITED BY
TIM MCLOUGHLIN & THOMAS ADCOCK

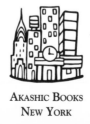

AKASHIC BOOKS
NEW YORK

Published by Akashic Books
©2008 Akashic Books

Series concept by Tim McLoughlin and Johnny Temple
Brooklyn map by Sohrab Habibion

ISBN-13: 978-1-933354-14-9
Library of Congress Control Number: 2007939598
All rights reserved

First printing

Akashic Books
PO Box 1456
New York, NY 10009
info@akashicbooks.com
www.akashicbooks.com

ALSO IN THE AKASHIC NOIR SERIES:

FORTHCOMING:

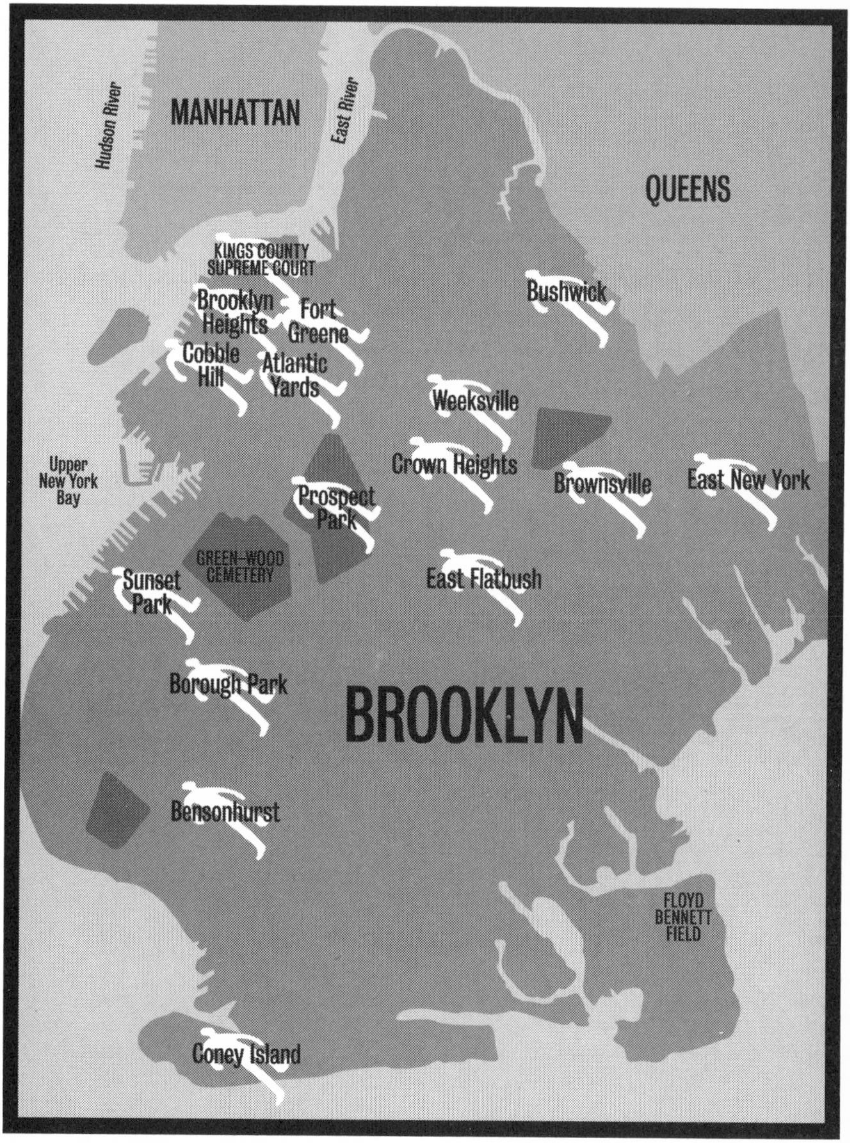

MANHATTAN
Hudson River
East River
QUEENS
KINGS COUNTY SUPREME COURT
Brooklyn Heights
Fort Greene
Cobble Hill
Atlantic Yards
Bushwick
Weeksville
Crown Heights
Brownsville
East New York
Upper New York Bay
Prospect Park
GREEN-WOOD CEMETERY
Sunset Park
East Flatbush
Borough Park
BROOKLYN
Bensonhurst
FLOYD BENNETT FIELD
Coney Island

TABLE OF CONTENTS

PART III: DEATH STEP

PART IV: SKELSIES

INTRODUCTION
STRANGER THAN FICTION

One sweltering evening a couple of years ago I was giving a reading at Tillie's, a café in Fort Greene, Brooklyn. It was part of a summer-long blitz to help publicize the first *Brooklyn Noir*. The contributors and I did forty-two readings in New York City that summer, all but six in Brooklyn. Predictably, a lot of them are now a blur. This one, however, stands out vividly in my mind. Patricia Mulcahy, the proprietor of Tillie's, welcomed me, and said, "I have a *Brooklyn Noir* story to tell you." She then related the tale that is included in this volume, about the killing of "Bobby from Russia."

"How does it end?" I asked.

"How does it end?" she said. "It's a true story."

I wound up at the Alibi Club that night, just down DeKalb from Tillie's, drinking and scheming with Akashic's publisher, Johnny Temple. We decided that at some point it would be interesting to do an anthology of true crime stories with the same mood and geographic structure as *Brooklyn Noir*. After all, it seemed as though every bar, bookstore, or library we read at had some connection to a sinister event. People were all too eager to point out back rooms or side streets where something had been heisted or someone had been whacked. What fun it would be to record those stories. What fun indeed.

As this book began to coalesce, the vibe of the project changed, in a small but steady way. It was insidious, like swimming in a deceptively gradual current.

There is a difference, as editor, between cheering the literary accomplishment of a fiction writer who has delivered a brilliant story about a serial killer or hit man, and reading the true account, however beautifully written, of a young woman raped, murdered, and forgotten. So this book, though it has its light moments (and thank God for those), is for me the darkest of the *Brooklyn Noir* series. These pieces remind us that crime is personal. It happens to us and to our neighbors. Sometimes it happens because we do nothing to prevent it. Life does not always offer the moral arc we so desperately crave in fiction. If it did, we'd have no need for myths and fables, religion or miracles.

Thomas Adcock was the first contributor to deliver a story, and I'm grateful that he then agreed to coedit the book; he brought aboard a posse of writers of which I could have only dreamed. Because the stories are about crime, about Brooklyn, and true, more than one ends in court proceedings. And because Brooklyn is the world's largest small town, real life overlaps in ways that fiction does not. My own reminiscence of events in and around the courts, "Snapshots," sits at the intersection of stories by Errol Louis, Dennis Hawkins, and Denise Buffa.

As with the two previous volumes, our emphasis is on the quality of the writing as well as the storytelling itself, and just as the earlier anthologies have done their bit to muddy the waters between genre and literary fiction, here we've done our best to blend reporting, personal essay, and memoir.

It's been an interesting few years since *Brooklyn Noir* debuted. That book, as of this writing, has just entered its fifth printing, with *Brooklyn Noir 2: The Classics* headed for its second. There are now more than twenty volumes of original fiction in the Akashic Noir Series, with another dozen in production.

That's four hundred or so stories that might not otherwise have been published, or for that matter written. No small feat given the paltry opportunities these days for publishing short fiction. So now let's see what we can do for true crime.

Read this book. Enjoy it. Be horrified by it. Carry it with you always. And the next time you're watching a particularly bizarre and salacious news item on the television set in your neighborhood pub, and the guy on the next stool says, "You can't make this shit up," smack him with it.

Tim McLoughlin
Brooklyn, New York
April 2008

PART I

RING-A-LEVIO

In which members of one group at one end of the block try to find and capture hiding members of an opposing group. A captured player is dragged into a chalk circle on the pavement at mid-block, by a hunter who holds him/her there long enough to holler, "Ring-a-Levio, 1-2-3!"

A SPRING AFTERNOON IN THE MEADOW, THAT "LONG, LOUD SCREAM"

BY CONSTANCE CASEY

Prospect Park

W ho" is important in this story: a man and four teenaged boys.
"What" is easy to answer: a bike and a gun.
"When" is a sunny afternoon in June.
"Where," in this case, is unusually significant.

Our location is Prospect Park, the green heart of Brooklyn. Of the five boroughs of the city of New York, Brooklyn is the one with the least green space per person. On a map, the park is a bit to the west of Brooklyn's dead center.

On the afternoon of June 1, 1993, a forty-two-year-old drama teacher named Allyn Winslow rode his new trail bike to a boulder near the top of Prospect Park's Quaker Hill, where he'd often gone for picnics with his wife and two children.

He may have stopped atop the hill to lean against the big rock and savor a friendly, familiar place. He may have noticed he was just up from the Quaker cemetery where fellow actor Montgomery Clift is buried. He may have paused to adjust his bike seat or take a drink from his water bottle.

There's no way to know.

Four teenagers surrounded him suddenly and tried to steal his turquoise bike. Winslow resisted by attempting to fend them off with a tire pump, and when he got on his bike and rode away, one of the teens fired a .22 caliber revolver—three shots into Winslow's back, one into his buttocks.

Winslow, who had run three New York City marathons, made it down the hill and into the park's Long Meadow—a bit less than half a mile—where he fell to the ground and died.

Three of the gunshot wounds were superficial. The fourth bullet angled up through his right lung to sever his aorta, the vessel that carries blood from the heart to the rest of the body.

"I was trying to scare him," said the shooter, sixteen-year-old Jerome Nisbett. This he told the police after his arrest a few days following the fatal shooting. His finger got stuck on the trigger and the gun just kept firing, he said.

At Nisbett's trial, a police ballistics expert effectively rebutted that excuse: "In a revolver, the trigger has to be pulled one time for one shot to be fired, and then pulled again for the next shot to be fired."

Winslow's death generated enormous publicity, as well as understandable sorrow and sympathy among Brooklyn residents. Especially for those who used the park, the killing also generated considerable fear.

That a pack of African American boys, albeit a small pack, attacked a white man hit a raw, racial nerve. Although four years had elapsed between the crime at Quaker Hill in Prospect Park and the 1989 case of a white female jogger in Manhattan's Central Park—in which a pack of five black youths out "wilding," as it was called, raped their victim and then beat her nearly to death—memories were quickly revived.

Amidst high public emotion around Winslow's death, arrests were made in a week and personally announced by the city's first black mayor, David Dinkins.

That the four suspects were so young, said the mayor, "boggles the mind and crushes the heart."

The murder of Winslow was a particular blow to those who lived on streets adjoining Prospect Park. Violent crime in their park had actually gone down in the 1980s and early '90s, a brutal time elsewhere in the city, and Brooklynites had begun to relax—and to enjoy the woods and hills and water and lush green of Prospect Park.

Frederick Law Olmsted (1822–1903) designed both Central Park, opened in 1858, and Prospect Park. Although the former is better known to the world, landscape historians consider the latter to be Olmsted's masterwork. When Prospect Park opened to the public in 1870, Olmsted wrote to a friend, "The park in all its upper parts in the East Woods, the Dairy District and the Nethermead, is thoroughly delightful, and I am prouder of it than of anything I have had to do with."

Both parks hit their nadirs in the 1970s. With the city's finances in disorder, park maintenance was down at the same time crime was up. The number of visits to Prospect Park hit an all-time low in 1979, a mark all the more dramatic when one considers that Brooklyn's population in the late nineteenth century was roughly a quarter of what it was in the late twentieth.

The salvation of both parks came about through the creation of public-private institutions—in Brooklyn, the Prospect Park Alliance—that raised endowment funds from government, community groups, and private donors to keep them from falling into disrepair again.

In an early account of the Winslow murder, a *New York*

Times reporter wrote that the teacher died "in a meadow." Gardeners and park historians know the place not as a meadow, but as *the* meadow—namely the Long Meadow.

Of all the fine features of Prospect Park, the Long Meadow most pleased Olmsted. (It still is the largest meadow in any U.S. urban park.) He was inspired by the grand sweeps of lawn designed for the landed gentry of eighteenth-century Britain. Olmsted modified the lawn idea, making the grassy area shaggier and edging it with native trees: oak, American elm, sugar maples, wild cherry, tulip, sassafras, and Osage orange. Before Olmsted, most European and American urban parks were more pavement than woods, usually focused on a fountain or statue surrounded by tight little combinations of domesticated ornamental plants, tidily fenced in.

Olmsted's idea was that the park would strengthen democracy; that in a leafy setting, under the sun and in the pure air, the divisions between rich and poor could melt away. His forests and meadow—wild-seeking, but actually planned down to the last shrub—would be a source of what he called "peace and refreshment" for all classes; a retreat from the crowding, dirt, and noise of city life.

Opponents argued that a wooded park with secluded areas would encourage, as one contemporary editorial writer put it, "riotous and licentious habits."

On the day of his death, Winslow's four-mile ride from his Bay Ridge home, past Green-Wood Cemetery to Quaker Hill, probably took about a half-hour.

His four assailants—Robert Brown and Gregory Morris, each fourteen, and sixteen-year-olds Chad Jackson and Jerome Nisbett—were supposed to be in school that day. They bumped into one another at a laundromat around 1 o'clock in the afternoon and decided to go to the park because, as they later said, Gregory Morris didn't have a bicycle whereas the other three did. In their minds, evidently, Prospect Park was the place to go to acquire a bike.

The group—three boys pedaling bikes with Gregory Morris astride handlebars, or sometimes just running alongside—first approached a woman practicing martial arts near the park's band shell. Morris started "messing with" her bike, Robert Brown said at trial. The woman told the boys to get lost and rode off quickly. Then the four thought of stopping a Latino on a bike, but he too hastened away.

About half-past 3, they walked up Quaker Hill and spied Winslow and his bike. Brown testified that Morris said, "Let's get him!" Brown further testified that Morris handed a gun to Nisbett.

There were no witnesses to the shooting, but people walking in the Long Meadow heard a popping sound.

"I hope that was fireworks," one man said to his friend as they sat beside a nearby pond. But, he added, "Then I heard that long, loud scream."

Allyn Winslow, who came to New York by way of Texas, was fully involved in the life of his adopted city. His two children, ten-year-old Jessica and eight-year-old Drew, attended public schools. On the morning of June 1, he'd walked his son to school from their Bay Ridge brick house—the one in which his widow, Marcy, had grown up. The couple had been thinking about moving to Park Slope in order to be closer to Prospect Park.

Winslow, who held a master's degree from Trinity University in San Antonio, had performed on stage in several venues, including the Dallas Theatre Center. He had also acted in small film roles and several television commercials. Of late, he'd been spending more energy on his teaching and journal writing. According to his journal, the New York City marathon in November 1993 would be his last.

Shortly before his death, Winslow had started a vacation from his job at the American Musical and Dramatic Academy, housed in the ornate Ansonia Building on Manhattan's Upper West Side. During the week prior to his death, he'd ridden nearly two hundred miles on his new bike—which he'd bought, along with one for his wife, in April.

Marcy Winslow was a legal secretary at the Manhattan law firm of Cravath, Swaine & Moore. In her statement at the sentencing hearing following the trial of her husband's killer, she demonstrated poise and familiarity with courtroom procedure as she broadened the picture of Allyn Winslow.

"The press only characterized my husband as a father of two and a drama teacher. He was more than that," she said. "At [the drama academy] where he worked, he was not only a teacher but he was a counselor and a mentor. He was the person who gave the first-year students their welcoming speech. Many of the students told me how inspired they were after hearing his speech and were excited about having him as their teacher."

Marcy Winslow concluded, "Jerome Nisbett will never know how much suffering he caused on June 1, 1993, and every day thereafter."

Could Frederick Law Olmsted, with his vision of the civilizing influence of his woods and meadow, have imagined a fourteen-year-old handing a gun to a sixteen-year-old for the purpose of robbery?

A year before Winslow's death, a published survey of New

York City public high school students carried out by the Centers for Disease Control and Prevention, found that seven percent carried handguns. One wonders about the truthfulness of the responses. Were some students afraid to admit they carried a gun, or were some ashamed to admit they didn't?

The U.S. arrest rate for juveniles climbed sixty percent in the decade before 1994, according to the Federal Bureau of Investigation. Youth crime of that period tended to involve wanting something in aid of popularity or prestige: A shiny new mountain bike made an even more attractive target than the latest pair of Nike sneakers.

As he delivered Nisbett's sentence, Brooklyn Supreme Court Justice Francis X. Egitto said, "I have seen youngsters in this courtroom take a life for designer jeans, for earrings, and now for a bike . . . I say this to young people: When you take a gun out on the street for robbery, are you prepared to pay twenty-five years to life for the crime that you commit?"

Which is exactly what Nisbett got as the trigger boy tried as an adult. He is today an inmate at the Eastern Correctional Facility at Napanoch, New York.

In return for agreeing to testify against the others, Robert Brown pleaded guilty to manslaughter and was sentenced as a youthful offender to sixteen months to four years. Chad Jackson likewise received a light sentence—two to six years—on his conviction for attempted robbery.

Fourteen-year-old Morris, the boy who wanted a bike, was convicted of murder and sentenced as a juvenile in Brooklyn Family Court, where the sentencing standard is considerably more lenient. Additionally, Morris benefited from an oddity in state law, whereby additional leniency is granted in the event a murder is committed during a failed robbery; after all, Winslow's mountain bike got away.

* * *

When Nisbett was taken off to prison, Marcy Winslow told a reporter that she was satisfied with the sentence, but no, she did not feel better: "My husband is dead."

Nisbett's court-appointed lawyer, Edward Friedman, has strong feelings about the trial after more than a decade.

"Who knows if he's ever going to get out of jail?" said Friedman of his client. "The ringleader was a juvenile," Friedman added, as if the trial had just ended. "My client had a bike; it was Morris who wanted a bike. Morris passes the gun to Nisbett and says, in effect, *Show you're a man*."

Friedman himself grew up in East Flatbush. He remembers being a kid walking home from summer evening concerts in Prospect Park in the late 1960s and feeling apprehensive, holding tight to his father's hand. He has moved away from Brooklyn to a suburban town on the south shore of Long Island. So has Marcy Winslow.

Jerome Nisbett was barely literate, as evidenced by his written confession introduced at trial. At the time of the murder, he lived part-time with his mother in Bushwick and part-time with his aunt in Crown Heights. His father was a minister somewhere in the West Indies.

Attorney Howard Weiswasser, who represented Robert Brown, was asked how fourteen-year-olds like Gregory Morris acquire firearms. "Often, they literally find them on the street because someone has thrown away a gun used in a crime," he said.

Attorney Howard Kirsch defended Morris. After trial, he said of young offenders in general, "These are the most dangerous kids in the world. They have no conscience, no control over their impulses. Their sense of morality hasn't developed."

Exactly how were Morris and his buddies caught?

"Like a lot of these kids, they couldn't stop talking about it," Kirsch explained. "They did it for street cred, to show how tough they were. If they had any brains, they'd keep it to themselves." He added: "Once they're caught, they sing like canaries."

Why?

"Because they're kids, because they're stupid. Basically, they're punks."

Is there any defense against punks?

Olmsted's biographer, Witold Rybczynski, was asked a few years ago what part of the designer's personality we should emulate today. He responded, "It would be this sense of time, this sense of both patience and looking ahead, of saying there are certain things that take time and you have to plan for them and you just have to be patient."

A park is a long time in the making, and is never complete. Olmsted planted many trees not much bigger than a broomstick; in placing them, he had to think years, even decades ahead. After construction and planting, Olmsted didn't walk away. He monitored park maintenance and fretted over any modification of his plans.

The design of a garden, let alone a whole park, is not a game for those requiring instant gratification. There's an old saw that defines gardening as the slowest of the performing arts—a philosophy that might surely have amused and pleased a drama teacher like Allyn Winslow.

Then there is Olmsted's philosophy, which in the context of Winslow's murder is ironic. For Olmsted once wrote:

No one who has closely observed the conduct of the people

who visit the Park can doubt that it exercises a distinctly harmonizing and refining influence upon the most unfortunate and most lawless classes of the city—an influence favorable to courtesy, self-control, and temperance.

SWEET CHERRY: R.I.P.

BY CHRISTOPHER MUSELLA

Sunset Park

S pider-Man was ready to save the girl again. Right there in front of the movie theater, the Cobble Hill Cinema. It was a warm night too; I don't know how he does it, wearing that mask, and I have to wonder if those tights are made of that breathable fabric pro athletes wear. Behind the barricades, beyond the movie cameras and production crews, throngs of Brooklynites stood patiently in the warmth of the first night of summer, just to catch a glimpse of the actor Tobey Maguire donning the web slinger's red and blue costume, and the damsel-cum-diva, Kirsten Dunst, waiting to be rescued. Meanwhile, in Sunset Park, not far from Cobble Hill, another piece of Brooklyn was waiting to be rescued that night.

Over on 3rd Street there was a block party. The johnny pumps were wide open. In Brooklyn, to beat back the clamoring heat of summer, we open up fire hydrants—what we call johnny pumps—and they spray out a stream of wet, cool relief, a break from the humidity and staleness called city air.

All along the riverfront—Brooklyn Heights, that is, where the famous span anchors us to lower Manhattan—families strolled along eating Grimaldi's pizza. (Okay, fine, call it Patsy's. The regulars have been fighting about that name for years.) And some were licking ice-cream cones. Everybody was taking in the last rays of the summer solstice, the longest day of the year. With the longest day of the year, you end up with the shortest of nights.

This was all happening on the night of June 21, 2006, in the greatest borough in the world—Brooklyn. Home to Coney Island, Di Fara Pizza (better than Grimaldi's), Prospect Park, and, if you believe a four-year-old named Gianna Maria, it's where they make the balloons.

But something else happened that night. Something happened in Sunset Park, a section carved out of the pavement, bordered by the million-dollar lawyers of Park Slope, Russian laborers of Bay Ridge, and the Orthodox Jews of Midwood. That night in Sunset Park, a strip club known as Sweet Cherry, a haven for Mafioso types, drug lords, and sex peddlers, was finally shuttered. The iron gates were pulled and locked for the last time, an ending that the politicians, community boards, and law enforcement agencies had fought to bring about for years.

Sweet Cherry—where dancers took their struts, drugs and money changed hands, and sex was brokered by murderous bouncers—sat in the shadows of religion and justice. Saint Michael's Roman Catholic Church, its high arching gothic entrance, cherubs and angels smiling on the rest of Brooklyn, was just an avenue away on 42nd Street. The Department of Justice, a square chunk of weathered cement and grimy blue tile, sits on Third Avenue and 29th, stoic and silent as you pass.

And there to complete the unlikely trinity was Sweet Cherry, keeping herself open despite all efforts to lock her down. It kept its stiletto heels dug into the pavement for more than ten years, remaining a growing community concern, with smarmy lawyers taking advantage of the political process that kept the sex trade alive. Heck, even old-time politicos need to cut loose now and then.

But in June of 2006, Lady Liberty, whose torch of justice and light of freedom is visible just a few blocks from the door—right there at the pier—had had enough.

A customer named Jorge misses the place. As he says—Sweet Cherry, rest in peace.

Remorse for a strip club?

Sorrow at the loss of a stage and a pole, strands of fake blond hair soaked with sweat whipping around in time to the shimmy of real live breasts? (No money for implants in this joint.) Sorrow at the passing of a place that inspired what some wags in criminal circles might call—heh-heh!—permanent violence.

How could there be remorse for all that? As we say in Brooklyn, fuhgeddaboudit!

I landed in Brooklyn in 1995. In Park Slope, where the young professionals were moving, where you can now rent a nice closet for about thirteen hundred a month.

Sunset Park is southwest of the Slope, set back from the East River's edge, its west-east borders resting on a pier at one end and Fourth Avenue on the other. Past Fourth is Park Slope South, as the realtors tout it these days, in hopes of boosting rents for unsuspecting Manhattanites looking to escape and to save some of their Wall Street bonuses for themselves. (Good luck.)

From the pier it is all warehouses, concrete, and pavement. Rail lines for bygone freight cars are exposed in spots, laid across streets with patches of cobblestones where pavement peeled away like so much industrial scab. The Brooklyn-Queens Expressway, a curvy swath of road peppered with potholes and cracks, juts through the neighborhood, veering and bumping riders on their way to or from the Verrazano-Narrows Bridge, gateway to Staten Island.

To the rear of boxy warehouses that sit like giant blocks piled up at the water's edge are a scattering of limestone and brick row houses; some wood frame ones too. The views are magnificent: New York Harbor, lower Manhattan, the Brooklyn Bridge, Lady Liberty, and Governors Island. All this in the panorama of Sunset Park.

The rising palisades of New Jersey lie on the horizon. And across the neighborhood, from Fourth Avenue down to the waterfront, apartments are perched over storefronts; some of the establishments gated in rusty aluminum, others open with vibrant neon, unchanged for years.

I always wondered what somebody's life would be like living above a storefront. A sense of privacy is lost, I imagine. But if you happen to own the business down below, at least you've got a really short commute. I read somewhere that John Gotti kept a little old lady in an apartment up over the Ravenite, a Manhattan social club on Mulberry Street in Little Italy. That's where Gotti held his secret meetings, when the old lady was out shopping. But then the little old lady agreed to cooperate with the feds. They went into her place when she wasn't home, wired a bug into a lamp so they could listen from a remote van, and that's how the feds taped his conversations; that's how they got Sammy "the Bull" Gravano to rat out his don.

In the case of Sweet Cherry, it wasn't so easy. No federal agent could put a bug in there and hear anything over the mega bump-and-grind decibels pumped out of the sound system.

Sweet Cherry occupied the ground floor of an unremarkable

building at the corner of Second Avenue and 42nd Street. Only in New York City, America's capital of irony, can there be two streets with the same names mere boroughs apart— the lesser-known address of Sweet Cherry versus the world-renowned main stem of Times Square.

The unremarkable building at the Brooklyn corner of 42nd and Second has an apartment upstairs with windows guarded by drawn shades pulled too far to one side, revealing only a slash of darkness beyond.

From the opposite side of the street, I'm walking by on a dreary February afternoon, assessing the remains of the strip club.

There's a big vertical sign, as tall as the building itself, with a curvy black-and-white silhouette of a dancer, set against a field of fuchsia, beneath the words *Sweet Cherry* in script. Another sign, this one running horizontal along the wall of the building, is smashed and cockeyed, with exposed dead fluorescent tubes. To the left of the tubes is a third sign with red lettering on a white board, also cockeyed and hanging from wires. It reads, *BUILDING FOR SALE BY OWNER*.

A delivery guy with a plastic sack of Chinese food dangling from his wrist is banging on the door of the apartment, checking the order stub for the address, looking up at the windows, waiting for some sign of life. Nothing.

I glance up at the windows again, and I can't believe anybody's inside of that apartment, or wanting to be. It's all the kind of charcoal-gray so thick you can practically feel it. I imagine cuts of light trying to pierce through the cloth shade of a lamp; the shade is streaked in cigarette-yellow. All in all, not my kind of room.

A man appears at the corner. A big guy, a Latino from the hood. He attempts to help the Chinese delivery guy by yelling up to the window, something indecipherable to me. No mat-ter how much the big guy hollers—nothing. The delivery guy gives up, disgusted at the waste of his time. I cross the street and ask the big guy what's up in my own weak Spanglish.

"Good place to let loose, you know, good times," he an-swers me in English.

I ask him his name. Jorge, he says.

"Some people got hurt here," I tell Jorge.

"I don't know about that stuff. Never happened when I was here."

"What about the bad stuff I heard about—murder, dope, sex for sale?"

"Ah, come on, man. This is a bordello, bad things can happen. You don't like bad things, you don't go, right? Besides, it's all dead and gone to me."

It wasn't murder, drugs, or intimations of rape that brought down Sweet Cherry. It was, ultimately, a decision—a coop-erative, multi-agency effort, according to law enforcement types—that finally did it.

To be sure, three homicides in as many months helped: Ir-ving Matos, manager of the club's bouncers, was shot dead in his apartment; Wayne Tyson, a club patron, met the same fate as his associate Matos, only Tyson was knifed; and Edwin "Eric" Mojica, who ran a security firm that pimped out work to bounc-ers, was killed a few weeks after his buddy Matos was cancelled.

Usually it's good things that happen in threes; at least that's what they taught me in Sunday school. The cops needed an angle to shut the club once and for all, and what better angle can you ask for than homicide-times-three?

Murder was grist for a community board hearing in early 2005. Angry residents—the hard-working, daily-grind subway-commuter types—stood, one furrowed brow after another, demanding that Sweet Cherry be shuttered. We've got respectable businesses and families working and living side by side, they all said. Our kids are not safe with drunks from the night before stumbling around in the morning.

On went the grievances, one after another after another, from the frightened families. The politicos offered up the standard retorts and compulsory agreements.

Then lawyers on the Sweet Cherry payroll had their say.

In the end, and very quietly, the board granted renewal of a liquor license for Sweet Cherry—good through October 2007.

And the families were left wondering, who's paying around here?

I ask my new friend Jorge what really happened in these parts.

"I used to go there a lot, to get away from the kids and the television," he says. "You know, in Mexico, we never had a television. I come to America and my wife, she wants two. There's one in the living room and one in the bedroom. I only watch soccer." He slurps from a paper coffee cup. "So, I like to come here and meet my friends, and have some whiskey, and watch some naked girls. We had a good time."

Didn't it get rough sometimes? Wasn't he scared?

"I seen some beatings, you know? Crazy shit, but you turn your head." He thinks for a second and reasons, "If you aren't getting hit, you stay out of it. But I heard stories, you know? You go anywhere long enough, you hear stories. They had one good fucking lawyer, I know that."

The phone rang in the Court Street law offices of Lance G. Lazzaro, counsel for Sweet Cherry. On the end of the line was

Jimmy DeNicola, owner of the club. After the hellos and bada-bings, the conversation probably went something like this:

> —*I kept the license for you. That was huge. Now don't mess it up.*
> —*I gotta keep my girls dancing, you hear?*
> —*The only thing that's gonna keep this place open is the grandfather.*
> —*The what?*

Lazzaro more than likely commenced to educate his client about the tide that turned sleaze to please in Manhattan's Times Square. Walk West 42nd Street from Seventh to Eighth Avenue in 1993 and you were greeted by *XXX* this and *All Nude* that. After the '94 mayoral election, Disney's mouse moved in and pretty soon the strip clubs, private viewing booths, and lap dances moved out—with many thanks going to the new Brooklyn-born mayor, Rudolph William Louis Giuliani, crusader for the quality of life he said New Yorkers wanted.

So, big showcase theaters for glittery productions such as *The Lion King* transformed old Times Square into the new Square Times. Out went the shops selling sex, in came Starbucks and lattes. Even the little old guy with a neatly creased paper hat who sold hot dogs and burgers under the marquee of a dilapidated movie palace got the boot.

But what about the local sex-flick joints that were already operating before the new zoning law went into effect? With their business permits protected by grandfather clauses, they could still peddle triple-X videos and DVDs so long as they also offered some movies you wouldn't mind taking home to the tykes. So, while a couple of wholesome titles were displayed in the windows, few copies were actually in stock. No such problem, however, with the likes of *Debbie Does Dallas*. Which could still be viewed in back if so desired, courtesy of a private booth. Just watch where you sit.

Likewise in outer-borough locales like Sunset Park, sex joints, so to speak, had grandfather clauses. They might be on Mayor Giuliani's radar, but they were still open and doing brisk business.

Sweet Cherry opened in 1996. Joe and Jimmy DeNicola bought the property from a Manhattan Beach businessman named Louis Kapelow.

It's been said that drugs killed the Mafia. The original bent-noses despised drugs. Colombo, Bonanno, Gambino, Lucchese, Genovese—none of them wanted their soldiers trading in dope. It was bad for business.

We all know what happened. As history tends to repeat itself, bad business came to Sweet Cherry.

Jorge tells me about a spring night in 1999, when Sweet Cherry was home to dancers with names like Chastity (really) and Jennifer (ditto).

"I liked it, you didn't have to wear nothing fancy. No jackets," explains Jorge. "I don't own a jacket . . . My brother Manuel, he comes in with me. In like two minutes or something, Manuel's off to the back room with a lap dancer. He comes out smiling about ten minutes later. Then this other guy comes in and walks up to the bar. He's a gringo. He goes to the back with another gringo. Leaves about five minutes later. That's when things started going wrong around here."

Later, I check out what Jorge was telling me. As the press reported at the time, the story goes something like this:

A stranger walks up to the bar, a small baggie of cocaine

is "exchanged with a patron" for twenty bucks. The stranger records the sale, and does so again on a number of successive nights. The stranger works for the NYPD Narcotics Division out of the Brooklyn South precinct.

Counselor Lazzaro gives his client a warning along the lines of, *They're going after the club, Jimmy.*

Jimmy's likely response? *What the fuck is that supposed to mean?*

It meant the cops never named an actual person or persons dealing drugs. They only named the place—Sweet Cherry. Narcs demonstrated a "pattern of activity," as prescribed by statute. In this case, the activity at Sweet Cherry was drug dealing. Establish that in a court of law, and the judge will say drugs, booze, naked women—they don't mix, so shut it down.

Jimmy might have wanted a personal meeting with this stranger from Brooklyn South. In which case Lazzaro might have told Jimmy that hostility would be bad for business.

Lazzaro's final advice? Probably: *Keep your mouth shut, don't do anything stupid, and we'll keep you open.*

An investigation proceeded, based on the narc's account and his catalogue of illicit drug sales. The district attorney of Kings County brought the matter to state court.

The argument Lazzaro and his cocounsels put up was simple: People in the club have their backs to the bar because they're watching the stage—and who wouldn't be when Chastity and Jennifer were performing? Consequently, house management was unaware of drug transactions since customers' hands were not observable.

On August 5, 1999, the judge ordered the temporary closure of Sweet Cherry and imposed a fine of $25,000. Big deal.

No doubt Jimmy DeNicola proclaimed his lawyer a genius. No doubt the genius told Jimmy to cool it.

Clients, a lawyer once told me, are the same as a doctor's patients: They don't listen to sound advice.

Staring at the gated front door, Jorge leans back, then forward, as if looking for something. He tells me, "It was like the judge took my hangout away. Then I seen this big dude out front one day. It was real hot. He was cleaning the front of the store. He says, 'Don't worry, we'll be back.'"

That was August. Late in September, Sweet Cherry reopened.

On December 8, 1999, nine-year veteran NYPD Detective Joe Continanzi double-parked his car on Second Avenue. It was well after midnight, moving toward dawn. The air that night was unusually mild for a New York awaiting Christmas. Later in the day, New Yorkers would gather in Central Park to celebrate the nineteenth anniversary of the murder of John Lennon. Continanzi's girlfriend, Michele Miranda, was in the passenger seat next to him.

I like to think that if they were listening to the radio, Lennon's "Instant Karma" was playing.

Michele slid out of the car to do what she came to do, which was to walk into Sweet Cherry and come back out with her friend, a dancer at the club. But when Michele returned alone, a group of loiterers in front of the club grabbed at her. Joe jumped out of the car. He didn't get very far.

At the hospital, Joe told his sergeant, *They jumped me.* The doctor told him to lie still.

Lucky, the doctor said. The stab wounds missed Joe's major organs. The doctor left and Joe finished telling his sergeant how he had been kicked, hit with bottles left and right, punched, and stabbed. The sergeant told Joe they nailed two of the droolers, and both had confessed.

Jorge was there that night.

"You spent a lot of time here, didn't you?" I ask.

"Yeah, I know, some people think me and my wife, we're not good," says Jorge. "But it's okay. She knows I don't do anything bad. I come home to her . . . But that night even I get scared. That was some fuckin' fight. Bitches slapping bitches, bottles breaking everywhere. I got out in a hurry. See, I was alone that night. Manuel was at work. That cop took a beating."

Officer Continanzi's lawsuit against the club failed. Lazzaro's argument this time, that the bouncer's responsibility ended at the door, prevailed. What happened outside the club, on the street, was not the club's responsibility.

Sweet Cherry, still alive.

March 8, 2004. A cold rainy afternoon. A sixteen-year-old girl walks into the club. She lies about her age to the manager, Gabriel Bertonazzi. She needs work, she says, and she can dance, she says. She can dance real nice.

At this, a grin may have found its way to Bertonazzi's double-chinned face. *Dance*, he might have said. *Dance for me.* He lets her know that he is the sole judge of talent for the club.

Inside, the smell of beer and liquor seeps from the floorboards in the heat and humidity of a place like Sweet Cherry, with its backlit mirror behind the bar revealing only the emptiness she feels as she removes her clothes.

Outside, the skies are steel-gray and cold as big trucks rumble through the neighborhood across broken cobblestoned streets. In the distance, salsa music plays on a truck radio somewhere.

Inside, a girl of sixteen shivers.

The man wants her to dance. In the world of third-rate strip clubs, it's the same old story. You have to show the man what you've got. She steps back and looks around. *This is what I have to do. Fine, this is what I'll do.*

Guitars rip through the silence of the bar. Like taking a bullwhip to a hummingbird, the guitar strings drown out the distant salsa. Stage music that twelve hours ago was in synch with the night is now out of sorts, like a bad suit at a black-tie affair.

She dances. She takes off her shirt.

She is alone in a room, with just this very large man watching her writhe to the music. In the same old story, she loses her dignity and whatever is left of her underage innocence as fast as she loses her clothes.

She dances in nothing but her g-string and spike heels, moving wildly to the syncopated rhythm, pretending not to look at the man's big eyes. Then the music stops. She turns her naked body, perspiring beneath hot stage lights, and there's a drop of sweat on a nipple, other drops between her breasts.

She's hired. She gets what she wants, a job dancing, where a friend told her she'd make good money. It's what she *didn't* want that would haunt her, she would later tell the cops. She didn't want him.

She had no choice, really. It's just part of that same old story.

She kept dancing there, and she kept making money. She kept taking the pill too.

And at Sweet Cherry, the beat went on.

Then, in November, the raid came down.

Vice detectives raid hard and fast. The music scratches to a halt. Patrons don't run as hard as they do in the movies. They think about it, but the place is surrounded by cops and you can't get away.

The cops only wanted to check the IDs anyway. They checked everybody, including the dancers. Vice cops asked questions quick and fast, no time to think about answers, leaving the truth nearly as naked as the dancer: *You're only sixteen, were you here against your will, were you forced to have sex with anyone, were you raped . . . ?*

During the course of the next few hours, she told an avuncular detective a tale of how she had come to this unfortunate station stop in her life. A true tale of family dysfunction—and whose family isn't dysfunctional? She told them about Bertonazzi, whom the detective was pleased to arrest on charges of rape and endangering the welfare of a minor.

A quick search online tells me that Bertonazzi made his $5,000 bail and was back to work a few days later.

I ask Jorge about the dancer. Jorge says that he remembers her. "She could dance. And let me tell you something, she had some pretty nice titties. They didn't bounce that much. We all thought the tits were no good—not real, you know? But Manuel used some of his paycheck for a lap dance from her, and he touched them and said they were some real titties. Manuel don't lie to me. He'd get smacked down if he did."

She was only sixteen, I think, just a girl.

"You know something I don't?" Jorge asks.

This is when it dawns on me that Jorge isn't just some local who used to drop by to watch girls dance. The guy is an informer for the cops and the D.A., and his name probably isn't Jorge.

"I think when you get into some sort of trouble, maybe you catch yourself and you make some changes," says Jorge, or whatever. "Maybe you behave a little better and you keep the heat off. That's how things work. Do your thing, just keep it quiet, keep the heat off. No one will bother you."

Logic evidently unheeded.

I checked the court records. In March of 2005, the drugs charges came back again. The "pattern of activity" allegation was once more lodged against Sweet Cherry. Undercover cops bought two bags of cocaine and a bag of marijuana. Also, according to the cops, another trade started to surface: prostitution.

"This guy starts working here," Jorge tells me. "His name is Irving. We call him Irv. Anyhow, Irv runs the door. He says if I need a girl, talk to him."

Irving Matos was in his early forties and a respected man of his community. He was a member of HANC, the Hebrew Academy of Nassau County. Vice president of the board of directors, no less. He was also manager of the bouncers at Sweet Cherry. Some guys, you never know what they have under their fingernails.

Irving had a friend in the club: Wayne Tyson, a run-of-the-mill hustler and sometime bouncer who ran a small prostitution ring out of his apartment in Brownsville.

Tyson was a frequent customer at Sweet Cherry. That's where he met Matos. And that's where the two of them met Stephen Sakai.

"I didn't like that guy Tyson. He dressed nice, but he never smiled," says Jorge. "I don't like him the first time I meet him. And he's the new bouncer. Sometimes he worked the door.

If he's got some freaky vibe or something, maybe I go in but maybe I don't."

Sakai, on the other hand, was a regular-looking guy, a tall black man, well-groomed. He got a bouncer job at Sweet Cherry through an agency that doled out that sort of work. The man who ran the agency was a guy called Eric Mojica.

During the course of a year, Matos, Tyson, and Sakai had their own inside gig operating out of Sweet Cherry, according to investigators for the Brooklyn D.A.

Bouncing at the door was their front, investigators claimed; steering patrons to prostitutes and skimming profits was the real action. The allegation went like this: Sakai got the nod from Matos and sent the patron his way; Matos sent him off to Tyson; Tyson got the john to the girl, collected the money afterward, and shared it with his partners.

But Tyson had his very own inside-inside thing, investigators said. A few of the girls interested in moonlighting on top of their moonlighting were given his address in Brownsville. No sense in Tyson passing up ancillary profits.

Somewhere along the line, it occurred to Sakai that he was getting burned. So say the investigators. He expressed his concerns to some of his Sweet Cherry colleagues and, as these things happen in the demimonde of bouncing, word got to the boss.

Eric Mojica controlled many of the bouncing gigs in New York City. He never cared much for Sakai—too cool for his taste. And just to show his regard, Mojica fired him.

After he lost his gig at Sweet Cherry, investigators said, Sakai was angry and took it out on Tyson—for reasons unclear to this day. He paid a visit to Brownsville, to a small apartment on Eastern Parkway, according to the investigators. He brought a knife, they said.

Tyson opened his door to Sakai, who confirmed his presence during questioning by police. Tyson had no reason to fear anything was amiss. The door closed. Tyson couldn't have anticipated Sakai's rage, investigators posit. Blood flew from Tyson's head and neck. He was left alive, but bleeding to death.

A few days later, police visited Tyson's neighbors in Brownsville to ask questions about the bloodied corpse they found in his apartment. Questions were also asked around the club, some of the replacement bouncers not seeming too disturbed that Tyson was gone. No one offered up anything. If you don't say anything, you don't know anything, and you don't get in trouble with anyone.

By November 2005, Matos had grown seriously worried. Tyson was dead. He hadn't seen Stephen Sakai in weeks. And there was no word on the street either.

For the time being, the johns kept coming to Sweet Cherry, and they kept getting what they were there for, and even if the business was slowing down, it now made up a trinity of sorts that was Sweet Cherry's economy: dancing, drugs, and sex.

And one regular patron dead—so far.

Irving Matos went home one night to his basement apartment and did what his sort of mogul does: He eased himself into a lazy-boy lounger and watched television.

There was a knock outside, and then an insistent doorbell. He got up to answer it. He saw it was Sakai, looking his usual cool. Matos invited him in. They sat there and watched the TV.

After some brief catching up on the news about Sweet Cherry, Sakai said it was time for him to shove off. *Don't get up*, he told Matos. *I'll show myself out.*

Then he pulled a pistol from his coat and fired into the rear of Matos's skull.

Sakai confessed as much to the police.

After a week or so, the DeNicola brothers began wondering about Irving Matos. Maybe he got the flu bug or something.

They called the police to investigate, after encountering an unbearable stench coming from his apartment. They found the decomposing body of Irving Matos, age forty-two, in front of the blinking television.

Brooklyn police put the Matos murder together with the Tyson murder: Both were no-forced-entry jobs, both were connected to Sweet Cherry, and the name Stephen Sakai was on the list of known associates of both corpses.

So was Eric Mojica.

Sakai found Mojica before the cops could.

A few weeks after Matos was found dead, Mojica turned up dead as well.

It took three murders to put the police onto Sakai's trail.

On May 23, 2006, the 11 o'clock TV news helped the cops find Sakai.

Stephen Sakai, with three alleged murders under his gun-holding belt, was working as a bouncer at Opus 22, a hip nightspot in Manhattan's Chelsea district. A couple of drunkards got into a fight outside the club, and Sakai would have none of it. He pulled out his .45 caliber and fired away. After the mêlée was over, the cops found four men shot, one fatally.

They picked up Sakai in Brooklyn a few hours later. He denied it all at first, but then a short time later, after some police persuasion, he admitted to being the gunman at Opus

22. He also admitted killing Matos, but denied killing Tyson. Still, they charged him with murdering Tyson and Matos—and Mojica.

By June of 2006, the ire of the people of Sunset Park had reached a boiling point, and now scorched the entire city.

Another bouncer had been accused of murder, this time by the Manhattan district attorney. A young woman named Imette St. Guillen had disappeared from a nightspot called The Falls, located in Soho. She was found dead the next morning, the alleged victim of a bouncer named Darryl Littlejohn, an armed thug with a criminal record. Thus did the city commence a crackdown.

Targets included the bouncers themselves and the hiring process clubs used—if any. The city urged greater background checks and tougher licensing procedures for both security and gun permits. Stephen Sakai had a security license, but not a gun permit.

And for Sweet Cherry, Lazzaro's streak of magic finally came to an end. With drug and solicitation charges pending against his client, the DeNicola brothers, Lazzaro cut a deal with the New York City Police Department, the Brooklyn D.A., and the New York State Attorney General's Office.

All felony charges were dropped and a civil suit was averted, while rape charges against Bertonazzi were also dismissed.

Robert Messner, assistant commissioner for the Civil Enforcement Unit of the Police Department's Legal Bureau, called the deal "a very good example of cooperation by multiple agencies." Sweet Cherry ponied up $50,000 in fines. No jail sentences, no probation. The DeNicola brothers pled guilty to misdemeanor drug charges, and were barred from ever again operating a nightclub in Kings County. All other charges were dismissed.

Stephen Sakai spent his nights on Rikers Island, awaiting trial in Brooklyn on three counts of murder in the second degree. He was later acquitted on one count and convicted on the other two; he now faces fifty years to life in prison. Meanwhile, he is still awaiting trial in connection with the fatal shooting at Opus 22.

Darryl Littlejohn, meanwhile, is also locked up, awaiting his day in court on charges of murdering Imette St. Guillen.

It was all over. The violence, the drugs, the sex—all of it over, just like that.

On the night of June 22, 2006, down on the promenade of Brooklyn Heights, families laughed and played and ate pizza and ice cream. The movie shoot in Cobble Hill was over, and Spider-Man slung his last web out of town.

Down under the Brooklyn Bridge, a newlywed couple held hands and had their picture taken.

In the neighborhood of Sunset Park, it was quiet on 42nd Street. The gates were pulled low on the entrance to Sweet Cherry. The lights were off, the deejay booth was silent, the bar was dry.

"It wasn't pretty, and neither were the girls," says Jorge. "But it was loud and it was fun, you know what I'm saying?"

He crushes his empty coffee cup, strolls to the corner, and flips it into a garbage can.

"I'm going to miss this." Jorge looks at me, then the club. As he walks off, he says, "Take it easy, my friend."

I think, *Remorse—for a strip club?*

EDITORS' NOTE: *Some of the information in this essay was originally reported in* "The Nine Lives of a Topless Bar: Complaints Hit a Wall of Law" *by Michael Brick* (New York Times, May 31, 2006) *and* "Strip Parlor Closes as Part of Plea Deal" *by Michael Brick* (New York Times, June 21, 2006).

THE GHETTO NEVER SLEEPS, MISTER POLICEMAN

BY ROBERT LEUCI

Atlantic Yards

My father was born and raised in East New York, on Hull Street and Hopkinson Avenue, one block off Fulton. He'd tell you he came from Brownsville; that's the way he chose to remember it, and he spoke of his neighborhood devotedly.

The only member of his family born in this country, Pop was one hell of a ballplayer and a devoted follower of the socialist and East Harlem congressman, Vito Marcantonio. Pop loved Brownsville and was proud of its socialist history. When I became a cop we hardly ever discussed politics; in the 1960s, we hardly spoke at all.

In the back of my mind where memories flourish, I often think of Brownsville. As a kid growing up in Ozone Park—Pop thought Queens, just across the Bayside and Acacia cemeteries from Brooklyn, was best for us—I went every weekend to the street markets of Brownsville to shop with my mother. Her name was Lucy and she called Brownsville "Jew-town."

One summer Sunday morning, I was playing stickball with my buddy Norman Bliestien. My mother drove by the playground to pick me up. In those days, going Sunday-morning shopping with my mother was at least as important as, say, going to the Crossbay Theater with the neighborhood guys to watch a movie. Or possibly my first sexual experience.

"Normie, I have to go shopping with my mom," I tell him. "I gotta go."

"Where you going?"

"Jew-town."

"Where?" says Normie.

"Jew-town in Brooklyn. Pitkin Avenue, Stone Avenue. Down there."

"That's Brownsville. What are you, a moron?"

I'd always thought that Jew-town was the name of the neighborhood, like Ozone Park where we lived, or Richmond Hill or maybe Polack Alley in Woodhaven. I was ten years old, so what did I know?

Brownsville in those years was awesome. On Belmont Avenue—Stone and Pitkin too—there were rows of push-carts heavy with vegetables and fruits and pistachio nuts and great round, thick, chocolate-covered halvah rings that were shoulder-to-shoulder with immense loaves of black breads, bagels, bialys, and pickles in enormous wooden barrels. In the shops there were appliances and clothing and shoes—special sample shoes, the only ones that would fit my mother, whose feet were tiny.

The shopkeepers loved my mother. They'd notice Lucy and shout her name; the commotion was unbearably loud and dazzling.

"Lucy, here Lucy—look what I got for you, only for you!"

My mother was beautiful. Small and beautiful with huge breasts. She was a Sicilian woman and they were Jews and the market women jumped for joy when they saw her. My mother greeted them as if they were family.

I learned how to slip and slide in and around fast-moving crowds as a little kid. Walking those streets, I worried that Brownsville's uproarious world would swallow us up. But that urgency in my belly passed soon enough when Lucy laughed. She laughed a lot, and anyone could see that she loved being there. The little lady could shop.

Her astute eyes missed nothing. Shirts for my brother, a dress for my sister, Keds sneakers for me—only half sizes, with soles so thick that when I wore them I'd feel as though I could jump over a building and back again.

I can still see the people, closely packed along the side-walk and overflowing onto the stone stoops that led to the shops. On the cold days in the winter it was a sight to behold, all those people warming themselves from the fires that rose out of black metal barrels, the fragrance of wood smoke mix-ing with the spicy essence of lox and salami. They are some of the most magnificent, clinging, and lasting memories of my childhood.

That was then.

Not until I became a cop in my early twenties was I to visit Brownsville again.

Years had passed and things had changed.

There were mountains of garbage in the little yards in back of the tenements where rats the size of small dogs prowled. No longer did I see women in ritual wigs, men in beards and long dark coats, boys with curls of hair dangling alongside their ears.

Brownsville faces were now black and brown and angry. It seemed new, but it was really the same old class struggle, only with different music. I was doing my best to understand the anger on the basis of hopelessly limited information.

During this rookie time, I was still living at home and the breakfast discussions with my father were becoming more and more heated.

"The yoms, Pop, they're crazy. They live like animals and throw shit at us from the rooftops. I mean bottles and bricks. You know what a bottle or a brick would do to you thrown from six stories up?"

"Yom is a dumb word spoken by stupid people," said Pop. "Don't ever use that word in this house again."

"Those people are crazy," I told him.

"They're not crazy. They're poor and oppressed, and they're angry. They take their anger into the streets. And let me tell you something, Mister Policeman, it's going to get worse."

My father was kin to all the demoralized and poor and out-of-work peoples of the world; his instinctive belief in the class struggle, back then, drove me up the wall.

"The bosses and landlords screw these people over in ways you could never understand," Pop said.

"You have to see how they live," I replied.

"I know how they live. You think we lived any differently?"

"Sure you did."

He smiled.

"Drugs, Pop. The drugs are everywhere—on the rooftops, in the basements, in the hallways. And where do they get the money for those drugs? They rob, they steal, they burglarize. Their women are prostitutes. It's a hellhole."

"Mister Policeman, who do you think brought all those drugs into that neighborhood? I wish you'd stayed in school."

In those days, I was assigned to the NYPD's Tactical Patrol Force. The unit had been formed in 1959, the creation of Police Commissioner Stephen Kennedy. At first, there were thoughts to simply name it Special Services. Except, having SS on the collars of New York City cop uniforms would have been less than wise.

TPF's nickname was Kennedy's Commandos. It was a specialized uniformed unit—most of the members were young and had been Marines or paratroopers. We patrolled across the city in high-crime areas.

Our special training focused on dealing with all sorts of civil disorder. Patrol in TPF was mobile and proactive and very aggressive. We all shined up our brass with silver polish. Our uniforms were always creased and unsoiled. It was there, in that unit, where I would draw my gun for the first time and shoot someone—in a place where I almost got shot myself, and the place where my first partner was killed.

In TPF, you carried yourself with poise, a kind of dignity and macho zeal. What I remember most about those years are the alleyways and backyards of the tenements, scary stuff, the sounds and smells and always the music—the sweet sound of salsa wafting up to the rooftops, how it made the scary stuff somehow go away.

Things happen quickly in the street, and as a cop you really don't know what you're doing most of the time. You're just doing. Afterward, you can tell yourself any kind of bullshit you want. Say that you handled it well, it didn't bother you one single bit, that you loved doing this or that, that you behaved heroically and you're proud of yourself. "You would not believe this shit," is what you tell people.

I had two partners, Dave Jackel and Pete Schmidt. Dave was six-foot-five and Pete was just about six-three. I was five-foot-nine, the smallest man in the unit; in my memory, we made a unique-looking trio walking our posts.

The TPF attitude was, action comes on so fast it's not smart or safe to involve yourself in tentative assumptions or too much scrutiny. Speed counts.

* * *

"Fuckin' muggers, I hate 'em." This was Officer Pete Schmidt talking. "We break out the gym set on those bastards."

Irony of ironies, after so many years I was back in Brownsville, standing with Pete Schmidt on the edge of a roof of a six-story tenement overlooking Pitkin Avenue. I tried to mentally reconstruct the street, as it had been in my youth. The shops and pushcarts and most of the Jews were gone. The neighborhood had changed; it was now one of the most dangerous, squalid, and dilapidated areas of the city.

Remember, this was the early '60s. A battle at the other end of the world was ratcheting up, and we had a drug war blazing in our backyard. At the time, even the most pessimistic observer could not imagine that we could lose both.

Most of time, when on patrol, I'd feel like the good yeoman crime fighter for the city of New York, the designated lightning rod for the madness that took place in ghetto people's lives. In a short time I learned that along with street criminals, there were hard-working, good people in these neighborhoods, people who counted on me.

When I walked patrol, I eyed the alleyways, hallways, and storefronts. I wasn't stupid, or very brave. I forced myself to go into the dark places, the long alleyways that ran between the tenements. At the end of those alleyways were doors that led to stairways that led to basements that were lit with candles, where mattresses were scattered on ice-cold floors, where rags were blankets and buckets were toilet bowls—the tenement cellars where desperate street people slept.

I could see faces at windows, shapes in hallways, forms traveling in and out of the darkness. Believe this when I tell you, the ghetto never sleeps.

I had been a visitor in many ghetto apartments—sometimes

invited, most times not. I knew that on the coldest of nights, ice formed inside the glass windows and on the sills of those apartments. I had seen ice on the floors and on bathroom mirrors. Slum landlords regulated heat in that part of town so that none rose after 6 o'clock in the evening.

My father was right. Small wonder these people wanted to burn those buildings, equipped as they were with rats and leaky faucets that ran ice water and ceilings that dropped lead chips of paint into cribs where infants slept. I once saw a baby girl whose toes had been gnawed to stumps by a rat. I saw that and wondered what in the hell country I was in anyway.

The next time, when I spoke to my father I said, "You were right. Were you ever. Jesus!"

He smiled.

A recollection. Voices and faces. Tales like threads over and around a piece of time. So mindful I am of my experiences in Brooklyn that nothing goes away. Now, I can see myself as I was then: None of it was real, like I was in a movie, some dodo up on the screen, some character in my skin making his way through a world he didn't understand.

I'm young and healthy. The drinking age in New York City was eighteen, but they wouldn't serve me without ID until I was thirty. Baby Face, they called me. The cops and the street people, they all called me Baby Face.

Today I look in the mirror. "Baby Face," I say to the reflection. "Yeah, right."

I see myself sitting in homeroom at William H. Maxwell Vocational High School in East New York one morning. A bright fall day in Brooklyn and the teacher walks into the room. Passing as a high school student, I'm there to buy dope.

The teacher smiles nervously at me, squints, turns around, then turns back and looks at me again.

The teacher's name was Veltri, I called him "Red" when I was the pitcher and he was the great glove and strong hitting shortstop of our own John Adams High School baseball team in Ozone Park. Later, in the boy's room, Red asked me, "How are you doing?" I said fine, that I was there to do something that had to be done. I told him I was a cop. He said, "Yeah, I figured."

After a week at Red's school, my job was done.

I was now standing in the principal's office. I remember how that dip-shit came at me, how angry he'd been that I'd bought drugs from fourteen of his students.

He was horrified. He unbuttoned his coat and loosened his tie and shouted that I'd crossed the inviolable threshold of his school.

A great sadness came crashing down on me. I thought I had accomplished something good, something worthwhile, something that needed to be done. It was the first time I realized that although the world's good people said they wanted evil exposed, in fact that was often the last thing they wanted.

The image I had of myself as a hero, as someone who was willing to do the work of an undercover cop—all of that was so much crap. This dip-shit principal didn't want the crap; he wanted me to go away. Rocking back and forth, getting reamed in that man's office, looking down at him seated behind his desk, I felt a swell of hopelessness; a claustrophobic sensation, as if I'd suffocate to death if I didn't get out of there.

He berated me, telling me that I was taking advantage of his students—his *kids*, he called them. This being the same man who only a week earlier was so happy to see me, so pleased that someone would come and help figure out if there was a drug problem at his school.

Full-blown into his rant, I got this picture in my head of a fourteen-year-old *kid* in jeans and a sweatshirt, a knowing smirk on his face. The little piss-pot telling me he could get all the drugs I wanted, whatever I wanted, as long as I had the cash. Guns he could get me too, this little shit, this tough guy with the long hair flowing over his shoulders. A good-looking boy, the image of one of my high school buddies from a few years back. But my buddy wasn't selling drugs, this piss-pot was.

Piss-pot's mother was the president of the PTA, an important person. As was this man, this dip-shit of a high school principal. As were the many others to come later: judges, prosecutors, politicians, chiefs of police, some of my family, my friends, journalists, television commentators, cops—so many cops. Faces in my not-so-distant future, scores of good citizens, my unborn children—all of them asking me about similar and different cases. Why didn't I mind my own business? I tried, trust me. I gave it my best shot. It just wasn't possible.

Imagine what arresting strung-out junkies would do to you. Or how depressed you'd get from collaring people who couldn't find their hands and feet. Between the crazy shit you saw both in the street and courthouses, and what you personally lost as far as moral perspective was concerned—being there, seeing it all up close and personal—well, if you had any brains at all you would see that it all boils down to a collective nervous breakdown of a person's system.

Your eye saw it but your brain couldn't really take it in. Like this one:

I've told it before—many times, several versions—but this is what actually happened.

It was late on a Friday when I walked into the Brooklyn arraignment court. It was a busy night, the place was jammed to the rafters and it turned the courtroom into a spectacle of craziness. It was a bazaar of victims and defendants, manipulators of all sorts.

I spotted Richard Smalls—"Sweet Dick," they called him. He was standing against a wall amongst a bevy of his working girls. Dick was an informant of mine, a "benevolent" pimp with processed hair and sharkskin suits. He looked to all the world like Sugar Ray Robinson.

Sweet Dick didn't bully or threaten his women so much as he charmed them. I guess he told them he loved them and made all sorts of ridiculous vows to protect them. Out of fear and loneliness a lot of street girls hooked up with pimps, slick guys who spared no expense or time winning and wooing them. Dick would keep at a new street girl with relentless pressure, over and over until she joined his crew. Most of these women didn't have much going for them in the way of self-reliance. Sweet Dick's women wore wigs and face paint and were street-pretty. They were heroin addicts, all of them.

I remember the way Dick put his hands on his hips, turned to look around the courtroom, giving the place his I-don't-need-this-shit look. Then he turned back to me and said, "Man, you gotta help me out here. My brother got busted by some precinct cop—bunch of bullshit. The kid didn't do nothing but ride in a car. The car was hot but he never knew it."

I asked, "What would you like me to do?"

The five women standing behind Sweet Dick, as if on cue, gave me perplexed, piercing looks.

"You can go and talk to the D.A., have his bail lowered or something," one of them said.

The assistant district attorney calling the arraignment calendar was—here, I'll call him "Joe." Joe was attorney for the state of New York, and that was unbearable to him. He longed to be in private practice and hauling down boxes of cash. Joe was an attractive guy, erudite in a Brooklyn sort of way. He knew his way around the courthouse, knew how to get things done.

Favoring navy blue pin-striped suits, off-blue shirts, and red ties, Joe had a full head of curly black hair. You'd make him as somebody who could work a lounge in Vegas.

"I have an informant here whose brother is on the docket," I said to Joe. "Can you help me out? I'd like to get his bail lowered."

He gave me a look, a supercilious grin, a look of both expectation and disbelief. I recall that it gave me a funny feeling, that look of his.

"Does he have any money?" Joe asked.

I went to Sweet Dick and asked him about money.

Dick inquired of his ladies, "Does anyone have any cash?"

The ladies searched their pocketbooks, by which I mean their bras, their panties. After much searching and shuffling about, they came up with about five hundred dollars in rolled-up fives, tens, and twenties.

I gave Joe what I thought was bail money—the whole rolled-up, scrounged-together hooker cash. He told me to go and get the prisoner. I just about lost it when Joe paroled the guy right there on the spot—into my custody.

"Whoa!" I said. "Wait a minute."

"Parole's better than low bail," said Joe, smiling again. "Or no bail at all."

The five hundred went south.

I left the courthouse that night and walked over to Court Street, to an Italian restaurant and bar called Café Roma. We called it "Chick's place" on account of the owner, whose actual name was Charlie.

There was hardly anyone there. Just Charlie—Chick behind the stick—and some guy at the far end of the bar sitting in semi-darkness, sipping an espresso.

Chick was the most urbane of bar owners, a Brooklyn guy with a good education. Something of a philosopher too, with a fine understanding of the city, how it worked and what it took to own a bar and restaurant and survive. We were pretty good friends, and he was willing to take my word for it when I told him that the courthouse was a zoo and the lawyers were all fucking thieves.

"What happened?" he asked.

"Charlie, it's complicated. But take my word, it wears you out."

He looked at me close, then turned and looked down the bar. He turned back to me and said, "You should tell that man at the end of the bar. He's a law professor."

"Really?"

The professor hunched forward over the bar. He was wearing a gray suit that covered up the broad shoulders of an athlete. This was my chance to say something indignant, my chance to hold forth with a resounding, irate speech. There were any number of bizarre stories I could have told the professor—some incredible, some beyond that, the absurd and the ordinary.

"I understand you're a law professor," I said. "Well, I'd like to know what the hell you're teaching these characters, because I'll tell you, you go into that courthouse, it's the same as the street. You need a scorecard to figure out the good guys from the bad guys. That's the truth, the whole truth, and nothing but the truth."

This professor had a way of glaring back at you when you spoke to him. Like he was calculating the right moment to cut in.

"Listen," I told him. "Lawyers run the show. They're the trendsetters, the role models. The prosecutors, judges, the defense counsels—they're all lawyers."

I remember how offended he looked as he explained to me that the vast majority of people practicing law were good people. They were dedicated, honest, and hard-working. So he didn't know what I was talking about.

Everything he said was said softly, as if he were talking to himself. He was not trying to persuade me, simply stating a fact.

"Look to yourself," he said. "How have you been behaving?"

The way he smiled made me think about the priests when I was a kid, how clean and innocent they all seemed. How they wouldn't believe any of this I was saying about lawyers. If you tried to tell a priest about a thieving lawyer, he'd answer you with a question: *So, tell me, how are you behaving?*

When I was leaving Chick's place, Charlie turned to me to ask, "So you talked to him?"

I nodded.

"That guy, the professor. He's someone you should know. He's going to be an important man someday."

"He's a professor, Charlie. Professors are naïve."

"Not him. He was one hell of an athlete and he's smart as they come. You remember what I tell you, this guy—this Mario Cuomo guy—he'll be an important man someday."

"Sure, sure," I said to Charlie. "I bet he'll be."

I would run into Mario Cuomo now and again at Chick's. We'd talk about the legal system, cops and lawyers, the court-house and the streets. Blah-blah-blah—as if I could really tell him what it was I did in the streets.

Mostly he told me things. He was full of humanity. He was an old-fashioned, incorruptible moralist. I remember wishing to God I could talk like him, then wishing to God I could un-derstand what the hell he was saying.

The brass were always telling us how we could win the war on drugs and wipe out the great plague. Their weekly memos and bulletins were quite inspiring.

I hasten to point out, we cops were not stupid. When we went out into the street up against that ocean of drugs, you couldn't help but swallow in shame and complicity. Even if you didn't pay attention you'd have to be deaf, dumb, and blind not to see that somebody was bullshitting somebody.

There are police stories and maxims that are passed down like legends from old-timers to rookies and from fathers to sons. For example: "You get pressed so hard they make you so crazy, they threaten and scream and call you motherfucker. You tell them if they don't back off, if they don't cool down, you'll take this stick and shove it up their ass."

I knew Robert Volpe, worked with him in the narcotics division. He was one of the kind ones, extremely talented. A fine artist, he had showings of his paintings at important gal-leries in Manhattan. There was not an ounce of white racism in his blood. His cop son Justin, a muscular guy with a Dick Tracy chin, is doing thirty years in prison for taking the stick end of a plunger to Abner Louima's rectum in a highly publi-cized police-brutality case in 1997.

Justin Volpe is now a legend. When you talk to cops,

and I do, they shake their heads when his name comes up. "Honest to God," they say, "who'd believe it. Was that crazy or what?"

There are no mitigating circumstances, but there are some points that few people understand. First, Justin was engaged to a black woman, so it's doubtful that racism played a role in his madness. Steroids, I think, may have played a role. But who really knows? His father, a truly decent man, dropped dead from a heart attack after visiting his disgraced son in prison.

The intersections of Fourth Avenue, Atlantic Avenue, and Flatbush Avenue constituted a drug marketplace that never shut down. An island stood at the heart of where those avenues came together, and on that island was a brightly lit stand where you could buy coffee, sodas, pizza, and soft-serve ice cream. There was an outsized Bickford's cafeteria across the street, and a block south on Fourth was a doughnut shop. The stand, the cafeteria, and the doughnut shop were gathering places for junkies that went strong twenty-four hours a day, seven days a week.

A short walk from the Bickford's was the Long Island Rail Road terminal, with tracks running under the streets of Brooklyn. Commuters—the good guys heading home to Mamma and the tykes in Massapequa and Hicksville—could stop for the lurid thrill of a quick ten-dollar blowjob, or else a ten-minute stand-up fuck from one of the dozens of hookers roaming those gathering spots.

I was an undercover narc and I could buy drugs all day and all night. Hordes of addicts and pushers were everywhere. Mostly I was buying dope from the walking dead, people so stoned that once they sold me drugs they might turn around and walk into an oncoming bus. It was no challenge at all. The dealers were ghosts who aimlessly walked the street. Fire your gun alongside their ears and they wouldn't even blink.

The closer I looked, the more I found the drug world a dark, painful, and unforgiving place, a world where only the strong and quick-witted survived. And when they survived, it was never for long. The plague was far and wide.

I was convinced that what we were doing was poorly conceived and just as poorly justified. Back then, I had neither the expertise nor the experience to come up with any real answers. But at least I knew this war-on-drugs business was bullshit.

I have always believed in the inevitability of personal fate. It's a paradox because although I was born and raised Roman Catholic, I do not believe in preordained destiny. I believe that if you find yourself in a serious trick-bag, that trick-bag is the ultimate manifestation of a series of behavior patterns. So if you can't do the time, don't commit the crime. You like playing in traffic? You'd better keep your head up and look out for the oncoming bus. I didn't, and that's another story.

Back in the day, as I am now able to say, those Brooklyn streets were a glorious show. When the full moon was out, there was no better place to be. You were in a place where you didn't belong, using new language. You saw and did things you would someday pay for. But at the time, it was one hell of a soirée. The world exploded around you, there was excitement, you'd get tremors and goose bumps; it was party time.

The streets themselves had names that raise hair on the back of my neck because of what it was I did there. Van Brunt Street—and Union, President, Columbia, Kane and Pacific, Sackett and Hoyt, Fourth and Atlantic, Flatbush and Atlantic. Just moving through those streets late at night, when the only people out and about were pushers and hookers and street gorillas and pimps. Everyone searching for the drug, hunting for heroin, the "white lady." I arrested a lot of drug dealers. As a cop, it was practically all that I did. But the number of dealers arrested meant nothing, changed nothing. There were always more.

Fyodor Dostoevsky, in his *Notes from Underground*, wrote:

> *Every man has some reminiscences which he would not tell to everyone, but only to his friends. He has others which he would not reveal even to his friends, but only to himself, and that in secret. But finally there are still others which a man is even afraid to tell himself, and every decent man has a considerable number of such things stored away . . . Man is bound to lie about himself.*

So it was for me on those Brooklyn streets.

THE MORGUE BOYS

BY THOMAS ADCOCK

Brownsville

1. La mise en scène

I t is best to plan your excursion to Brownsville for a warm Sunday morning. This is when the neighborhood churches open their stained glass windows and the creamy-voiced tambourine ladies carrying on inside have a way of soothing the savage breasts of certain blasphemers on the outside—the ones loitering in dubious doorways, like spiders hungry for flies.

To get to Brownsville—which nobody in Manhattan nowadays has ever heard of, never mind that it was home to the departed pugilist Al "Bummy" Davis and later two other heavyweights by the names of Mike Tyson and Riddick Bowe—you must catch the Brooklyn-bound 3 train. Hang onto your snatchables for the next thirty to forty minutes and you should arrive at the elevated Saratoga Avenue station relatively unmolested.

Now then, descend two flights of tired-out stairs. Feel the grooves beneath your feet, created over time by the lunch bucket hordes. Decades ago there was a lively after-shift crowd, too, arriving in Packards and Imperials and Cadillacs. The *shtarkers* and Mafiosi of Manhattan, all dressed up in their spats and sharkskins for copious meals in the trattorias of Mulberry Street, would slum it across the East River to

Brownsville for dessert: a nice plate of biscotti maybe, washed down with genuine Brooklyn egg creams. Also maybe some business.

Upon reaching the sidewalk, the first thing you see is the Shop Smart Mini-Mart. In another day this was a round-the-clock pastry shop and candy store known as Midnight Rose's. That and the headquarters of Murder Incorporated, which in truth was not, in the commercial sense, a kosher establishment.

The proprietor of Murder Inc. was a Brownsville homeboy by the name of Albert Anastasia, a.k.a. "Lord High Executioner." He was a short, fat man with cold eyes and a habit of telling smutty jokes at the dinner table with his mouth full of food. He insisted that his Christian name was Albert, which sounded to him more American than what his birth certificate read: *Umberto Anastasia.*

In the enterprise directed from Midnight Rose's, Umberto/Albert Anastasia was assisted by Louis "Lepke" Buchalter. In contractual association with Charles "Lucky" Luciano and Meyer Lansky, Messrs. Anastasia and Buchalter undertook approximately 800 acts of permanent violence before the count was forever lost on October 25, 1957.

At 10 o'clock a.m. on that date, a red Cadillac sedan containing a debonair Brownsville candy and pastry merchant pulled up in front of the Park Sheraton Hotel in Manhattan, which is now the Park Central but still situated at 870 Seventh Avenue. Mr. Anastasia slid out from the back of the Cadillac and strolled into the hotel barbershop for his daily shave and shoeshine. And on that particular morning, his weekly haircut.

He parked his blue chalk-striped suit in a plump barber's chair of maroon leather, reclined, and closed his eyes. Mr. Anastasia was said to have been chortling under a hot white towel dropped across his moon face; he might have been plotting a preemptive strike against a certain business rival on the Italian north side of Brownsville who had whispered something about how the fat man at Midnight Rose's was headstrong.

Unaccountably, Mr. Anastasia's chauffeur sped away from the curb outside two minutes after that towel went down.

The Negro shoeshine kid started up with his brushes, as well as the song Mr. Anastasia got such a kick out of: *Shine and shine / Fifty-cent a boat / Make you look like a New York s'poat . . .*

The Italian barber started in with his scissors where the flesh pooched out from his customer's collar line. But when several gentlemen suddenly piled through the door, all wearing sunglasses and fedoras and bulky coats and waving large pistols, the barber and the kid took a break.

A barrage of bullets found their way into Mr. Anastasia's chest, arms, head, and left rib cage. The fusillade was of such weight and velocity as to propel him out of the plump chair and down to the tiled floor, where he died in a crumple amongst his hair clippings.

There were no arrests following the assassination of Albert Anastasia. But it was generally accepted by police and wiseguys that the late Joseph "Crazy Joey" Gallo, along with four helpers, did the deed. Before Mr. Gallo likewise succumbed to a notable shower of lead—while dining at a Mulberry Street clam house called Umberto's, of all names—he often referred to himself as a member of "The Barbershop Quintet."

Crazy Joey (probably) whacked the Lord High Executioner at the behest of the late Carlo Gambino (more than likely), who looked and sounded like everybody's *nonno* despite his being the namesake of what remains as the most prominent of New York's five traditional mob families. As a lad fresh off the boat, Mr. Gambino had peddled Italian ices on Brownsville's main stem, Belmont Avenue.

Mr. Gambino died of old age in 1976. His elaborate send-off was orchestrated by a society funeral parlor and attended by a number of respectable New Yorkers, after which his body was buried in St. John's Cemetery in Queens.

On the other hand, few had mourned the rude demise of Mr. Anastasia, largely due to his disgusting table manners. The Lord High Executioner lies below the sod of Brooklyn's Green-Wood Cemetery.

The Brownsville district of central Brooklyn is slightly more than two square miles in size. It is located downwind from the old bone-boiling glue factories of Jamaica Bay, which accounts for the fact that nobody with serious money ever lived in the neighborhood.

It has always been a tough place, Brownsville. Full of tough characters hanging out on the corners, glaring at you and spitting on the sidewalks. Tough gets you respect.

Sometimes respect grows, and festers, and turns to fear. People who can will leave a neighborhood at this point. They will tell new neighbors in new places about the glares and the spit they left behind. And soon enough the whole city is scared of a place like Brownsville, and content to let it rot.

The local police precinct, the 73rd, routinely tops New York in uniform crime statistics measured by the Federal Bureau of Investigation. Unsurprisingly, Brownsville ranks dead last in expenditures for city services—medical clinics, street sanitation, health inspections, public schools, housing code enforcement.

Emotionally inclined immigrants almost anywhere else in the fable of New York, New York say the city's streets are paved with gold. On sunny days, when the sidewalks of Gotham sparkle like gemstones, they swear they hear Frank Sinatra crooning, *If I can make it there / I'll make it anywhere* . . .

In Brownsville, there is no percentage in looking for sunny lyrics in sidewalks as gray and dull as thrown-away chewing gum.

Before World War II, Brownsville was mostly Jewish and Italian, with an enclave of Syrians along Thatford Avenue and a longtime Moorish colony on Livonia Avenue. Today it is predominantly black, largely poor, and frequently combustible.

Many African Americans consider the ambitious neighborhood newcomers—working-class Caribbean strivers and entrepreneurs from Senegal, Burkina Faso, Mali, and Mauritania—as yet another reminder of how they have been profoundly shortchanged.

On busy Belmont Avenue, a fresh-cooked meal of *tiebou djen* may be enjoyed at the several lively Senegalese cafés. The fragrant bowls of steaming hot fish and saffron-laced barley have become as ubiquitous in Brownsville as red beans and rice on paper plates.

You used to hear English on Belmont Avenue, even if the people speaking it used some other language at home. The people spending money today on Belmont mostly speak French.

Those with little to spend dream of hitting a good number and leaving Brownsville. When slim hope is dashed, there is always something to smoke or drink or inject in order to keep the faith.

Getting out is elusive. Getting high is total victory.

2. "Amy Fisher popped some bitch in the head . . ."

The plague came early to Brownsville. In the 1970s and '80s and '90s, the streets were conveniently full of decrepit buildings favored by crack cocaine dealers who could hole up inside, unseen by the twin threats of cops and hinky customers, and trade their poison for cash slipped through chinks carved in the walls.

An Amazon River of money and crack surged through Brownsville, flooding the neighborhood with fast profits and even faster degradation.

In the early winter of 1994, powerful forces in City Hall and the federal government accused officers of Brownsville's virtually all-white occupation force—the 73rd Precinct—of being participants themselves in the chaos of crime and shame in those plague years.

The mostly young and tender officers of the 73rd did not live near their place of work. Save for fifty-three-year-old Patrolman Frank Mistretta, they did not even live in the city. Instead, most commuted daily from Long Island cop suburbs where they were born and raised.

In the early days of the plague, Patrolman Mistretta was one of two men determined to rid Brownsville of evildoers. Nobody actually heard him say "evildoer," a word freighted with righteousness, but he might as well have; the basis of Frank Mistretta's self-respect was his being a street cop in the neighborhood of his youth.

He was proud of his five hundred arrests and sixty-seven department medals. But over time, Mrs. Mistretta would come to despise her husband's professional dedication.

She told him one day that while she loved him, she had no affection whatsoever for the NYPD. After which, Mrs.

Mistretta grabbed her husband's .38 caliber police special, swallowed the barrel, pulled the trigger, and was no more.

Brownsville's other would-be savior is recollected for a charming smile that seemed to say, *Would I kid you?* Among other things, he was a minister of the Lord, which made him an easy man to clock. But in Brownsville, being a suspicious character is not necessarily a cause for alarm.

He had green eyes, strong coffee–colored skin, and magnolias in his voice. His name might have been what he said it was, Pastor Billy Rich.

According to the old domino players I spoke with on Herzl Street, the pastor led a congregation of exuberant worshippers from a rented storefront, a few blocks down from Brownsville's last remaining synagogue and a few blocks the other way from a squat, shuttered factory where pine boxes for dead people used to be manufactured.

On the Sabbath, an elaborate crucifix shone in Billy Rich's store window: a life-sized plaster Christ on His terrible cross, with red lights throbbing from the places where He was punctured with thorns and pierced with nails. Shouting and stomping behind the crucifix, Pastor Billy's flock would implore Heaven for a miracle that would drive the crackheads out of Brownsville, just as Jesus had driven money changers from the temple.

On weekdays, the window contained a sign of shiny gold letters: *GET RICH QUICK!* Inside, the part-time ecclesiastic peddled life insurance policies of debatable legitimacy, though personally blessed. After business hours, clients were invited to enjoy cut-rate libations in the cellar bar.

In the spring of 1993, a felonious incident unreported to the police took place in that cellar. At half past 2 o'clock on an April morning, a non-investor walked right in and sat himself down at the bar. The interloper stood apart from the all-black crowd of woozy barflies not because he was white, but because he was seven feet tall and togged out in the impressive leathers of a motorcycle club.

Billy Rich, it was learned, was somehow in arrears. Details are murky, but the matter of serious delinquency was apparent by the determined presence of the giant in leathers. He took a hatchet from his belt and chunked the blade a full inch down into the mahogany and said to Pastor Billy, with a snort, "Get Rich quick, that's real freakin' funny."

The barflies winced at the sound of splintering wood as the giant yanked his hatchet free of the wound he had made on the bar. He asked Billy Rich for a nice foamy draught, and said he expected "payment in full" within the time it took him to smoke a Camel and kill a brewski.

No doubt it was a mistake for Billy Rich to have responded with, "Forgive our debts, as we forgive our debtors."

And most surely it was a mistake for him to have flashed his Would-I-kid-you smile as he drew one from the tap and set it out before the debt collector. Irritated, the giant again employed the hatchet, this time whomping it across the back of Billy Rich's strong coffee–colored hand.

The barflies talk of how Pastor Billy's broken hand shot up to his forehead like the distressed heroine of a silent movie, and how he fainted away to the beery floor. They talk of how his right pinky and ring finger remained on top of the bloody bar, twitching.

Billy Rich skipped out to whereabouts unknown, leaving Frank Mistretta as the sole guardian angel of Brownsville.

Knowing that evil lurked in the darkest and damnedest places, and without a wife anymore to complain about the exigencies of his calling, Patrolman Mistretta put in for the graveyard shift.

* * *

On February 2, 1994, one of first newspaper articles about the shame of Brownsville's finest was published in the *New York Times*:

FIVE BROOKLYN OFFICERS
SUSPECTED OF DRUG SHAKEDOWNS
by Clifford Krauss

Five Brooklyn police officers suspected of shaking down drug dealers for cash, guns, and cocaine have been removed from active duty in anticipation that they will soon be arrested, police officials said yesterday. The officers, who are attached to the 73rd Precinct in Brownsville, first came under scrutiny last summer when a former officer testified to corruption investigators that the five often broke down the doors of known drug dealers, and then divided their stolen booty in an abandoned coffin factory. Though known to other officers as "the Morgue Boys" for their choice of a headquarters, the five have not been publicly identified . . .

Soon enough, the names of cops scrutinized that previous summer during Judge Milton Mollen's hearings on citywide police corruption would come to blazing tabloid light.

According to the interim Mollen Commission report of December 1993, a pattern began emerging in the department of "invidious and violent character: police officers assisting and profiting from drug traffickers; committing larceny, burglary, and robbery; conducting warrantless searches and seizures; committing perjury and falsifying statements; and brutally assaulting citizens."

Under favorable plea deals or outright grants of immunity

from prosecution by Zachary W. Carter, then the U.S. Attorney in Brooklyn, two officers of the 73rd wasted little time admitting their own guilt—in return for testifying against three of their comrades.

In police parlance, they were rats. The U.S. Attorney's Office referred to them as government cooperators. Cooperating were Daniel Eurell, 29, and Christopher Banke, 25. Along with confessed dirty cops from other precincts—notably Michael Dowd and Philip Carlucci—Messrs. Eurell and Banke had been interrogated by the Mollen Commission. Also interrogated was Officer Kevin Hembury, yet another confessed Morgue Boy who had bitten the government's cheese.

In an audio tape not heard at trial, but later quoted in the *New York Daily News*, Mr. Hembury is heard telling his fellow cooperators that they stood a good chance of making money from *Hard Copy* or some such tabloid TV show.

With reference to the televised interview of a teenager in love who went to prison for shooting the long-suffering wife of her middle-aged paramour, Joey Buttafucco, Mr. Hembury's precise words were, "Amy Fisher popped some bitch in the head and got five grand. We're the Morgue Boys. You don't think we could get fifty grand?"

In addition to similarly florid testimony, the Mollen Commission staff and investigators for the Brooklyn D.A. and U.S. Attorney's Office assembled numerous boxes of documentary evidence in support of narcotics conspiracy charges against the remaining three alleged Morgue Boys.

Accordingly indicted and bound over for trial were Officers Keith Goodman, 29, who operated a part-time insect extermination company; Richard SanFilippo, 28, a bazooka-armed body builder; and Frank Mistretta, known behind his back as "the oldest rookie."

3. "Look, we're doing God's work."

When Mr. SanFilippo was unable to afford the continued expense of the high-profile criminal defense lawyer who counseled him during the run-up to trial, he turned to a young, good-looking attorney nobody had ever heard of outside of Brooklyn: Joseph Tacopina.

Mr. Tacopina was familiar with the territory. For young Joe Tacopina, Brownsville was an irresistible walk on the wild side, a short ride down Flatbush Avenue on the B33 bus from his parents' respectable home in Sheepshead Bay. As a prosecutor with the Brooklyn D.A.'s office, he was assigned the borough's most deadly turf, what his colleagues called the "gray zone" of Brownsville and neighboring Crown Heights.

Recently resigned from the D.A.'s office, Mr. Tacopina had accumulated splendid résumé credits for winning thirty-seven of thirty-eight homicide trials, efforts that were richly educational but which earned him less than $30,000 a year. He decided to switch to the more remunerative field of criminal defense.

When Mr. SanFilippo came his way, the closest that attorney Tacopina had come thus far to actually handling a defense case was carrying the bulging leather exhibit bags for his clients' original choice of representation—the legendary Bruce Cutler, once banned by a judge from defending John Gotti, the deceased Gambino family don. (In so many words, the judge had accused Mr. Cutler of being the family *consigliere*.)

When not toting bags, Mr. Tacopina nursed coffee in midtown Manhattan diners and read the tabloids and hoped somebody would ring up the answering service he checked frequently. (Operators were instructed to explain that Mr. Tacopina had just stepped out of the office but would call right back.) Besides perusing the crime blotters, he spent his time worrying about where the money was supposed to come from to support a wife and two babies, not to mention a third one on the way.

So he took a night job at a private club, which allowed him to collect tips for checking coats in an airless room with a Dutch door. Behind the suspended minks and cashmeres, Mr. Tacopina pored through sixteen cartons of evidence in preparation for arguing his maiden defense case.

At trial, star prosecution witness Danny Eurell outlined the Morgue Boys' modus operandi in rousting the proprietors of neighborhood crack dens and stealing money, merchandise, and available bling-bling.

"Sometimes we got in by verbally threatening people," he said. "Other times, we would break in using any tools we had—battering rams, crowbars."

The loot was divvied up before sunrise at the Herzl Street coffin factory. Assistant U.S. Attorney Charles W. Gerber told jurors that the graveyard shift officers "thought they had a license to steal."

In an interview, Gerber spoke of a precinct house atmosphere that might account for the attitude. "The average age of the police officers was some incredibly low number, like twenty-five," he said. "You had a lot of kids who grew up on Long Island who had no stake in the community, had no common experiences with the people, no common upbringing. That, to some extent, is a recipe for disaster.

"It's important that a cop is doing a job because he's trying to help all those people who every day get up and get into the subway and go to work and make a living and raise families in a tough environment. People who go to church and do the right thing. This is the kind of case you prosecute because it's the right thing to do."

Counsel for the Oldest Rookie was Edward P. Jenks, who

had grown up in the Williamsburg section of Brooklyn. Which in his youth could not be imagined as the hipster magnet it is today.

"My parents bought this brownstone on Bedford Avenue for seventy-nine hundred bucks. I am not kidding you. I loved it there because the weather didn't matter, I played handball off the brick wall in the basement," said Mr. Jenks. "And there was a joint everybody went to called Teddy's Bar. They kept a pail of wontons you could eat for nothing.

"This'll blow your dress up. That brownstone I grew up in? It's going now for a million-two. The owner's some guy probably down in his wine cellar where I played handball, probably having a pinot grigio.

"And the other day," he added, "I see in *New York* magazine that a beer at Teddy's gets four-fifty now."

Outside the courtroom, Mr. Jenks and his client would engage in such reminiscences. And sometimes Mr. Mistretta would admit to the difficulties of being a beat cop in Brownsville, old enough to be the father of the youngster cops from Long Island, who didn't know from handball.

On his client's behalf, Mr. Jenks explained, "There was some feeling of mistrust from those younger cops. Like, what's his story?"

Counsel for Mr. Goodman was Stephen C. Worth, a son of Brooklyn who was the borough's district attorney in the late 1970s. In an interview, he spoke of the disgraced Michael Dowd, the first cop to rat on other cops before the Mollen Commission.

"It was no surprise to me there were drug-using cops like Dowd," said Worth. "By the sheer force of numbers and the availability of drugs, you couldn't be surprised about some cops turning out like Dowd.

"You had drugs literally on every corner. There were a million burned-out buildings. It was unbelievable how blatant it was."

Worth, who spent a considerable amount of pretrial time riding in squad cars with the officers of the 73rd Precinct, added, "If I was a cop, I could have made twenty arrests a ride. But it would have just been shoveling against the tide. My guy Goodman and the other two who went up with him, Mistretta and SanFilippo, they're saying, 'Look, we're doing God's work.'"

4. "You knew I was a snake . . ."

Joe Tacopina figured he was smart enough to be a trial lawyer, even if he did not happen to possess the finest mind of his fraternity.

He learned something new and unexpected—and something very intoxicating—on the afternoon he delivered closing arguments for the defense in the trial of the Morgue Boys. The lesson serves him well today as one of the city's most prosperous criminal defense attorneys and a frequent TV talking head on legal topics.

But there he was back in '94, a hungry criminal defense lawyer who checked coats by night, arguing his maiden case—all alone in the courtroom well, with a stone-faced judge eyeing him from the bench, with the prosecutor pouncing at every opportunity to object, with the press out there still trying to figure out how to spell his name, and with the jurors thinking who-knows-what of him.

For a couple of awkward minutes, Joe Tacopina was scared. But as he warmed to his argument, he learned that all the pressure somehow made him at least ten percent smarter than he otherwise would have been.

And that got him flying high. Waving sternly at the government cooperators, he told the jurors:

Their testimony, their stories, remind me of an Indian warrior called Cochise. I don't know if you ever heard of him, but he is allegedly a fierce warrior.

One day out in the plains, he comes across a snake. Cochise is going over to kill the snake. The snake won't move. The snake was frozen. Cochise raised the weapon to kill the snake, and the snake made a plea: "Please, Cochise, don't kill me, spare my life. Warm me up and I'll never bite you."

Cochise took the snake back to his tent, warmed him up, thawed him out. The second that Cochise sat down, the snake bit him.

"What did you do?" Cochise said to the snake. "You promised you'd never bite me."

And the snake said, "You knew I was a snake when you warmed me up."

I think we've seen, ladies and gentlemen, that immunity is an open invitation to perjury. I know the government was giving out immunity letters in this courtroom like lollipops.

Ladies and gentlemen, if the prosecutor can convict on the words of Eurell, Hembury, and Carlucci . . . on this type of evidence, contaminated by their motives, their lies—then the government can convict any of us. Our daughters, our sons, our neighbors—we are all at risk!

God gives us freedom, and Danny Eurell takes it away. God gives us liberty, and Philip Carlucci takes it away. God gives us life, and Kevin Hembury takes it away.

I'm going to tell you something, ladies and gentlemen. What happened here is not right.

In addition to the rat cops, Mr. Gerber called forward a small parade of Brownsville crack cocaine dealers, whose civil rights had allegedly been violated by the three alleged cop assailants.

Jurors wasted little time in voting to acquit. Mr. Gerber acknowledged, "Some of the witnesses were not terribly sympathetic, like the street dealers with huge rap sheets."

His investigator on the Morgue Boys case was Anthony P. Valenti, who had grown up in the Red Hook district of Brooklyn, which he described as a place where a young man had three career paths in life: "The cops, the clergy, or the cons."

Investigating a Brownsville case, he said, is complex. "You're operating in a neighborhood where the good guys don't want to help and the bad guys for sure don't want to help," said Mr. Valenti in an interview. "It's tough."

With the plague now gone, where does this leave Brownsville? "I don't know if it's better or worse," said Mr. Valenti, "or any different at all." For four years—through the Mollen Commission hearings, the investigations, the trial—the three Brownsville cops were put on what bureau cops call modified duty. Street cops know this humiliation as the rubber gun squad.

Officers Goodman, SanFilippo, and Mistretta sought redemption through departmental administrative hearings. "I want to get back out there again, on patrol," Mr. Mistretta told the *Daily News*. "This is what I am, what I do."

His gun and badge were returned, and Frank Mistretta was back on his post. He filed suit against the city in the amount of forty million, but a judge dismissed the action. He remarried and retired from the force and now lives in Florida.

Mr. Goodman was not so lucky. The department cut him loose. He became a full-time killer of household pests. Mr. SanFilippo won back his job, but eventually left town—and an apparently resentful ex-wife, who answered a telephone inquiry by asking, "You're suing him too, I hope?"

She would not divulge his whereabouts any more precisely than, "He's not here. He's in Mexico." In unmistakable terms, as the vocabulary of scatology allows, the ex–Mrs. SanFilippo offered fair warning of her litigious impulse.

5. Crime Scene

The coffin factory on Herzl Street is layered in four spray-painted gang graffiti, making it difficult to determine exactly who is in charge: *Syc* or *Cripp 2XSS Gang* or *2-S Deuce* or *Royal Deuce*.

At the end of the block, the elevated subway tracks of the 3 train provide shelter for a colony of hard-faced individuals who will sell you dope or themselves.

One of them, a fellow named Daisy, said, "Yeah, I heard of the Morgue Boys." So, were they guilty or innocent? "Man, it don't matter," said Daisy. "It's Brownsville."

PART II

JOHNNY-ON-THE-PONY

In which two teams compete. One team crouches into a single-file line, each person holding the waist of the person ahead. Members of the second team try one-by-one to hop atop the "pony" and to stay on for a certain amount of time before they're shaken off.

FUN-TIME MONSTERS

BY ERROL LOUIS

East Flatbush

*All of us had worked hundreds and hundreds of cases but never
seen anything this horrible.*
—Detective Mike Hinrichs, NYPD's most decorated officer

Kayson Pearson and Troy Hendrix, already convicted
of first-degree murder, spent their final moments in
court in one final show of murderous bravado.

"I have no regrets," said Hendrix.

"Me and my brother, Troy, we're the fun-time monsters,"
said Pearson. He was smiling.

Pearson was still grinning when New York State Supreme
Court Justice James Starkey ordered the pair to serve another
twenty-two years in prison on top of the crushing murder sentence they had already received—life plus twenty-five years.

The sentence meant that even if some legal fluke nullified
their life sentences, Pearson and Hendrix would spend forty-
seven years behind bars. Neither man is eligible for parole.

It's about as much prison time as you can get in a state
like New York that has effectively abolished the death penalty.
(New York has not executed anyone since 1963. The state still
has a death penalty law on the books, but in June 2004 it was
declared unconstitutional by the state's highest court. There
are no prisoners on New York's death row.)

As of this writing in late 2007, Pearson and Hendrix are being held in solitary confinement—locked down for up to twenty-three hours a day. They will almost certainly die behind bars. But it's not an excessive punishment, considering the vile and vicious things they did.

On April 24, 2003, Pearson and Hendrix abducted a pretty, petite twenty-one-year-old college student named Romona Moore off the street in Brooklyn's East Flatbush neighborhood. She was walking along Kings Highway, a well-traveled road, around 7 o'clock that evening.

It's not clear exactly how Pearson and Hendrix got Romona off the street and into the basement of 5807 Snyder Avenue. The most likely scenario is that they simply attacked and dragged her into their lair—a move that might have been risky, given how many cars travel along Kings Highway and its side streets, but not impossible.

It's likely, too, that the monsters employed a wicked charm in luring Romona to the vicinity of the small house where they attacked her. Both men, it turned out, were good at sweet-talking young women. They had a knack for appearing normal and friendly just long enough to put their prey at ease—before erupting in savage violence.

Pearson was twenty-one, Hendrix was nineteen. They knew nothing about the young woman they would butcher, although she lived only a few blocks from Hendrix.

Romona, the only child of Elle Carmichael, arrived in Brooklyn at age four when her mother moved from Guyana, part of a tide of Caribbean newcomers who turned East Flatbush into a bustling black neighborhood full of ambitious entrepreneurs and hard-working civil servants.

The deal was simple, and understood from the slums of

Kingston to the hills of Trinidad: You could trade status in the Caribbean for opportunity in the States. It was common to find men and women who had been engineers, administrators, or bankers in the Caribbean working as maids, cooks, janitors, and cab drivers in Brooklyn, often with the prickly impatience of people eager to regain their stations in life.

They bought homes, started families, joined churches, and saved their pennies. Some kept two passports, and thereby dual citizenship, sending their children to stay with relatives in Jamaica, Trinidad, Haiti, Barbados, Grenada, or Guyana every summer—all with an eye toward a triumphant retire-ment someday back on their sun-drenched islands. What be-gan as a small Caribbean colony in Brooklyn at the turn of the twentieth century grew by leaps and bounds over the decades; by the 1980s, East Flatbush was an island community with its own robust civic associations, political clubs, restaurants, and grocery stores.

The proud islanders who built the community never let the West Indian lilt leave their voices. But many grew to love their new home, and either sank roots in Brooklyn or joined New York's age-old, working-class pilgrimage to the suburbs.

Romona was part of this immigrant journey, growing up with five cousins in the heart of Caribbean Brooklyn. She was dark-skinned with a bright, warm smile. One of her profes-sors at Hunter College called Romona "very proper and very formal" in class. "She was the type of student who you would feel wouldn't answer your questions but suddenly would come with a very smart response," he said.

In her third year at Hunter, Romona didn't have a special boyfriend, although she did have plenty of friends, along with a 2.8 grade point average. She was studying psychology and preparing to vault her family forward with a career in medicine. Romona was going places.

All that came to a halt on April 24, when Romona went to visit a male friend in the neighborhood and trade some music CDs. From there, she planned to walk to a Burger King on the corner of Church and Remsen Avenues, about a block from her home.

She never made it.

After grabbing her off the street, Pearson and Hendrix held Romona prisoner in the filthy basement apartment for at least three days. They stripped and bound her, putting a heavy chain around her neck and connecting it to her hands behind her back. Then they took turns beating, raping, and sodomizing her between bouts of swilling booze and smoking marijuana.

The basement was a house of horrors. Police found rubber monster masks hanging in the apartment, along with pinup photos of women in chains.

In that same room, Pearson and Hendrix burned the young woman with cigarettes—three circles just under her eye in a triangle meant to look like a dog's paw, a sign of the Bloods gang the monsters claimed to belong to.

Pearson and Hendrix weren't hard-core gang-bangers: In fact, Brooklyn is a world away from cities like Los Angeles and Chicago, where highly organized sets hold and defend turf. More likely, the pair were playing at being tough guys, knowing just enough gang lore to think burning Romona's face might be a cool thing to do.

Later, at trial, the burns didn't get much attention; the focus was on other brutalities inflicted by Pearson and Hendrix. They mutilated Romona while she was alive, hacking at her hands and feet with a saw.

"Classic sociopaths," is how Brooklyn District Attorney Charles J. Hynes would describe the pair.

At least one person saw Romona's agony unfolding.

Ramondo Jack, a childhood pal of Hendrix's, had moved from Brooklyn, but was in town visiting his uncle and other relatives in the old neighborhood when he ran into Pearson and Hendrix. The pair brought him into the basement, poured a few drinks, and displayed their handiwork. They showed off Romona like a trophy, pulling back a sheet to display the innocent woman they had defiled and brutalized and chained like a dog.

"He lifted up the covers and I saw this female laying there," Jack later told a reporter. "She had a bruise on one of her hands and one of her feet. She had bandages on one of her hands and one of her feet. And she was bleeding from the middle of her face. And one of her eyes was swollen. I couldn't believe what I was seeing."

"Say hi, bitch!" Pearson ordered Romona, according to Jack.

"Her voice was low—teary. One of 'em tried to saw one of her hands and her foot," Jack later told a jury. "They both had smirks on their faces, like no cares."

Romona Moore, three days into her ordeal, bloodied and beaten, quietly begged Jack to help her. The psychology major even kept her composure enough to try and play on Jack's sympathy.

"You seem nicer," she told the last outsider to see her alive.

Romona was wrong: Jack was not nicer. A nice person— hell, a normal, compassionate person—would have walked out of the makeshift torture chamber and immediately called the cops. Not Ramondo Jack. He'd moved out of the tough Brooklyn neighborhood years ago and started a family in Maryland. But he clung to the idiotic, immoral code of the street and its first commandment, *Thou Shalt Not Snitch*.

"I left," he would later tell the jury. "I went home. I wasn't happy about it. I was bothered."

Just not bothered enough to tell anybody who could help.

And so Ramondo Jack put the incident out of his mind and went shopping, he told cops.

He will go through life knowing he lacked the spine to make an anonymous 911 call that might have saved a desperate girl's life. Jack's refusal to act reflects a shocking moral collapse in inner-city neighborhoods from coast to coast, in which witnesses to vicious, inexcusable crimes keep their mouths shut and refuse to notify police or cooperate in any way.

For a few witnesses, silence is borne of the legitimate fear of being harmed by drug dealers or other urban predators. But for many others, like the cowardly Ramondo Jack, silence is immoral apathy—a desire to appear cool and tough like the neighborhood gangsters, but in reality a weak-minded refusal to take responsibility for stemming the violence and chaos that have claimed countless lives and even entire neighborhoods.

The syndrome was on display in Baltimore in 2004, where drug dealers brazenly sold an underground video titled *Stop Snitchin'*. The video featured dealers flashing guns and openly threatening to kill anyone who might dare to testify against them. Startled cops used the video to round up and prosecute the dealers, but not before *Stop Snitchin'* and a companion T-shirt became runaway hits in inner-city neighborhoods from coast to coast, including Brooklyn.

"The most frustrating thing is while you're pulling your hair out of your head looking for the girl, these people directly across the street know—saw and know that a girl's being tied up and held in the fuckin' basement," said Detective Mike Hinrichs, who took charge of the Moore case. "And nobody calls the police. Where are their heads? So far up their asses, I don't know."

About the only thing Ramondo Jack did for the doomed girl was to gently chide her captors.

"I was like, 'What's wrong with you all?'" he said.

Pearson and Hendrix just shrugged, and told him, "It's already said and done. There's nothing we can do about it now."

Pearson and Hendrix were uneducated losers, the product of families so failed and broken that Hendrix's grandmother did not know, or never cared to ask, about the makeshift torture chamber in her own home. Not even when Hendrix and Pearson lured a second woman off the street and raped her in the Snyder Avenue basement near Romona's dead, battered body.

On the morning of April 28, 2003, the second victim, a fifteen-year-old student, arrived at school too late and found the doors locked. Hendrix was hanging around the building.

"He said, 'Do you want to come and hang out with me and chill with me? It's just one block in between the school and the house,'" the girl later recounted.

With that deadly snake charm the monsters could turn on, Hendrix persuaded the teenager to come with him. When the pair got to the basement on Snyder Avenue, the girl saw Pearson, the taller of the two, standing near a futon bed.

"The taller guy came behind me. I thought he wanted to come into the room, so I just moved aside," the girl later testified. "And then he put the pillowcase on top of my head. They pushed me on the floor. They cut my book bag off, and they was taking, from what I felt, my shoelaces off my sneakers."

She continued, "I was yelling for help. They told me that I should be quiet and that I shouldn't act up because if I acted up they would have to kill me like they did the girl the night before because she was feisty. I stopped yelling and gave them my arms. They just tied me up and put a sock in my mouth and took the pillowcase off."

The monsters told the girl about Romona. "While I was sitting in a chair, they had tape over my mouth and my eyes," she told police. "He said that the girl's body was behind me. And he asked me if I smelled it. And so he turned my head so I could smell it. I don't know. It was a funny smell. I don't know exactly what a dead body smells like."

After raping the schoolgirl, Pearson and Hendrix fell asleep. Their victim managed to free herself, licking the adhesive off the duct tape that covered her mouth and loosening the ropes that bound her.

"I saw the taller guy by the futon [asleep] with a gun in his hand, and the shorter guy right by the door with a knife," the girl said. "It was like a big kitchen knife. It wasn't a steak knife. I tippy-toed out of the room."

And finally, someone called the cops.

Police didn't connect the fifteen-year-old's rape story with the disappearance of Romona Moore until an anonymous tipster called Romona's mother, Elle Carmichael, with chilling information.

"He told me that he heard a girl screaming a few nights ago. Then he told me something about Snyder Avenue. I was overwhelmed," Carmichael testified. "I was hearing him, not hearing him. He was being really specific. He said they wrapped her up in plastic, and I think they killed her."

The caller was the uncle of Ramondo Jack, the visitor who'd seen Romona in her final hours alive. Jack, who never contacted the police, eventually told his uncle what he'd seen, and the older man called Carmichael to tell her where to look for her daughter's body.

Carmichael notified the police, then set out for the place the tipster had indicated, an abandoned house on Kings Highway. She got to Romona's body minutes before the police arrived.

All this happened on May 11, 2003. Mother's Day.

The most veteran, crime-weary detectives assigned to the Romona Moore case were stunned by the violence she had suffered.

"They shattered her jaw. Completely almost knocked it off her head," said Detective Wayne Carey.

"Her whole face is gone between the maggots and everything else," said another detective at the crime scene.

According to the medical examiner's office, the cause of death was blunt force trauma to the head and chest, the result of being assaulted with a hammer.

"They had a hammer and a saw, and they used it on Romona. Well, all of us were starting to feel sick," said Detective Hinrichs of the Brooklyn South homicide squad. Hinrichs is the NYPD's most decorated officer.

"Getting killed is one thing," he said. "But when you start to think what could have happened to this girl—what did happen. All of us have worked hundreds and hundreds of cases and had never seen anything this horrible."

* * *

As Carey and Hinrichs began the grim task of working with NYPD forensics experts to find blood, teeth, and bone fragments to serve as evidence, Caribbean community leaders began taking the cops to task over how the case was handled.

For Carmichael, the problems began the minute she reported her daughter's disappearance.

"It was total disrespect. All I got from the police was that if my child is out there and she don't want to come back, you know, she don't have to come back. No one came. No one called," she told ABC News. "They had already said there was nothing they could do. And there was nothing they would do because she was twenty-one."

Patrick Patterson, Romona's uncle, said no amount of arguing by family members could convince cops to mount an immediate, sweeping search for Romona.

"They just brushed us off," he said, "telling us, 'Look, she's gone somewhere with some male companion, she's an adult.' We kept on pleading with them, telling them she's not the kind of person who would do such a thing. We pay taxes like everybody else. Why is there a double standard?"

By double standard, Patterson put his finger on a long-standing grievance in black communities: The police and New York media often give saturation coverage to missing-person cases when the suspected victim is young, white, wealthy, and living in Manhattan. In neighborhoods like East Flatbush, the treatment is very different: Pictures of missing black girls do not get splashed on the front pages, and police task forces do not instantly spring into action.

The police, of course, see things differently—and have their own complaints about a lack of cooperation from the community. NYPD Commissioner Ray Kelly said Brooklyn detectives did all they were supposed to do when Romona was first reported missing.

"We would have had Romona alive and this [second] girl never attacked if these people would have picked up the goddamned phone," said Hinrichs.

Things came to a head during an angry demonstration across the street from the 67th Precinct. "You sent fifty officers to Romona's funeral. Not one officer looked for her. Not one!" shouted a young woman protestor. "All we wanted you to do was look! *Look for her!* She was right there, look for her! Her mother's only child. Shame!"

"There's an old saying in the [Police] Academy," said a rueful Detective Ken Silvia, Hinrichs's partner. "If you want to be a hero, go join the Fire Department."

Recriminations quickly took a backseat to the search for Romona's killers. It didn't take long to find Hendrix: He was already in jail on Rikers Island on an unrelated charge. Hendrix quickly named Kayson Pearson as his accomplice. But Pearson was nowhere to be found.

Hinrichs's team launched a manhunt, banging on dozens of doors all across the city, especially in Brooklyn and Queens. A tip led them some hundred and forty miles north of New York City to the state capital, Albany, where Pearson had once been busted on drug charges.

While looking for Pearson's brother, a low-level Albany dope dealer, the cops found his wife—Kayson's sister-in-law— who was on the outs with the Pearson family, saying she'd been raped and beaten by her husband. She gave the cops an earful, including the fact that the fugitive Kayson had sent her an e-mail asking her to send his Social Security card, birth certificate, and other identification to an address in Georgia.

That sent cops racing to the airport to catch the first available flight to Georgia. They had no authority to make an arrest out of state, but Georgia cops accompanied them to the small house where they were sure Pearson was hiding. He wasn't there.

Flying back to New York—and closing in on a hundred hours without sleep—cops followed a fresh tip to a house in Yonkers where Pearson was staying with an eighteen-year-old girl he'd recently met. (The deadly charm had worked once again.)

Cops staked out the building and intercepted the young woman as she returned home. They showed her a picture of Pearson. She confirmed that he was inside and gave them a key to her apartment.

The capture was violent. Pearson had barricaded himself inside the bedroom, pushing the bed against the door. When cops burst in, Pearson lunged at them with a knife. A Yonkers cop shot him twice in the leg before he was taken into custody.

Back in Brooklyn, Hinrichs and his team were still shaking their heads.

"If you told me it's two young kids snatching girls at random off the street and raping and killing them, I'd think you're crazy," said Hinrichs. "You know, this shit happens in fucking Idaho or some shit."

Like everything else about the case, the trial was dramatic, violent, and sickening. Pearson and Hendrix each accused one another of murder, leading the court to pick two juries to hear the case—one to judge whether Pearson was guilty, the other for Hendrix. It made for long, complicated proceedings: It took twice as long as normal to find twenty-four jurors; every time evidence came up that might unfairly prejudice one set of jurors, the proceedings would stop and twelve people would be hustled out of the courtroom until the evidence was heard, after which they shuffled back in.

On January 19, 2006, several days into the trial, Pearson showed up in court dressed in white and wearing a yarmulke. Ever the charmer, he'd told his lawyer, Mitchell Dinnerstein, that he planned to convert to Judaism.

"We even recited some Hebrew blessings," Dinnerstein later said.

It turned out to be just another con job by the murderous Pearson. A few minutes into the proceedings, members of Romona's family noticed Pearson and Hendrix winking at each other. Both men saw they were being noticed, and accordingly brandished Plexiglas shivs, the nasty homemade blades inmates fashion out of jailhouse debris. The monsters had secreted the knives in their underwear before coming to court. Now they used the weapons to make a bloody bid for freedom.

Wheeling on Dinnerstein—the man he'd prayed with just minutes earlier—Pearson slashed him across the face. At the same time, Hendrix leaped over the rail separating witnesses from spectators, pouncing on a court officer and grabbing for his gun.

All hell broke loose.

There was blood everywhere. Dinnerstein's shirt quickly became soaked in red. He would later need stitches to close the gash in his face. A fifty-eight-year-old court officer, Sergeant James Gorra, sprinted toward Pearson, who kept trying to stab Dinnerstein.

"I saw a weapon, and when he got close I gave a forearm as hard as I could and grabbed him. I couldn't let him get behind me because the judge is behind me," Gorra said later. "He hit me with the shiv twice, and then I flipped him over my side and then he hit me the third time. We were rolling around. I remember screaming out, 'He's going for my gun!'"

Albert Tomei, the sixty-six-year-old judge hearing the case, was at first puzzled by the chaos.

"While I was watching all this, I heard, 'Gun, gun, gun!'" he said. "As soon as I heard that, I said, 'I'm outta here!'"

Judge Tomei tried to leap from his perch on the bench and get to safety. "I'm not very good at jumping," he said. "I missed the first time."

Hendrix missed too. Officers swarmed over him, kicking him to the ground and hosing him down with pepper spray before he could get his hands on a gun.

Spectators fled the courtroom. Jurors dove to the floor. Romona's mother, Elle Carmichael, was rolling on the ground, crying hysterically.

"They could have killed everybody in that room!" she screamed. "Hang them right now by the neck!"

Minutes after the escape attempt started, it was all over. Hendrix was wheeled out to an ambulance on a gurney, his face covered with an oxygen mask. He gave reporters the finger.

"In all my time on the criminal bench, it was the most frightened I've ever been," Tomei later told colleagues. But there in the courtroom, amid the pandemonium, he was more blunt, looking at Dinnerstein's soaked bloody shirt and voicing the feeling of everyone present.

"Holy shit!" said the judge.

Tomei had no choice but to declare a mistrial, which he did the following week. The juries that watched the escape attempt would be hopelessly prejudiced against Pearson and Hendrix. The judge also excused Dinnerstein from the case, assembled two more juries, and resumed the trial in February.

Anna-Sigga Nicolazzi, the prosecutor assigned to the second trial, squeezed Elle Carmichael's hand, then began explaining to the jurors what had happened to Romona.

This time, Pearson and Hendrix were banned from the courtroom and made to watch the proceedings via video feed to the Rikers Island lockup. On the rare occasions they were brought to court individually to testify in person, each man's arms and legs were shackled, their hands encased in mitts and surrounded by twenty officers.

"Any outburst on your part, any showing of your hands or shackles on your part in order to create a mistrial, will not result in a mistrial," Justice Tomei told Pearson.

The trial dragged on for weeks, but the outcome was never in doubt. Both juries convicted the monsters on all counts.

At sentencing, Judge Tomei told Pearson and Hendrix he would not call them animals.

"That word is not appropriate because animals do not torture each other," he said. "You are a deadly human virus . . . a deadly vessel of human terror."

Then he sent them to jail forever.

"You're going to be consigned to a place where there is no love, there is no compassion—[a place that is] cold and lonely. And you'll be consigned to that place for a very, very long time," he said.

Elle Carmichael sued the city for more than a million dollars, claiming that delays in searching for her daughter—along with the fact that the police closed the case while Romona was still alive—contributed to her death.

But for Carmichael, money is the least of her concerns.

She moved from the home she shared with her daughter and went for months of psychological counseling. She carried a picture of her smiling daughter as a kind of talisman to ward off thoughts of Romona's final terrible days.

"The one question I always ask is, *Why did it happen?* I feel like at my worst times, when I feel most helpless, that's the question I ask," she told a reporter. "It puts me into a trance sometimes, so I try to avoid that question. But I still wonder, *Why did this happen?*"

The killers have their own chilling answer to that question.

"We did it for fun," Pearson said at his second and final sentencing, when he got an extra twenty-two years for the bloody escape attempt. "It was fun to see a system that has so much power and control lose it in a second. The judge—he's the one with all the power—was running away, bumping his knee. That was the most fun I've had all my life."

GETTING TO KNOW MAD DOG

BY ROBERT KNIGHTLY

Bushwick

I t is a convention of crime fiction that the detective is haunted by the case he did or didn't solve. Me, I never was a detective. Too many off-duty incidents in bars.

But I did have some memorable moments, as in hair-raising, as a patrolman in the 1970s in Bushwick specifically, the self-styled "Fighting 83rd" Precinct. And not without justification.

The '70s in New York City was the worst of times, in that crime was rampant. The city was on the brink of bankruptcy, had laid off a quarter of the police force, and arsonists—for profit or revenge—were busy burning down the wood-frame tenements of Bushwick, to the point where whole blocks had the look of a lunar landscape.

But the '70s were also the best of times, in that a cop never had a dull moment. Cops of the Fighting 83rd were a tight band of brothers; female officers had yet to debut in the patrol precincts. We were bound together by the shared perils of the street.

On the night of July 13, 1977, the lights went out in Bushwick and everywhere else in the city. In what the media has referred to as "blackout looting," larceny commenced forthwith along a two-mile stretch of Broadway, the main shopping artery dividing Bedford-Stuyvesant from Bushwick. Bodegas, supermarkets, discount furniture emporia, a gun shop, jewelry, clothing, and shoe stores had the gates ripped from doorways, and the contents inside were carried off into the night. For extra measure, the stores were then set afire.

All that night and into the next day, we cops roamed streets that looked like the siege of Atlanta as pictured in the movie version of *Gone with the Wind*. And yet, despite the *Sturm und Drang*, it is not the events of that blackout night that remain in the forefront of my memory. That place of honor belongs to Joseph "Mad Dog" Sullivan.

Mad Dog and I met in an after-hours Puerto Rican social club on a cold January night in 1977 when neighborhood cops—myself among them—were motoring through the streets of Bushwick in what was known as a "precinct conditions car," an umarked Plymouth sedan, a.k.a. the "brown car," the scourge of drug dealers, gunsels, chop shop operators, counterfeiters, and after-hours social clubs that catered to the ungodly.

Shortly after midnight, we exited said vehicle and burst through the barred front door of the Puerto Rican club on Jefferson Street, just off Knickerbocker Avenue.

As we made our entrance, glassine envelopes and various drug paraphernalia floated to the floor like autumn leaves. But what caught my attention was two white guys sitting by themselves in a corner, the only non-Latinos present. So my first words to the two, as they sat at the table looking up at me, were, "On your feet and against the wall."

I gave the muscular guy to my left a little push against the wall, off which he bounced, spun around, and stood stock still, staring at me. He was Irish-looking, five-foot-ten with a mustache and chiseled features.

Thus, without benefit of names, did I make my initial acquaintance with Joseph "Mad Dog" Sullivan.

The first thing I noticed about Mad Dog was his flat, dark,

dead eyes, with which he assessed me for a long minute, then slowly turned around and assumed the position. His Italian-looking tablemate did the same, without objection.

Looking down at the floor, I found something that didn't surprise me—a Beretta semi-automatic, which, I would later discover, was loaded with seven live rounds, one in the chamber. I hollered "Gun!" whereupon the four other cops with me focused attention on the two guys I had on the wall.

I didn't find out who these desperadoes were until we got back to the precinct house for arrest processing. We had a dozen other patrons of the bar for various drug possession counts, but only Mad Dog and his companion for the gun.

In those days there were no computers. You made a phone call to the Bureau of Criminal Identification at NYPD headquarters in downtown Manhattan. BCI eventually identified one Joseph Sullivan, a.k.a. "Mad Dog," on lifetime parole as a convicted murderer. His Italian cohort was Anthony "Snooky" Solimini, a Genovese soldier out of place here because around the corner on Knickerbocker Avenue were the Bonanno lads sipping espresso and plotting mayhem.

In those days, everything was done manually. You took a prisoner by the hand and rolled his fingertips over an ink pad and then pressed each one onto a print card. Then you handcuffed the prisoner and went through his personal effects. Then you vouchered (recorded and packaged) drug evidence for the police lab and the gun for ballistics, after which you transported the guy downtown to Central Booking, which back in the day was on Gold Street in downtown Brooklyn. There he would be processed further, and a cop like me would be interviewed by an assistant D.A., who would draft charges based on what I told him.

With these particular arrests, both my prisoners stood to

be charged with felony possession of a loaded gun if I wanted to go by the book—but it was a tenuous charge to lay against both. What I had to do, practically speaking, was select the one more likely to have possessed the weapon. Based on my estimation of Mad Dog's background, he was elected as the guy who made a motion under the table to toss the gun. A complete fiction, but no more of a fiction than those invented by prosecutors and judges in criminal court, where they are known as "legal fictions."

Although my statement to the assistant D.A. could be seen as a lie, it was in fact expected as a professional courtesy. The last thing a prosecutor or judge wants to hear in a criminal case is what actually happened. What they wanted was what they could put together to make a solid case against whomever the perpetrator was that I had dragged downtown. So every cop in my day would say what he was expected to say in order for the wheels of justice to grind exceedingly slowly and for no bad guys to escape. This is no doubt true even today, as I do not expect anything has changed.

So, the D.A. was pleased to accept my legal fiction that I saw Mad Dog ditch something under the table. After all, he had Mad Dog's complete and lengthy history on his yellow sheet, so-called because a criminal record was then printed on yellow paper. Mad Dog had been paroled after being sentenced to twenty-to-thirty years in 1967 upon conviction of manslaughter. Yet there he was in 1977 in my clutches. Which was a mystery to us all.

What was known, though, is that we had a very bad guy on our hands. As the D.A. said, "We're gonna stick it to this guy, he's going back upstate."

I could certainly endorse the sentiment. So I gave the D.A. a story he could live with.

We then adjourned to the courtroom. By this time, the sun had risen and day court was in session. In those days, the arresting officer actually went to court with the prisoner for arraignment. Not so today, as the police department, in its wisdom, has found a way to avoid all the overtime wages involved in having a police witness to a crime appear in court with the perpetrator.

So there we were, waiting for the case to be called so we could stick it to Mad Dog and send him back upstate where he belonged. Then Mad Dog's lawyer appeared—Ramsey Clark, the former attorney general of the United States.

I recognized Clark, even if some of my partners didn't. Certainly the court did, and so did the D.A., and he and the judge fawned all over the ex–attorney general. Of course, Clark didn't have a clue as to criminal court procedure. However, the Legal Aid lawyer on arraignment duty couldn't do enough for Ramsey, leading him by the hand through an unfamiliar process.

Oh! By the way, how was it that Mad Dog Sullivan got lawyered up with the former attorney general of the United States—?

Ramsey Clark had evidently been instrumental in gaining parole for Mad Dog in December 1975.

Since 1967, Mad Dog had been incarcerated at Attica Correctional Facility, which is so far upstate you can hear Canadians hiccupping on the other side of the border. Maybe Canada is where Mad Dog had been heading when he escaped from Attica in '71 by hiding in a delivery truck on its way out of the penitentiary gates; thus goes the honor to Joseph Sullivan as the only inmate in the history of Attica to ever have busted out.

But he wasn't missing for long. Two months after his departure from the pen by truck, Mad Dog was captured on West 12th Street and University Place in Greenwich Village by agents of a state task force. A judge slapped an additional ten years onto his sentence and he was returned to prison.

Ramsey Clark was, at the time, active in the prison reform movement, and Joseph "Mad Dog" Sullivan became something of a movement poster boy. Just as the Brooklyn novelist Norman Mailer was attracted to the late murderer/writer Jack Henry Abbott, author of the acclaimed *In the Belly of the Beast*, so too was Ramsey Clark fascinated with Mad Dog Sullivan.

And just as Jack Henry Abbott had failed to mend his homicidal ways while on parole—thanks in part to Mailer's efforts in creating a cause célèbre, Abbott was free to fatally stab a young waiter at the Binibon Café in the East Village—Mad Dog Sullivan also eschewed the path of redemption.

Some time after Ramsey's intervention on behalf of inmate Joseph Sullivan, the newly paroled Mad Dog was a suspect in the execution of Mickey Spillane—ex-boss of the Irish mob in Hell's Kitchen, not to be confused with the nom de guerre of a certain crusty pulp novelist. Spillane was shot dead on May 13, 1977, outside his hideaway apartment in Woodside, Queens, where he mistakenly believed he was living under the radar. Mad Dog was never charged with the hit, nor was anyone else.

As it happens, Mad Dog's youth was spent in the vicinity of Woodside. He grew up in Richmond Hill, Queens, where he committed his first murder.

His last recorded murder occurred on December 17, 1981, when Mad Dog took a shotgun to John Fiorino, a reputed Mafioso and vice president of Teamsters Local 398. Mad Dog was convicted of killing Fiorino outside the Blue Gardenia restaurant in upstate Irondequoit, near Rochester.

Mad Dog is today a sixty-nine-year-old resident of the Sullivan Correctional Facility in Fallsburg, New York, eligible to appear before the New York State Parole Board for the first time in the year 2069.

Jack Henry Abbott died in the Wende Correctional Facility in 2002. Unless Mad Dog Sullivan sees his 130th birthday, his fate is likewise sealed.

—And so there I was in the courtroom with Ramsey Clark and his toady from Legal Aid. I sat and listened with foreboding. With an inkling that Mad Dog might not have to go north after all.

As it happened, my instincts were correct.

Later on, out in the hallway, the D.A. approached me and said, "Ah, we didn't have a case anyhow." I didn't bother pointing out that he'd said earlier we had a very solid case.

Then Ramsey and Mad Dog emerged from the courtroom. Mad Dog had the grace and style to ignore us cops. Ramsey, being a gentleman, came over to me with a look of compassion and said these words I will never forget:

"Officer, I think justice was done."

To which I replied, "I doubt it, Ramsey."

Well, Mad Dog has stayed with me all these years and I have followed his career as best I can. I have discovered both what he'd done before we met in January of '77, and what he did after. Most of this I learned from Mad Dog's autobiography, entitled *Tears & Tiers*, a seminal book self-published by Mad Dog and his wife, Gail Sullivan, and first released in 1997.

One thing I learned from the autobiography was that before we met in '77, Mad Dog had been paroled from Attica in December 1975 despite a murder conviction and, as mentioned, his being the only escapee from Attica back in '71.

An extraordinary guy, this Joseph Sullivan, and an inscrutable situation from a legal point of view.

Not long after his parole, in May of '76, Mad Dog had a relapse. He hooked up with an old comrade—a made member of the Genovese crime family—who brokered gainful employment as a hit man. Mad Dog was to be under the direct supervision of Anthony "Fat Tony" Salerno, top boss of the Genovese organization.

On July 20, 1976, Mad Dog did his first job for the family by executing Tom Devaney, an enforcer for the Mickey Spillane mob, forerunner of the more famous Westies gang of Hell's Kitchen.

Mad Dog put a bullet in Tom Devaney's head as Tommy was drinking at a Hell's Kitchen bar. After which, on a sunny day in August of '76, he did the same to another Spillane enforcer, one Eddie "the Butcher" Cummiskey, in another saloon. In his autobiography, Mad Dog tells us that he also did three or four subsequent hits, but he doesn't identify the bodies.

Then Mad Dog and I met, on January 29, 1977. A week prior to our evening meeting, in the daylight hours of January 22, Mad Dog gunned down Tom "the Greek" Kapatos on a Midtown Manhattan street, according to the autobiography and T.J. English, author of *Paddy Whacked: The Untold Story of the Irish American Gangster* (HarperCollins, 2005).

When he walked out of court a free man, thanks to Ramsey Clark, Mad Dog was given a new assignment by his handlers within the Genovese family: the cancellation of Carmine "Cigar" Galante, boss of the Bonanno crime family who, ironically, began his career as a hit man for the late patriarch Vito Genovese (1897–1969).

Up through the summer of '78, Mad Dog was running all over the city trying to corner Carmine Galante and knock him off. He explained in his book that he regrettably was unable to do so on account of being called off the job by Fat Tony.

On July 12, 1979, however, Galante was sent to his maker at the hands of others: murdered by close-range shotgun blasts just as he finished eating lunch in the back garden of Joe & Mary's restaurant at 205 Knickerbocker Avenue, Bushwick. He'd been dining with his cousin, Giuseppe Turano, and his bodyguard, Leonard Coppola.

Then along came the shooters—Anthony "Bruno" Indelicato, Dominic "Big Trin" Trinchera, Dominick "Sonny Black" Napolitano, Cesare "CJ" Bonventre, and Louis "Louie Gaeta" Giongetti—and the rest became pictorial history. The tabloids captured a photograph of the late Mr. Galante sprawled in his own blood in the garden at Joe & Mary's, cigar firmly clenched between his teeth.

Considerably irritated at losing the Carmine Galante project after so much investment of his professional time, Mad Dog did a few robberies and freelance killings until he was arrested by an FBI task force in Rochester in early 1982; they collared him for an alleged bank job. The feds were confident they could send Mad Dog out of the state, namely to the U.S. penitentiary in Marion, Illinois, where John Gotti was incarcerated until shortly before his death in 2002.

Mad Dog credited an excellent pair of lawyers—recruited by his friend Ramsey Clark, naturally—for getting him acquitted on the Rochester bank robbery charge. But he would not so easily escape state prosecution.

The state hauled Mad Dog back into court for several homicides and assorted other violent crimes, culminating in a long murder trial in 1982, which ended in conviction and his being sentenced to eighty-seven years and six months, plus ninety-nine months to life.

But this is not the end of my story. There's an epilogue.

What goes around comes around. Every cop subscribes to this philosophy. Which is relevant here because of an Irish cop I'll call Danny.

When I was working the Bushwick precinct, Danny was assigned to the 9th in the East Village, my own first assignment in 1968–69. We used to drink together in Murphy's Bar in Greenpoint, the very Brooklyn neighborhood where we were both raised.

Danny was a big, gentle guy who shouldn't have been drinking; he couldn't handle it. Neither could I. I quit the drinking life on New Year's Day 1980. Danny didn't.

Some years later, while he and his sergeant were bouncing in bars in Manhattan on St. Patrick's Day, Danny fell into an alcoholic blackout and shot the sergeant to death.

Danny had no recollection of the shooting and put up no defense at his trial for second-degree murder. He was convicted and sentenced to fifteen years to life in prison.

State prison is a hard road for a police officer. Normally, a cop inmate is kept segregated from the general population. But Danny chose not to be confined to his cell for twenty-three hours a day. Instead, he went into general population and was soon confronted in the yard by a wiseguy of the Genovese persuasion, whose ass he proceeded to kick.

This earned Danny a mob contract on his life, whereupon the prison authorities transferred him immediately to another maximum-security facility—where, as fate would have it, he met Joseph "Mad Dog" Sullivan.

Mad Dog approached Danny in the yard to tell him that he'd heard how he kicked the wiseguy's ass, and to tell Danny that he heartily approved. If the story he'd heard was true,

Danny was further told, then he could take his place on Mad Dog's personal work gang.

To go it alone in prison is to invite rape or death. Danny quickly confirmed the story.

Danny survived, unmolested. Actually, he was freed after eight years in prison when his conviction was overturned because of errors at trial. Instead of another trial, he was allowed to take a guilty plea in return for time served.

What motivated Mad Dog to save Danny's life? Was it their shared Irish heritage? Or the fact that Mad Dog's father was, of all things, a first-grade detective with Brooklyn's 78th Precinct in Park Slope until his early death by natural causes in the 1950s? Or was it Mad Dog's disdain for the Genovese family, which had turned a deaf ear to his appeals for help when the FBI task force was closing in on him back in Rochester?

Who knows.

One more thing, which is a grievance I have with Gail Sullivan.

In her book, she wrote that many law-abiding citizens, including an investigator for ex-Mayor Rudy Giuliani, describe Mad Dog as "one of the most respected inmates" in the New York State system. That may be so, and I accept that Mad Dog has done many good deeds while behind bars upstate; the rescue of my old pal Danny, for one, was a corporal work of mercy, as Roman Catholics say.

But just how is it that while Mad Dog lives so vividly in my memory, our fateful meeting rates nary a line in his autobiography?

Makes you feel like a blind date, a one-night stand, you know?

TRUE CONFESSIONS

BY DENNIS HAWKINS

Brooklyn Heights

Have you ever heard a retired cop or prosecutor tell a war story, or write a memoir, where he wasn't the hero? I haven't and I'm tired of listening to all the air-bags blather on for fun and profit.

So I'll tell you a tale of failure, with all the hope that confession is good for the soul. Bless me Father for I have sinned:

There was a time before I became a legend in my own mind for my piece of the action in the 77th Precinct investigation, the Howard Beach case, the capture of "Gaspipe" Casso, the first death penalty case in Brooklyn, the Colombo wars—yadda, yadda, yadda.

Back in spring of 1988 I was a green prosecutor, and I failed miserably during a trial called *The People of the State of New York v. Gilbert Ortiz*, this being the case of an alleged 77th Precinct grass-eater, which is a term of art in the police profession meaning a cop of ordinary corruption as opposed to a meat-eating hog.

And Gil, let me apologize now for telling this sad tale.

It's the mid 1980s in New York City. Mayor Ed "How'm I doing?" Koch appoints Ben Ward as the city's thirty-fourth police commissioner in early '84. According to *Jet* magazine, *"Ward oversaw the nation's largest police department during the rise of the crack cocaine epidemic and a sharp increase in crime and murder."*

What an understatement. The way I remember it, the city was a sewer, the precincts in the poorest neighborhoods were free-fire zones, and no one gave a shit about crime in the ghetto because the social scientists absolved us from effective law enforcement by telling us that the only way to cure crime was to remedy the root cause—poverty. Don't hold your breath.

Imagine for a moment being a cop in one of the precincts in the heart of Brooklyn during those times—the 75th in East New York, the 73rd in Brownsville, the 77th in Crown Heights. Brian O'Regan, who committed suicide rather than surrender at the end of the 77th Precinct investigation, wrote in the note he left behind, "The precinct is hell." And it was hell, in Brian's opinion, because no one really cared what happened in the ghetto. I think he was correct.

If the 77th Precinct was indeed hell, the lords of hell were two sets of partners, so far as I know from evidence uncovered: William Gallagher and Brian O'Regan, and Henry Winter and Anthony Magno. They were the veterans, the leaders—except for O'Regan, the ultimate follower—and they set the standard for corruption in the precinct. It was a very low standard, nickel-and-dime compared to the thieves of Enron and thieves of Baghdad yet to be discovered in Iraq.

Petty the officers were, but so very corrosive to the oath they took to uphold the law. They robbed from the drug dealers, from the dead, from the violated. As a fireman of my acquaintance once said, they would steal a hot stove with both hands.

Into this hell comes Gilbert Ortiz, a twenty-two-year-old when he was arrested in 1986, a police officer since only two years before that. You didn't stand a chance, Gil. No one in the police department was looking out for you. And you became my target because you were there—in the wrong place at the wrong time.

As I think of you now, I think of the kid who shows up at a pickup softball game and is the last one chosen for the team. He's stuck in right field. Maybe nobody will hit the ball to him. Unfortunately for you, Gil, this was the corruption team of the precinct from hell and because you're stuck in right field you get tagged with the loss.

But the tale I tell reveals itself not at a game, but at trial. So let us proceed.

In the spring of 1988, I took the short subway ride from the Office of the Special State Prosecutor at 2 Rector Street in lower Manhattan to the Brooklyn Supreme Court at 360 Adams Street, a trip I had made many times, though never before to try a felony case. Exiting the train in Brooklyn, I walked through the large, sterile plaza dominated by the State Supreme Court, built in the 1950s and designed by the same architects who created the Empire State Building. I drew no inspiration from the long, squat structure that would house the case of *People v. Ortiz* for the next week or so. While the Empire State Building raises the spirits with its soaring reach to the skies, this functional mausoleum of a court flattens all hope. It was here that defendants saw their last glimpse of a tired-out urban downtown before going upstate for their incarceration. And it was here that the hopes of prosecutors, who could not make their cases, were dashed.

As I walked up the courthouse steps, I remembered that it was also here, eighteen months earlier, that Charles Joseph Hynes, the New York State special prosecutor for the city criminal justice system, scheduled the arraignment of the "dirty dozen" cops from the 77th Precinct in Brooklyn.

It was a most extraordinary arraignment in which Joe Hynes, after addressing the judge in a stately manner—"May it please the Court"—made an elegant opening speech about the entire investigation and the reason we the prosecutors, the twelve defendants, their defense attorneys, and a full house of journalists were in court that day.

Joe had a commanding presence in the courtroom, and neither the judge nor defense attorneys objected during his speech. He talked about the scope of the corruption that led to the arrest of defendants who had betrayed their oaths as police officers. When he finished, he sat, leaving the "technicalities" of the arraignment to me and my colleagues, who had presented the cases to a grand jury for the return of indictments.

One by one we stood to present the charges, only to have the reading of them waived by defense counsels. One by one the defendants pled not guilty and we made bail arguments. Return dates and a schedule for motions and discovery were set.

I recall nothing from that day of police officer Gil Ortiz, charged with five counts that ranged from conspiracy in the fourth degree, an E felony, all the way down to a trespassing violation. Perhaps I should have paid more attention, because this was the case I would ultimately try. But my thoughts were on the charges against Officer William Gallagher, charged with eighty-six counts, ranging from criminal sale of a controlled substance, an A-II felony, down to the A misdemeanor of official misconduct. Gallagher's was the case I had hoped to try—the first and most important case of the lot.

I also wondered, *Where the hell is Gallagher's partner, Brian O'Regan?* He had been scheduled to surrender with the rest, but had not reported to Internal Affairs division headquarters that morning. Was he in Ireland? That was surely where I would have been if I were he.

But those arraignments were long ago. Since then, O'Regan killed himself rather than surrender; Gallagher and three others pled guilty before trial; two other defendants were tried and convicted, two were acquitted after trial; and two others had indictments dismissed. Three defendants were left: Gil Ortiz, plus two others involved in the theft of precinct garbage cans—the bottom of the barrel, so to speak.

Today was my turn in that barrel, as prosecutor in *People v. Ortiz*. I was not looking forward to the trial, given that the evidence was a single taped conversation between Ortiz and Henry Winter, one of two dirty cops who had flipped at the beginning of the four-month investigation. Winter was possibly one of the most corrupt cops in the precinct, although he had denied it in an earlier trial, accusing Gallagher and O'Regan of being even more corrupt.

Ortiz was represented by Barry Agulnick, an experienced defense attorney who specialized in representing police officers. He was one of the defense lawyers in the high-profile Michael Stewart case back in 1985, resulting in the acquittal of all the transit police officers accused by the Manhattan district attorney of killing Stewart during his arrest for writing graffiti in the subways. I knew Barry because he had represented Gallagher and had negotiated a realistic plea agreement for his client. The evidence in that case was overwhelming, and Barry knew it; he obviously had a different read on the Ortiz case.

This trial would only be my fifth; my first two as second seat counsel had resulted in convictions, my next two as lead prosecutor the same. I was not cocky about my skills, but thought I made a nice appearance, spoke well, was organized, and had done the prep work needed. I also knew the central weakness of the case: Henry Winter versus a good-looking rookie cop, namely Gil Ortiz.

We assembled in a large courtroom on an upper floor of Kings County Supreme Court to select a jury on that beautiful spring morning. I still did not fully understand the science of jury selection, and to this day wonder if it isn't all just a crapshoot.

How do you tell in a few minutes if a jury prospect will be fair, if he or she will truly listen to the facts of your case and do the right thing? There are attorneys who wax poetic about their ability to identify a juror who will be good for the prosecution or good for the defense. There are old wives' tales about the predilections of accountants, social workers, and church ladies. There are jury consultants who will tell you that if a juror grows roses, it's a sure bet that person is patient and discerning. I didn't know then and I don't know now if I buy all that. What I did know is that I wanted smart people who could get along with their fellow jurors, make a group decision, and not hate my star witness—Henry Winter, a guy known to cops as a "rat."

I prepared the prospective jurors to the extent that I could during voir dire interviews. They would be hearing from a witness who committed many other crimes himself before finally being caught and offered a deal for his cooperation, I informed the prospects. I then asked them if they could listen carefully to the testimony of such a witness, if they could fairly assess the truthfulness of his testimony, and if they could reserve judgment until hearing all the evidence. Both Barry and I explored prejudices that might get in the way of their rendering a just verdict, which is another way of figuring out if they could buy into the theory of our respective cases.

Jury selection was uneventful, with a minimum of postur-

ing by either Barry or myself. Along with the judge, we ultimately believed we had a competent panel. For my part, I was
happy with the twelve jurors in the box because I thought I
had connected with a number of them, and that they considered me trustworthy. I'm sure Barry felt the same way.

After our jurors were told when to return for trial, Barry
approached me to say, "I've never seen a prosecutor do what
you did today."

My first thought was that Barry was trying to play head
games with me, even though that had not been my experience
with him in the past.

"What do you mean?" I asked him.

"When you asked some of the jurors whether they would
stick up for their views—even if all the other jurors disagreed—
you were asking a defense attorney's question. What are you
looking for, Dennis? A hung jury?"

If I were not olive-skinned, Barry would have seen
my blush. To any other attorney, I might have said, "Fuck
you."

But to Barry: "I just want strong, independent jurors."

And Barry's hunch was sound. I was indeed going for a
hung jury. One of my colleagues on an earlier case had been
stung with a not guilty verdict in ninety-six minutes flat. I was
not about to let that happen to me.

Childish? Absolutely. But unlike the paragons of prosecu-
torial virtue we see in fiction, or in self-congratulatory mem-
oirs, I had flaws and they were evident in this tactic. Certainly
to Barry.

At some level, I believed in the case, even though I knew
it was very weak. I had invested too much of my life in the
investigation to just walk away.

Ultimately, it was my faith in Henry Winter and the investigation that inspired me to proceed to trial. Perhaps that was a mistake. But you can be the judge.

I met Henry after he'd been "flipped" by Joe Hynes, when I talked my way into being part of the investigative team that would run him as a confidential informant for an extraordinary four months.

Having a mole inside a notoriously corrupt police precinct was an investigative attorney's dream. The role of investigative attorney—my job—is rarely portrayed by TV dramas that prefer to organize their shows law-and-order style: the cops investigate, the prosecutors bring police cases to trial. My job was and is the missing dimension in TV-Land. I actually ran the investigations I brought to trial.

True enough for the tube, most prosecutors "catch" cases brought to them by the police. Which is interesting, but nowhere near the excitement of building the case yourself. Investigative attorneys are thought to be wannabe cops. While there might be some truth to that, it's too simple a notion. A good investigative attorney is always thinking about how the evidence gathered can be used at trial. Unlike the cops, our work is not over when the arrest goes down.

And so, as an investigative attorney for the New York State Special Prosecutor's Office, I got to shape the investigation that would lead to the indictments and trials. Perhaps that is why I went astray in the 77th Precinct case. Chief John Guido, legendary head of the NYPD's Internal Affairs Division, used to say, "Don't fall in love with your investigation."

But I thought the investigation was so good. I thought the sum total of the evidence would overwhelm even the least culpable defendants.

* * *

Soon after Henry Winter and his partner, Anthony Magno, agreed to cooperate with my office and NYPD Internal Affairs, we sent them back into the sewer of the 77th Precinct to catch more corrupt cops. As part of the investigative team of prosecutors and Internal Affairs detectives, I met with Henry and Tony at least once a week for the next four months, and almost every day listened to the hours of tapes they secretly recorded while on duty in the 77th.

I got to know them more through these tapes than from our personal meetings: Henry, the smooth talker, full of fun and credible to cops, crooks, and the community; Tony, a man of few words, direct, tough, and angry. Henry delivered the evidence right from the start, Tony dragged his heels. Henry understood he had to work off his time in jail, Tony was reluctant. In time, I realized that Henry was a natural undercover operative and investigator. He was inventive and helped create scenarios that captured other corrupt cops on tape.

I have often wondered since those heady days of the investigation whether we were too much like the scientists who go out into the field to make objective observations but "contaminate" the environment by our mere presence.

Did we make it too easy to be corrupt by providing a convenient way to dispose of illegally seized drugs and guns, though our undercover buy-back program?

And was it the flagrant, seemingly undetected corruption of Henry and Tony that inspired Gil Ortiz to spend too much time with them? Was it unreasonable for him to consider them the true leaders of the precinct?

When the investigation abruptly ended due to a leak that we never traced with certainty (though we had our suspicions), I would spend hours with Henry and Tony going over the tapes, refining the transcripts, getting a better understanding of the crimes. We were never buddy-boys, but I did respect their work.

And my respect for Henry increased when he agreed to testify in this one last trial, even though the police department had told him he would be terminated after it was over. Henry always held the hope that the department would let him and Tony stay on the job long enough to retire with a pension. Fat chance.

Henry could have walked away from the trial and not testified, and I could have subpoenaed him. But how would that have looked to the jury, and what kind of testimony would he have delivered? The time for threats had passed. Henry had been the star witness in three previous trials and I, for one, did not believe we should send him to jail for his failure this last time to live up to his agreement.

But it never came to that. When I called Henry to tell him about the trial date, he came in and got down to business. He told me that he was pissed that the department had decided to cut him loose.

I told him, "You know, Henry, we have no control over what the department does."

I started to remind him of our deal: Cooperate fully and he would never see the inside of a prison because we would make the extent of his cooperation known to the department. But he stopped me.

"I know what the deal is," Henry said. "I promised to see this through till the end and I'm keeping my word."

The "Thanks, Henry" that followed was difficult because I had learned that he had worn a wire against me and another prosecutor during preparation for an earlier trial in order to try and get us on the record making a better deal than the one we had actually made. We had restated our understanding of the deal and Henry thereby got no additional leverage. So it was hard to accept that the ultimate rat was doing the right thing. But that appeared to be the case.

With jury selection out of the way, I would have a chance to tell the panel just what the *People* planned to prove—a conspiracy involving Henry, the defendant, and another cop to "hit" a known drug location, steal the drugs and money, and divide the proceeds of the crime. I told the jury that they would hear the testimony of a corrupt cop who had agreed to cooperate, and that, most importantly, they would hear "with your own ears" the money being split after the hit—where no drugs were found. This was the core of my case.

Barry underscored the weakness of my position—the ambivalent taped conversation, called a "conspiracy" by the prosecutors, and the failure of the tape to demonstrate that his client had accepted any share of money at all.

No one wins a case during opening arguments. But the stage is set and the jury is given a road map of where it will be going. We all agree that the burden of proof is on the prosecutor to prove each and every element of the crime beyond a reasonable doubt—a heavy burden indeed.

After openings, I began with an Internal Affairs witness who could tell the jury that he met with Henry Winter on the day of the crime, provided him with a fresh tape, and put the appropriate "header" on it—identifying himself and Henry, as well as date, time, and place. Also that soon thereafter, he retrieved the tape from Henry, and that the money was taken from the location. He testified that he vouchered both tape and money and had brought the very same tape and money to court today to be introduced into evidence as *People's* exhibits.

Another police officer provided the basis for the introduction of evidence that Ortiz was on duty that day in the same sector where the hit occurred. I had a police witness introduce a map drawing of the location in question so that Henry could show where the defendant and he had been during the incident. All this testimony went smoothly and, I hoped, showed the jury the competence of our investigation. But as we used to say in those days, *Where's the beef?*

Henry was the beef—or sacrificial lamb, I should say, given my experience watching him cross-examined at previous trials. But Henry was no lamb. In fact, it was open season on rats who testified against those presumed to be innocent.

Henry and I had agreed that I would do an abbreviated direct examination of his past crimes and bad acts. Having seen Henry subjected to an all-day direct examination of his entire oeuvre of bad acts—dating back to when he worked in a Modell's sporting goods shop as a teenager and marked down the price of baseball gloves for his friends—I decided to spare him the double-dose of confessing first to me and then to Barry. No matter, Henry still faced days of withering cross-examination by defense counsel to show him for a liar, a cheat, and a thief beyond compare.

When Henry took the stand, I quickly established that he had been a crooked cop, that he'd stolen money and drugs, that he'd resold the drugs, protected some drug dealers and extorted others, that he was not beneath stealing from the dead, and, significantly, that he'd been caught and had made a deal with prosecutors to avoid jail. Barry did not raise any objections to this testimony. After all, I was doing his job—undermining the credibility of my own witness. The theory here is that it's better for the jury to hear it from the prosecutor, who is hiding nothing, than for the defense counsel to expose a cover-up by the prosecution.

I wanted to get as quickly as I could to the facts of the case—what Henry had done on the day of the crime, and what the defendant had said and done. And this is where I ran into trouble. Barry had an objection to every question I asked. And while some were legitimate, I thought others were meant merely to disrupt the flow of the testimony. Each time he made an objection, he asked for a sidebar conversation up at the bench with the judge outside of the jury's hearing.

But soon our sidebars became so loud and heated that the judge moved us to the corridor. I became more and more frustrated as the frequency of the objections and sidebars grew. Barry was clearly setting the pace and controlling the courtroom and preventing me from presenting my case in a coherent manner. We seemed to fall into a pattern of me asking a question, then Barry making an objection and calling for a sidebar. After the pattern has been set, Barry would just make the objection, get out of his seat, and walk toward the corridor for his sidebar, followed by the judge.

Too much, I thought. *This has got to stop.* The next time the migration began and Barry was out the door and the judge was approaching the door, I held my ground behind the prosecutor's table, looked at the jury, and said in loud voice, "Who's running this courtroom anyway?"

Big mistake. Not only did I insult the judge, who let me know that she would not tolerate that kind of behavior, but I undermined her authority in front of the jury. We all know that jurors tend to have great respect for the judge and look to them as the fount of justice in the courtroom. I lost my temper, squandered some of the dignity of the prosecutor's position, and may have jeopardized my case. I had acted unprofessionally. Nonetheless, while Barry continued to make objections, the processions to sidebar talks decreased significantly and I proceeded with my direct examination.

Henry testified about his tour of duty the day of the crime, his conversation with the defendant about hitting a drug location and splitting what was recovered, and that he had captured the conversation on tape. He testified that he had given the tape to IAD, initialed it, and had subsequently listened to the tape in order to confirm it as a full and accurate representation of the conversation that he'd had with the defendant. I asked him if the tape that had been introduced into evidence earlier was the same tape that he had made and listened to and he answered affirmatively.

"May I play the tape for the jury, your honor?"

"Yes, Mr. Hawkins."

This was supposed to be the evidence that would prove beyond a reasonable doubt that the defendant entered into conspiracy with Henry to possess and sell the "found" drugs. Of course, it was Henry who would steal the drugs, if any were found, and "sell" them to us in order to receive money to split with his coconspirators. We had devised this plan in order to keep other cops in the precinct from selling it to their sources and putting the drugs back on the street. It was an excellent investigative move, but during this type of trial it was not always clear if jurors bought into our deception or even thought it was fair play.

Not really a problem in this case because no drugs were found, only money.

Once the jury, judge, attorneys, and defendant put on their earphones, they heard Henry speaking, laying out a plan to hit a drug location, suggesting that if he found drugs he knew where to sell them and that he would share the proceeds. It was clear that the defendant was present but not so clear that he agreed with Henry, an essential element of the conspiracy charge. Ortiz was told that he should cover the back exit of the apartment building to prevent drug dealers from escaping—the usual role for a junior police officer—and that Henry would go into the apartment and conduct the search for drugs and money.

Ortiz seemed to agree to cover the back exit, which in legal terms is an overt act in furtherance of a conspiracy. "Seemed" is the operative word. No clear agreement, no conspiracy. I knew I was on shaky ground with my agreement, but I thought that the conclusion of the tape could put me over the top and beyond reasonable doubt.

Ten minutes of tape went by as judge, jurors, and counsel heard Henry tromp around the empty apartment searching for drugs and money—and commenting from time to time about what a "shit-hole" the place was. Then we heard Henry discover some cash, with his comment on the find: "Not much, but better than nothing."

The tape concluded with Henry apparently meeting the defendant outside the location and reporting better-than-nothing. In a clear voice, Henry counted out Ortiz's share: "One, two, three, four, five, six, seven—buy yourself a beer." Henry laughed in his good-natured way. And we heard the rustle of the bills as they were being counted out. This constituting my "gotcha" moment.

Unfortunately, there was no taped response from the defendant. Dead silence.

I looked at the jury panel. Some jurors looked back at me with expressions that said, *Is that all there is?* So I switched off the tape, turned to Henry on the witness stand, and asked him to fill in the blanks with specifics.

"What, if anything, did you find at the location?"

"I found twenty-one dollars."

"And what did you do with that money?"

"I gave the defendant seven dollars and kept fourteen to divide between my partner and myself."

"And what did you do with your share?"

"I turned it in to IAD at the end of my tour."

"And is this seven dollars, previously marked as *People's Exhibit Three*, the money that you gave to IAD?"

"Yes."

"How are you able to identify it?"

"I put my initials on the money."

"Your honor, I ask that People's Exhibit Three be moved into evidence."

The judge said to Barry, "Any objections, Mr. Agulnick?"

"No, your honor."

I continued questioning Henry.

"Now, could you describe what it is that you are doing at the conclusion of the tape with respect to the remaining money?"

"I'm counting out seven dollars to give to the defendant."

"And did you in fact give that money to the defendant?"

"Yes, I did."

"That concludes the *People's* questions for this witness, your honor."

I glanced at the jury and once again got the feeling that some were asking, once again, *Is that all there is?* Unfortunately, yes. That's the case against Gil Ortiz. You either believe Henry or you don't. You have a tape that is, at best, circumstantial evidence. Or you have no real evidence at all.

For me it was easy to believe Henry. For months he had trolled for evidence of corruption in the 77th Precinct and I'd never caught him in a lie. Most of his allegations were backed up by taped evidence—including assertions of corruption by Gallagher, Rathbun, and Spivey.

But as I look back now some twenty years after the events, I ask myself whether we should have charged the kid—a twenty-two-year-old who, at the time, was younger than my youngest son. I don't know the answer, but I do know that I think about it more than any of the so-called successes of my career.

I had done my job and presented the evidence I had; now it was Barry's turn. And did he ever do his job. He flayed Henry over the course of the next two days and made him admit that he was a liar, a thief, a man of no conscience, and someone who would do anything to avoid prison. To this last point I objected.

There was little I could do to protect Henry. He knew it and I knew it. He was a corrupt cop by his own admission. From time to time, I would object: "Argumentative, your honor," or, "Assuming a fact not in evidence." But these were bullshit objections, meant to give Henry brief respite from the onslaught of Barry's cross-examination.

After a particularly grueling series of questions from Barry, I saw that Henry needed a real break; he was turning bright red with the embarrassment of his position. So I objected by employing Barry's tactic: I asked for a sidebar.

As Barry and the judge moved toward the corridor, I collected some papers I thought I might need for the argument and saw Henry look at the jury, shrug his shoulders, and wiggle his ears. Some jurors laughed. No one seemed to notice and I kept it to myself. Here was Henry trying to reach out to the jury and portray himself as a human being. I probably should have informed the judge so that she could admonish him about inappropriate communication and instruct jurors that they were to disregard it as a prejudicial attempt. But I said nothing, deciding that if that's what it might take for Henry to reestablish his humanity, so be it.

At lunch that day, after a recess in the cross-examination, I bought sandwiches for Henry and me and we went to the Promenade overlooking New York Harbor. We couldn't talk about his testimony because that's against the rules, and at this point in our careers we didn't want to break them.

Henry was a wreck. He'd forgotten how difficult cross could be. I told him that he was doing fine and that he was doing the right thing. He was close to tears and I had to use all my professional skills to keep from joining him. I thought about the quiet, dark boxes of the confessional, where I secretly told my sins to a priest, who would absolve me by prescribing a simple penance of Hail Marys and Our Fathers. How perfect those confessions are—expiation without too much pain. God love the Catholic Church. But a public confession on the witness stand is something quite different, namely a public humiliation.

Barry ended his cross when it was clear to all that neither Henry nor my case had any credibility whatever. All that was left were closing arguments.

Barry led by declaring what any defense attorney would under the circumstances: Henry was a liar, a thief, and a cheat all of his life, and his "performance" in this trial was payment for his do-not-go-to-jail ticket. He called my evidence worthless, and maintained that his client was a good and honest young cop who happened to be in the wrong place at the wrong time.

All that was left was for me to make a compelling closing argument and pull the conviction rabbit out of the hat. I spun the usual prosecution bullshit: If the *People* wanted to make up a story to frame the defendant, we would have done a much better job of it, and Henry had nothing to gain from accusing the defendant.

"What did he do?" I asked. "Take his own money into the drug spot and then pretend to count it out for the defendant's share?" I worried that some jurors might be thinking exactly that.

The judge gave instructions to the jury and sent them out to deliberate, just before dinnertime. Which I considered a nice break for me: With an extra hour or so to eat before deliberating, the jurors just might be kept overnight.

The judge told Barry and me to be available in case of an early verdict. As the age of cell phones had not yet dawned, we gave beeper numbers to the clerk. I decided to have a bite at a local Irish pub rather than go back to the office. Some colleagues from the Special Prosecutor's Office joined me. Foregoing food, we had a beer or two.

As time went by, I grew convinced that I had the jurors struggling with the evidence. I thought I must have done something right and ordered another beer, convinced that the jury would retire for the night without rendering a decision.

At about 10 o'clock, my beeper went off and I called the court—expecting to be sent home for the night. But no, there was a verdict.

There goes my hung jury, I thought. I returned to the courthouse hoping for a miracle. I ran into Barry in the corridor and he said that I tried a good case, given what I had to work with.

I replied, "You kicked my ass, Barry."

The jury returned to its place in the courtroom, with nobody giving a sign I could detect of what their decision was. The judge asked the foreperson if a verdict had been reached and she said, "We have, your honor," and passed the verdict sheet to a clerk who gave it to the judge. I noticed no extra court officers in the room—a telltale sign of a guilty verdict.

The judge read the verdict sheet and returned it to the clerk, who returned it to the foreperson. My heart raced as it always did right before a verdict, and I listened as the judge asked the foreperson, "On the first count of the indictment, how do you find?"

"Not guilty, your honor."

Which was the same response to the remaining counts. And so, the last trial in the 77th Precinct investigation ended.

The judge thanked the jurors for their service and I asked if I could speak with them—customary practice for attorneys who want to know how jurors analyzed the trial. I moved to the jury box, from which most good citizens had fled but a few remained. I approached an attractive young woman whom I thought had listened with close attention during my closing arguments.

Before I could ask a question, she said to me, with some hesitation, "We tried, Mr. Hawkins, but there really wasn't evidence." I thanked her for at least considering the facts.

Another juror said, "We just could not believe Winter. He is so bad." A few others offered their thoughts and I thanked them all before leaving.

Barry and his client were talking in the corridor as I headed for the elevators, which even during the day took forever to arrive. Normally, I would walk down the stairs to avoid running into the defendant, but tonight I waited, thinking the stairways might be locked due to lateness of the hour.

When the elevator finally came, I entered, alone. As the doors closed, there stood Barry and his client, taking a pause from their conversation. The defendant grinned. I pointed my finger at him and said, "Get ya next time."

Nice work, Dennis. Very professional, especially since the system worked exactly the way it's supposed to: I brought a case I could not prove beyond reasonable doubt and the jury found the defendant not guilty.

There I was, playing the *Dirty Harry* version of a prosecutor and making threats to a kid who smiled his awkward smile because he was relieved and didn't know how to relate to the guy who just tried to send him off to jail.

It may not have been the last time I acted like an asshole, but it's the time I remember best.

The next day, Barry called to ask what the district attorney's office planned to do about the other indictments. I told him that we would have to review the situation. (We ultimately dismissed those indictments and referred the cases to the Police Department for administrative hearings. I was told that Gil resigned before those trials.)

"And Dennis," Barry said, "you really shouldn't have said that to my client."

"I know, Barry, I know. Would you please tell him I'm sorry?"

Ah yes, confession is good for the soul. As is an appropriate apology. But some confessions do not absolve the guilt.

Gallagher's partner wrote page after page of confession in the hours before he killed himself. Henry Winter confessed his sins three times over while sitting in the witness box. Some years later, he hanged himself at his home in Valley Stream, Long Island.

Today, I still carry their confessions with me, along with my own smaller sins, but sins nonetheless.

And I remember what Joe Hynes said to the *New York Times* some years ago on the subject of investigating cops: "[It] is the saddest job I've ever had. It destroys lives. If you enjoy it, you're sick. If it gets to you to the point where you have trouble sleeping at night, you ought to be out of it."

Thank God I'm out of it.

THE BODY IN THE DOORWAY

BY PATRICIA MULCAHY

Fort Greene

I never saw the body. I found out that Vladimir the antiques dealer, a.k.a. Bobby from Russia, had been shot in the head at point-blank range in the doorway of his shop at Vanderbilt and DeKalb because the drums were talking. This is how it went in Fort Greene, Brooklyn, in the mid-1990s.

Friends called friends to alert them to the fact that there'd been another mugging in Fort Greene Park, or gunshots heard from an unknown source on Adelphi at 3 a.m. A mention of Fort Greene on the news usually meant that another four-year-old had been shot tragically in drug-related violence in the Walt Whitman Houses. Myrtle Avenue was referred to as "Murder Avenue" by all and sundry. The local citizenry protected each other with all-points alerts about crime in an area labeled up-and-coming, yet still on its way to that elusive goal, whatever it meant to anyone who wasn't a real estate broker.

Burnt out on tourists, nonstop street spectacle, and rising prices in Greenwich Village, I'd moved to Brooklyn in 1990, thrilled by the beautiful architecture, the wide, tree-lined streets, and the warm and generous spirit of the people who lived here. Hell, I got a free dessert the week I moved in. Christine, a Caribbean woman who ran a bakery at the corner of Carlton and DeKalb, told me, "Watch out going by the park after dark," as she welcomed me with a delicious rum pudding. No one had given me free anything in the twelve years I'd lived in Manhattan. This was Fort Greene in a nutshell: *Welcome, and watch your back.*

Taxi drivers told me I was crazy to live in a neighborhood like this. Unspoken was the fact that I was white and the area was predominantly African American. Perhaps I was naïve, but I didn't worry. In the nine years I'd lived on Jones Street between West 4th and Bleecker, I'd been mugged in broad daylight in the lobby, burglarized by a guy who called on the phone a week later to let me know he could come back anytime he wanted, and terrorized by a drug-and-booze-addled jazz musician neighbor whose friends I passed shooting up in the hallway on my way to work. How much worse could it be in Brooklyn?

It was tough in New York then, and things could happen anywhere: This was the common wisdom passed from one nervous neighbor to another. Watching your back was a way of living, the price of being in the big city, with all it had to offer. The worst thing that happened to me in Fort Greene was being labeled "white meat" by a bunch of teenaged boys eager to look tough for their cohorts. But if I stayed out late I hoped and prayed I would find a parking spot close to my apartment. Muggers exercised equal opportunity in their choice of targets.

In truth, I learned that for all its tough-talk swagger and reputation, Brooklyn had a big, warm heart. Living in Fort Greene and Clinton Hill felt like being in a village where everyone knows your name and people stop on the street to exchange pleasantries along with the latest news on tire slashings. We even had a plant thief on Washington Avenue who was fencing window boxes somewhere in South Brooklyn. My next-door neighbor, a divorcée with a BMW, a very active social life, and no visible means of support, left town one day and never came back, taking with her a baby who'd arrived under mysterious circumstances. Later, I found out that she had tried to sell the child back to the doctor who delivered her. There was never a dull moment.

Which brings us back to Bobby, shot dead in the doorway of an emporium crammed to the rafters with lovely chests of drawers and old Tiffany-style lamps and antique dining tables. The tall, rangy Russian, who was in fact from the Republic of Georgia and usually wore a broad-brimmed leather hat, à la Crocodile Dundee, was one of the many "gentlemen friends" who'd been seen coming and going to the house next to ours. I doubted that he was the one who threw a rock through the window at 6 a.m., necessitating a visit from a patrolman, or the one who set the fire in the foyer. But who knew?

At the time of the murder, rumors flew up and down the streets of Fort Greene and Clinton Hill: Bobby had been shot by his former brother-in-law, with whom he'd been in business until recently; it was someone from the Russian mob in Brighton Beach, from whom he'd borrowed money; it was the husband of one of his paramours—my next-door neighbor was just one of many.

Tillie Asnis, the landlady, had discovered the body in the doorway of the store. I met her when she was selling furniture, emptying the place for a new tenant. As I recall, she said little about the murder itself that day, and instead gossiped about the Russian's way with the local ladies. That, too, was typical of the neighborhood then: Once a crime had been broadcast on the local grapevine, it was rarely discussed further. Better to keep a lid on things.

A frizzy-haired woman of Russian Jewish ancestry who'd moved to Brooklyn from the Bronx, Tillie lived above the shop with her children and grandchildren. A two-pack-a-day smoker, she reminded me of the characters on *The Honey-mooners*, with her husky voice and no-nonsense demeanor. After running a dry cleaning store on the premises with her late husband for many years, she'd let the space to her son-in-law for a bike shop and a locksmith's business before leasing it to Vladimir. Given his untimely departure, she was back to square one. Life went on, as did the need to pay the bills.

Though horrified by the manner in which the store had been vacated, I asked Tillie about the rent on the space after buying two chairs for fifteen dollars. At the time, I was a book publisher with no experience running restaurants, though I'd worked as a waitress in a country club, a truck stop, an ice-cream parlor, and an Italian restaurant in high school and college. The oldest in an Irish Catholic family with six children, I was as chronically overscheduled as the West Indian characters in the old *Saturday Night Live* skits.

In an effort to meet people in my new neighborhood, I'd volunteered as a writer and editor for a local quarterly called *The Hill*. A look at back issues alerted me to the previous existence of an espresso place in an old carriage house on Waverly Avenue run by students at Pratt, an art school situated in the neighborhood. What a brilliant idea for a shop in an area full of graphic and fashion designers, architects, and other people who worked at home and had no place to hang out other than the local Greek diners. And the corner of Vanderbilt and DeKalb was just three blocks from the Pratt campus. Didn't art students and their teachers need cappuccino to fuel their creative efforts?

Though I loved working with writers, I was becoming increasingly disenchanted with corporate publishing, which had its own version of sword-and-knife play. In addition, I had come to relish my involvement in the Fort Greene community, and wanted to make a contribution to a place I felt had a bright future in so many ways, with its diverse population, its proximity to Manhattan, and its history-filled beauty. And if I didn't take the space, it might become yet another real estate office, of which we had a plethora already.

I put my nest egg where my heart was: Hands shaking, I wrote Tillie Asnis a check for a security deposit and set out to convert an old antiques store into a cozy neighborhood café named in her honor. While I was out of town on a publishing trip, the Jamaican contractor and his Trinidadian crew performed a ceremony involving white rum and chicken feathers to purge the space of any bad spirits left over from the murder of the previous tenant. Despite the Caribbean version of an exorcism, predictions of failure were as common as rain in April. Word on the street was that no one in this neighborhood would pay $1.50 for a cup of coffee when they could buy it across the street at the diner for sixty cents. At the time, DeKalb Avenue had just one restaurant, the beloved Cino's, a red-sauce fixture since the 1950s, and Starbucks was just beginning its retail march from sea to shining sea.

Fast-forward to the new century. I'd left publishing for freelance life. We'll move right through the years of light foot traffic, employee theft and subterfuge, and near-bankruptcy at the store. Nothing I'd done in my life had elicited such an honestly enthusiastic and truly grateful response: Area residents stopped me on the corner, in line at the grocery store, and in the post office to tell me how much they loved my shop. Even in Manhattan, people I'd never met called across subway cars, "Hello, Tillie!" By the time we celebrated our tenth year in business in 2007, Tillie's was considered a neighborhood institution, which made me feel both proud and definitely older.

Though friends and family members saw me as a Pollyanna when I opened the store, the survival of my risky venture validated my view of the neighborhood as a place filled with genuine potential, despite its dicey reputation. I wasn't getting rich, but nor was I spending my days listening to my boss cavil about so-called "big books."

By then, many more restaurants and coffee joints had opened not just on DeKalb, but all over the area, and real estate prices in Fort Greene had increased by such leaps and bounds that the *New York Times* real estate section could barely keep up. In 2006, a photo of the side of Tillie's illustrated an article in the *New York Times* magazine about the death of bohemia and the invasion of the stroller brigade. How far we'd come from the days of Bobby the Russian's sad demise.

Fears of rapid change—of the Manhattanization of Brooklyn by condo and office tower—now fuel the local rumor mill. Friends call friends to discuss not the latest shooting, but the sale prices of houses and coop apartments, and whether or not the area will change irrevocably for the worse when the Atlantic Yards development is built. After years of peace and quiet, there's been a recent blip upward in the local crime rate, as the "have-nots" eye this newly fertile hunting ground of "haves." Still, the neighborhood remains positively bucolic in comparison to the bad old days, which some longtime residents refer to with a sense of rueful regret. Though no one condoned burglary or car theft, there was a sense then that we were in it together, battling for a better future. Now that it has arrived, we aren't all sure we like the way it looks. Fairy tales don't start with bodies sprawled in doorways.

References to the Borough of Kings now connote not working-class pride or even street style, but a certain kind of city life that is artistically astute, relatively well-off, politically correct, and, yes, self-satisfied. For a taste of the old ways, you have to go further into what friends call "deepest Brooklyn," where even in an era of drastically reduced crime all over the metropolis, there are still bodies on the ground, almost all dark-skinned.

At the funeral of one of our first customers, Frank Giaco, who sat in front each morning sipping coffee and smoking a smelly cigar, I nearly lost it when I saw a Tillie's card in his coffin: *Buy ten, get one free.* In the best Brooklyn tradition, we hang on.

PART III

DEATH STEP

In which players who are not faint of heart assemble atop a structure of any sort—a fence, low building, rock, etc. One by one, they step forward to the edge and close their eyes while those behind give a sudden shove. As the game continues by round, the ultimate winner is the one player no longer afraid to take a blind leap.

SNAPSHOTS

BY TIM McLOUGHLIN

Kings County Supreme Court

I have worked in the New York City courts for more than twenty years. All of that time in Brooklyn. All but one year in Criminal Court or the Criminal Term of Supreme Court.

My coworkers and I have borne witness to a generational slice-of-life of the criminal underclass. One of the things we have learned is that siphoning the antisocial actions of any individual through the filter of a government bureaucracy—however well-intentioned—turns even the most evil behavior into mundane drama.

Most of the defendants I've encountered are life's losers: lost souls who, through bad choices, bad company, or just bad luck, are destined to spend their unhappy lives in courthouses, social service offices, rehab facilities, homeless shelters, and Rikers Island—in such an overlapping, dizzying whirl that I'm certain they often can't remember which building they're in on a given day, or why.

Then there are the bad guys: predators whose casual cruelty is too often mistaken for cool in their communities and emulated by kids a few years younger. But their stories, even the worst of them, are drained of passion in the halls of justice. The antiseptic nature of ritual proceedings will inevitably do that. Think of weddings, graduations, religious services, or oaths of office. Even being inducted into the Mafia is probably boring.

But what still gets to me are the snapshots—sucker-punches, facial expressions, snippets of conversation. The snapshots will catch you off guard. Sometimes they will shock and enrage you. Sometimes the snapshots will break your heart.

It can be the look on a mother's face when her son is denied bail, or on a father's face when his daughter's rapist is released on a technicality. It can be the tense moment an innocent man spends in front of the bench pleading guilty to a crime he did not commit, knowing that he cannot roll the dice in hope of an acquittal because of his past record.

There are the elevator stories—complete novels played out in thirty or forty seconds while traveling from courtroom to lobby and back. I've made copious notes on them in the tiny spiral-bound journals I've always kept tucked in my jacket pockets. As I flip through them now some are meaningless, the memories lost. Others are so vivid I don't need the prompt. These are the earliest and latest entries.

My fourth day of work:

Still unsure where most courtrooms and offices are, riding to the lobby to meet the kid who is delivering lunch for a deliberating jury. There is one other occupant, a young woman in a business suit with an attaché case. The elevator stops and she greets another young woman who steps in, similarly dressed.

"Hey, how are you?"

"Great! I just got a rape and kidnapping knocked down to unlawful imprisonment."

"You're kidding."

"Nope. Thank God I had a brand-new A.D.A. who didn't know his ass from a hole in the ground. My guy was

guilty as sin. No way I thought he was walking out of that room."

The elevator doors open. They give each other a high-five and walk off in different directions.

Last month:

Riding down to get a cup of coffee. Two women and a toddler on the elevator with me. The women stand silently and the toddler cries. One of the women looks down suddenly and screams, "Shut up! Shut the fuck up!"

The little boy looks like he's been struck open-handed, and is immediately quiet.

"He's just hungry," the other woman says.

"I know," the first woman says. She looks down at the child. "We gonna go get dollar pizza," she says to him. He is looking at the elevator floor.

After several seconds of silence, the first woman says, "I pray Jesus, Jesus, Jesus, Jesus, Jesus; pray that lady can't identify him."

"Thought he said he wasn't there," the second woman says.

"He wasn't," the first woman replies. "Fuckin' cops lie. Besides," she adds as the doors open, "he say it was dark and she old."

Both women laugh as they walk away.

I am reminded of my first few years on this job when I worked in uniform, searching members of the public as they entered the building. I was shocked at the number of young women with infants, and remarked about it one day to an old-timer.

"Twenty years from now," he said, taking a slow drag on his cigarette, "I'll be long gone and you'll be searching those kids."

He retired seven years ago, and died a year later, and those infants are in their early twenties now. The ones that haven't already been killed are coming through my doors, and the only thing that feels different is that you can't smoke in the building anymore.

In March 2006, two high-profile cases were heard on the same day. One was the arraignment of Darryl Littlejohn, a nightclub bouncer accused of the torture and murder of a young woman named Imette St. Guillen, who had been drinking at the bar where he worked. That case had dominated the tabloid headlines and local news shows for weeks following her death. The other was the trial of two men, Troy Hendrix and Kayson Pearson, for the rape, torture, and murder of another young woman, Romona Moore.

Although Ms. Moore's murder occurred almost three years before Ms. St. Guillen's, it had only recently become famous. During their trial, her killers attempted to escape from the courtroom, using plastic knives to stab one of the defense attorneys and making a grab for a court officer's gun. They were unsuccessful, but their efforts gave Romona Moore something that being abducted, raped, and murdered hadn't provided: attention.

Though Romona Moore and Imette St. Guillen shared tragically short lives and sickening deaths, their backgrounds were quite different.

Imette St. Guillen was American-born, from Boston, living on Manhattan's west side and attending graduate school.

Romona Moore was black, poor, and an immigrant. She

was East Flatbush by way of Guyana, rather than Williamsburg by way of a trust fund, so even her Brooklyn pedigree was not newsworthy. There had been some notice granted due to her family's grassroots campaign to locate her while she was missing. But as news items go, the discovery of her dead body was just a blip on the radar.

On the day of Darryl Littlejohn's arraignment in one part of the courthouse, a jury in another part returned a guilty verdict in the Romona Moore case, convicting the murderers Troy Hendrix and Kayson Pearson.

I was standing in front of the building, waiting to meet a friend for lunch, when Romona Moore's mother, Elle Carmichael, stepped outside with a few family members and friends. Dozens of reporters and cameramen surrounded her, calling out questions and requests for comments.

Ms. Carmichael composed herself, then spoke. She talked about her relief that the verdict had been what it was, and about her anger and frustration with the police department and the media. She sounded angry and frustrated; she sounded tired, although calm and resolved. She had been through an ordeal that few of us will ever have to endure, and finally, at the end of it, someone was paying attention to her daughter.

While she was speaking, the family of Imette St. Guillen emerged from the building. Almost every reporter immediately turned and walked away from Elle Carmichael. Her voice faltered a bit as she watched the parade of microphones and bobbing cameras moving away from her. Then she continued, concluding her statement to the four or five journalists who remained. When she finished, they too were gone in a flash, eager to catch up to their colleagues. Ms. Carmichael and her family were alone on the sidewalk.

I will never forget the look on Elle Carmichael's face when she felt that, finally, her daughter was getting the notice she deserved. And I will never forget the look on her face when that moment ended. Sometimes the snapshots will break your heart.

NO ROSES FOR BUBBEH

BY REED FARREL COLEMAN

Coney Island

I once wrote that there were certain comforts to middle age. That just surviving till forty imbues you with a sort of weary serenity. You don't sweat the small things quite so much. You've survived acne, probably marriage, maybe kids, and surely jobs you've hated. You realize that neither the loss of love nor your hair is apt to be fatal and that the kind of panic you felt every day in high school was now a distant, almost fond memory.

There is another aspect of middle age, however, that is of no comfort at all: things fade. As your eyes lose focus, so too does your memory. You can no longer recite the entire roster of the '69 Jets or recall which games Art Shamsky started in the '69 World Series. For that matter, you have trouble remembering kids on your block or who your seventh grade history teacher was. Until forty, your memory is like a vivid and complete jigsaw puzzle. About ten years later, pieces have gone missing. You scramble to replace them. Those replacements you do find are never quite as vivid. Others are lost forever.

Some things in a man's life must not fade: the feel of his newborn children in his arms, his first Little League home run, his first taste of a woman. There is pain too that must not be forgotten: the agonizingly slow death of his mother, for example, or the murder of a nameless stranger.

* * *

For most of my early life, criminals were just a colorful part of Coleman family lore. The gangster, murderer, and world-class sociopath, Dutch Schultz, né Arthur Flegenheimer—a maniac who made even a homicidal lunatic like Ben "Bugsy" Siegel seem judicious—had a wicked crush on my *bubbeh* (that's Yiddish for grandmother). Apparently, my grandfather, my *zaydeh*, whose blue eyes I inherited, owned a small grocery store in Hell's Kitchen when they first came over from the old country. Back then, Hell's Kitchen was part of Dutch Schultz's territory and he ruled with an iron fist. Every business—Jewish-owned or not—was forced to pay heavy protection money. But because Dutch was so smitten by my *bubbeh,* he never made my *zaydeh* pay up. For a time, the story goes, Dutch sent roses to my grandmother every day.

Of course, I've always had a little trouble with this story. You see, I was very young when Bubbeh was very old. And even though everyone told me that back in the Ukraine, Anna Dukelsky was the greatest beauty in all the Jewish settlements, I had difficulty picturing my sweet, Chiclets-chewing *bubbeh* as Miss Shtetl of 1895. To me, she was a grandmother with thick-heeled black shoes and false teeth, a woman in a frock who spoke almost no English. Who could have a crush on my grandmother?

In the intervening years between Bubbeh's death, a week or two before my brother David's bar mitzvah in 1963, and that fifteenth or sixteenth summer of my life, I had a fair amount of exposure to petty crime of one sort or another. I'd had two bicycles stolen, gotten assaulted for lunch money, had my butt kicked a few times for no good reason by the neighborhood tough guys. I too had broken a few windows, helped myself to a few candy bars, kicked some undeserving ass. I suppose that was just sort of the price of doing business, part of the coming-of-age thing in Brooklyn.

In the '60s and early '70s, serious crime, even in Coney Island, was usually experienced at arm's length. It was something that happened to a friend's cousin or a friend's friend. Sure, this guy I sort of knew from junior high, Mark Donchek, had been stabbed through the heart. One Monday morning the principal got on the P.A. and announced to the school that Mark had been murdered, but his death was like an extended absence. He was there on Friday and not on Monday. He might just as well have moved to Valley Stream over the weekend. Like I said, arm's length. I haven't thought about Mark Donchek for more than thirty years.

There was this other thing that happened, once. I think about it sometimes to remind myself that arm's length is a myth, a lie we tell ourselves to feel secure. I tell it to myself when I'm on the road and away from my wife and kids. It helps me sleep.

Anyway, yeah, I was fifteen or sixteen. Like I said, things fade. We still had troops in Vietnam. I was working my second real job; my first with legitimate working papers. The year before I had gotten a job at the Carvel on Coney Island Avenue and Avenue Y by forging stolen working papers. So the next summer, the one I'm talking about now, I was working at Baskin-Robbins on Sheepshead Bay Road. I think I was making a buck seventy-five an hour, but in those days, one hour's pay would've purchased at least three gallons of gas. A pity I wasn't yet driving.

It was one of those scary gorgeous Brooklyn days when the sky is cloudless and endlessly blue. There was little humidity. A breeze was blowing in off the Atlantic and I could smell the ocean in the air, almost taste the salt on my tongue as I walked up Avenue Z from our tiny garden apartment on Ocean Parkway. I was at the age when a boy begins to notice the beauty in things: in the shape of a woman's mouth, in the structure of an iris, in the way your father smiles. On most days I rode my bike to work, but that day I walked.

It's odd now when I think of it, how walking up Avenue Z was like tracing a timeline of my early life. Although I wasn't born there, Coney Island Hospital loomed large over the neighborhood. I tried not to notice. I hated hospitals. When I was four, my dad was diagnosed with bone cancer. He was in and out of hospitals so much that I thought the revolving door was invented to accommodate him. Next, there was the basement apartment on Z between East 6th and Hubbard Streets. It was the first place I remember. We moved three blocks away to the garden apartment when I was, like, three.

A few blocks up, there was P.S. 209 and the Avenue Z Jewish Center. P.S. 209 was built in the '20s or '30s, one of those beige brick behemoths that dotted the landscape of the borough. Unlike today's user-friendly, welcoming school buildings, 209's institutional look lent it a certain gravitas. Besides, its light brick walls were perfect for chalk stickball boxes and its prisonlike cyclone fencing made hitting a home run somewhat challenging. Though I couldn't swear to it, I'm sure there were kids playing stickball and softball with Clinchers when I walked by that day. It was 1972 or '73, before *Metal Gear Solid 3* had replaced street games and made ghost towns of schoolyards.

Across the street was the Avenue Z Jewish Center. My *zaydeh*—yeah, the Ukrainian grocer from Hell's Kitchen who had long since moved his family and business to Brooklyn— was one of the temple's founding members, though there's no plaque with his name on it. God, how I hated Hebrew school.

During my bar mitzvah ceremony, I did my section of the To-
rah from memory. *Judo Jack*—that's what we called our rabbi
for the marshal art–like hand gestures he made during his
sermons—had some sage advice for me that day.

"Coleman," he whispered, "look at the back of my head
when I speak. This way you won't look like so much of an
idiot."

Nice, huh?

Next up was Coney Island Avenue, the unofficial border-
line between Brighton Beach and Sheepshead Bay. On my
side of Coney Island Avenue, the kids went to Lincoln High.
Across the street, you went to Sheepshead. On my side, you
went to Goody's Luncheonette. On the other, you went to
Z Cozy Corner Luncheonette. On this side of Coney Island
Avenue, I had one group of friends. On the other, a different
group of friends. Even at fifteen or sixteen, I thought it was
weird how arbitrary and artificial borders can have such a pro-
found effect on our lives.

So, what's any of this got to do with anything? What does
where I went to elementary school or my rabbi's nickname or
bone cancer or blue skies or roses for Bubbeh have to do with
the point of this essay? Well, everything. On this day, something would happen to someone else that would change me
forever, recolor my perceptions. I would have to relearn whole
sections of what I thought I already knew. I would have to
reexamine assumptions and presumptions and question where
the borderlines were really drawn.

It happened across the border. When I headed beneath
the shadow of the el, past the newsstand that had the best
vanilla egg creams in Brooklyn, and I reached the bend in
Sheepshead Bay Road where it turned to the water, I heard
something. There was a pop, a crackle, like a firecracker, but

not a firecracker. A gunshot! The wind carried it to me, a siren's song. I followed it to its source.

Never the fastest guy in my neighborhood, it took me ten seconds to get to the post office on Jerome Avenue. At least I think it was Jerome Avenue. Like I said, things fade. A few years later, as I recall, the post office moved around the corner. But that day, in front of the old post office, there was a man. He lay on his back, head nearly in the gutter, his chest heaving, his arms and legs unmoving. I was about three feet from him, frozen.

Let me tell you what I remember about him. He wore heavy-rimmed glasses and his hair was stringy and unkempt. He was a thick man with a fat belly. He wore a short-sleeve shirt. It might have had stripes on it. I know for sure the shirt had a red spot on it where the bullet had bored into his gut. I recall thinking that there wasn't much blood, that such a little hole couldn't kill a human being. I was wrong. For a time, the world was deafeningly, torturously silent. I was not alone in my inability to move. The crowd around me was inert. I think we were trying to read his eyes through his glasses. *Does he know he's dying?* Or maybe we just wanted him to ask for help. It was as if we were waiting for permission to move. *Simon says, help the dying man.*

Finally, someone came to him, propped a sweater or newspaper—I can't remember—under his head.

"Call a fucking ambulance, for chrissakes!"

The fat man's chest was still heaving when the ambulance from Coney Island Hospital got there. It seemed to have taken hours. That deadly silence long broken, the crowd buzzed in my ears. I strung together a narrative out of loose bits and pieces of conversation.

The man on his back was the manager of Wolfe Motors,

the Ford dealership on Coney Island Avenue and Gravesend Neck Road. He had picked up payroll cash at the bank across the street and then gone to the post office. When he emerged from the post office, a white guy, or maybe Spanish—that's what people called Puerto Ricans then, when *spic* seemed inappropriate—ran up to the fat man, shot him in the belly, grabbed the mail and the money, and ran. Sometimes when I think about that day, I imagine that I caught a glimpse of him or heard his frantic footfalls as he fled. But I didn't.

The guy's chest stopped heaving. The ambulance men—I don't think anyone had yet coined the term Emergency Medical Technician—tried all sorts of things to revive him, to get his chest to move even a little bit. The ambulance men lifted the fat guy onto a gurney. One put a stethoscope to his chest. The other did something that is so ingrained in my memory that I can't imagine forgetting it, ever. He removed the fat man's left sock.

The sock was black Banlon and thoroughly worn, most of elasticity gone. With the sock removed, the ambulance man ran a tongue depressor along the naked sole of the fat guy's pale foot. Even in the midst of it all, I thought that tongue depressor thing was bizarre, almost medieval. I've since learned he was checking for something called a Babinski reflex. As it happens, newborns and dead men don't have them. To the ambulance men, the fat guy, once declared dead, was an object, no more worthy of their attention than the crumpled sock on the sidewalk.

He lay on the stretcher wearing one sock, his shirt with the little red dot, torn open. The entrance wound, now clear to see, was tiny still. There just had to be more blood, I thought, for a man to die. But the fact remained unchanged: The man was dead. I didn't yet have an understanding of internal bleeding or of how bullets, as they slow, chew up human tissue. When, in a daze, I left to go to work, I noticed it was still a beautiful day. The world had not stopped turning. Yet everything was different.

I never knew the dead man's name. I suppose I might have known it for a brief time and forgotten. There were posters put up around the neighborhood by his family and the cops. But the posters faded and frayed and fell off the telephone poles like the ones for missing pets or the guy who'll rake your yard for ten bucks. To the best of my knowledge, the murderer's never been apprehended.

Near the conclusion of my novel *The James Deans*, the protagonist-P.I., Moe Prager, having learned the truth about a thirty-year-old murder, goes to reveal that truth to the victim's long-suffering mother. But as he steps out of his car to confront the dead boy's parent with the truth, he stops himself and returns to his car. For at that moment, Moe learns the lesson I learned over thirty years ago.

In my writing, I try always to keep that day in mind. Whenever the urge strikes me to get too flippant or fanciful about murder, I remember. I remember that this nameless man had a family, and that for them his loss is nothing like the extended absence of a vaguely known kid from junior high. For them there is no such thing as arm's length or closure or justice. Serious crime is not about glamour or fame or gangsters with funny nicknames. Murder is about pain and loss. Murder is no roses for Bubbeh.

THE BROOKLYN BOGEYMAN

BY C.J. SULLIVAN

Bensonhurst

The Bogeyman came to life in New York City in 1977. The fiend was born in Brooklyn in 1953, an unwanted child who was put up for adoption because his biological father—a well-off Long Island businessman screwing around with a Brooklyn housewife—would have nothing to do with this unwanted progeny. The kid's penniless mother had no choice but to dump him on a family that wanted a child but were unable to conceive. Little did the couple know that the bundle full of joy they took out of Brooklyn was a monster.

The Furies must have been full of wicked humor as they walked the halls of that Brooklyn hospital on June 1, 1953. As soon as the Bogeyman was born he was taken out of Brooklyn. The Bronx and later Queens would have to deal with him as he morphed into a psychopath. In 1976 and '77, as the evil started to cut short the lives of young kids from Queens and the Bronx, the people of Brooklyn thought they had dodged a bullet.

"Son of Sam is too scared to come into Brooklyn," was a common boast of young Brooklyn men.

But like the Bogeyman of legend, he waited until everyone figured they were safe. Then he sneaked in during his last stages of malevolence and broke out his final act of wrath. And there have been rumors that Berkowitz's killing in Bensonhurst may have been recorded and made into a snuff film.

* * *

David Berkowitz, a.k.a. "Son of Sam," appeared in 1977 New York City as the place was at its nadir. His killing spree added to the woes of a seemingly dying metropolis. It was a city that was told to—in a famous *Daily News* headline—"Drop Dead" by President Ford. The coffers of the treasury were empty. Crime was rampant and the city's answer was to lay off cops. Arson became pandemic, and with the ruined budget new firemen couldn't be hired to help already overworked smoke eaters. If you were in New York in 1977, you knew murder and mayhem. Not much scared you, because if it did you would have moved out.

In fact, between 1970 and 1980 the population of New York dropped by 800,000 people. Many left, few moved in. New York was not a choice destination in those days. In 1976, when the Bogeyman started to come alive, he killed one person. Others, full of passion, jealousy, viciousness, evil, poverty, and anger killed another 1,621 people in New York that year. In 1977, the Bogeyman killed five and other killers came up with 1,548 murders. In those two years, 3,175 people were murdered in New York, yet it was the Bogeyman's six killings that made the headlines. People couldn't get enough of the story once it broke in the daily papers.

Everyone knew about muggings, shoot-outs, and drug wars. But for someone to come out of the shadows at night and gun down innocent girls and boys, well, that was beyond even a New Yorker's ken. In the Big Apple, you're usually killed for a reason, not just randomly picked out by a madman and slaughtered.

The origin of the word Bogeyman is hard to trace. In the southern regions of America, he is called *Boogerman*—elsewhere the standard appellation of Bogeyman applies. Some think it came out of Indonesia where the word *bugis* means pirates. Pirates were known to steal children and take them away from their homes to work on their ships. So parents would warn their children to be good or the Bugis would get them.

The Bogeyman's legend has lasted and thrived for hundreds of years. Sam Raimi, the director of *Spider-Man* and one of the classic horror films of all time, *The Evil Dead*, is fascinated by the Bogeyman. Raimi once said, "He's a mythical character that is the stuff of stories of generations. He is a horrible creature that consumes human beings . . ."

William Safire, the noted wordsmith for the *New York Times*, traced the oldest form of the word Bogeyman to thirteenth-century France. The word they used was *Bugibu*. In the later Middle Ages, Satan became known as *Old Bogey*. Safire suggests that there is a link between Satan and the Bogeyman. And some people—including Berkowitz himself—believe that Satan and the Son of Sam are also connected.

Safire explains how in Iceland the Bogeyman is *puki*, in Scotland he is called *boggart*, and in Germany he is *Boggelmann*. He also has theorized that the scarifier *Boo* comes from Bogeyman.

Writer Sharon K. West once did an essay on the fiend. "Bogeymen have no distinct habitat and can appear out of nowhere," she concluded.

Well, New York had its own Bogeyman. No one knew where he lived and he did appear out of nowhere.

It was on April 17, 1977, that the Son of Sam came out of his lonely and twisted closet to show all of New York City just who they were going to have to deal with.

On that early Sunday morning at 3 a.m., a young couple, Alex Esau and Valentina Suriani, coming home from a date in Manhattan, were parked in a Mercury Montego along the lonely service road of the Hutchinson River Parkway in the Pelham Bay section of the Bronx. As the couple hugged and kissed, David Berkowitz sneaked up to the car and shot them through the passenger-side window, killing them both.

He walked away and dropped a note addressed to NYPD Captain Joe Borrelli. In simple block letters, the message read:

> I am the "Son of Sam" . . . I am the "monster"—"Beel-zebub"—the "chubby behemoth" . . . I am on a different wavelength then [sic] everybody else—programmed to kill . . . to stop me you must kill me . . . I'll be back! I'll be back!

After thirty years he has never really gone away.

In the summer of 1976, I started hearing some disturbing rumors about Satanic cults operating in the wooded sections of Orchard Beach in the Bronx and up in Untermyer Park in Yonkers. After Son of Sam's arrest, it was revealed that his home address was a short walk from Untermyer Park.

I was employed that summer as a parkie at Orchard Beach, and one day as I was raking sand, a fellow worker said, "Yo, man, stay out of those backwoods here, they're dangerous! Especially at night. There's some sick shit going on out there with these devil-worshipping dudes. I think they kill dogs and drink the blood."

I had been going to Orchard Beach since I was a kid and I couldn't see devil-worshipping going down there. It was a place my father called the Bronx's Riviera. The beach had seen racial wars, when whites would wander into what the Puerto Ricans had claimed as their section, or vice versa. But it is a big leap from stupid territorial brawls to Satanism.

Even so, I could believe it was happening up in Untermyer Park. That was in the suburbs and home to most of the heavy metal heads in the metropolitan area, including many who were interested in the occult. Back then I thought New York City kids were just too jaded to be into Satan. God has trouble drawing an audience in New York, never mind a second-rate deity like Old Scratch.

Untermyer was a weird park, though, and a lot of Bronx kids would go up there to cop marijuana or acid. The park was a former rich man's sprawling estate located above the Hudson River. There were old, creepy Gothic towers with gargoyles on top and abandoned stone buildings throughout the grounds. It was thick with overgrown brambles, gardens, and woods. I could imagine, in the more secluded sections of the park, a band of hooded Satanists sacrificing dogs on nights when the moon was full.

Satanism did seem to be *in* back in those days. The movie *The Exorcist* was in rerelease (this was before video) and one of the most popular films of the summer in 1976 was *The Omen.*

I was having a hard enough time just getting by in 1976. Teenage years are tough everywhere, but in New York they can be particularly brutal. And one of the things I had never seen in New York was devil worship, so I was a bit intrigued. Every morning before work I would think about my Orchard Beach coworker's warning, "Stay out of those woods, man."

I would look into those foreboding trees on the other end of the beach and wonder. Then I would forget about it. Until one July 1976 morning when the night watchman at Orchard

Beach was getting off duty and called me over to his car. He told me that at midnight he had seen a bunch of people on the beach wearing hooded black robes standing in a circle. He moved closer and heard them chanting and staring up at the full moon. He ran back to the parkie house, locked himself in, and called the cops. The figures were gone by the time the police arrived. We both shook our heads and I swore I'd never let the sun set on my ass at Orchard Beach.

On July 30, 1976, I was on a break from my parkie job. I sat in the shade of a locker room sipping a coffee and reading the *New York Post*.

One story on the front page caught my eye. A mile from Orchard Beach, in a neighborhood known as Pelham Bay, two young girls, Jody Valenti and Donna Lauria, had been shot the night before while sitting in a 1974 Oldsmobile Cutlass. They were talking about their night at a New Rochelle disco when a lone gunman sneaked up on them and started shooting. He killed Lauria and badly wounded Valenti. She later recovered.

Wild story, I remember thinking. I finished the article and cynically thought it was a mistaken mob hit. The Pelham Bay neighborhood was no stranger to Mafia shootings. I figured the long-haired girls had been mistaken for some hippy drug dealers working the forbidden zone of a good Italian neighborhood.

The only problem with that theory was that when the mob boys hit, everyone dies. There are no witnesses left. In this shooting, only one girl died. Jody Valenti was able to give the police a good eyewitness sketch of the gunman.

After a day or two all the local dailies dropped the story. There were nearly twenty thousand murders in America in

1976. Poor and dead Donna Lauria was forgotten. (Though not by her father, who publicly threatened to kill Berkowitz in 2006, years after he was convicted of the murder.) What no one knew then was that the girls would later become immortalized as the Son of Sam's first victims.

In 1953, Son of Sam was given the name David Richard Berkowitz. He was born Richard David Falco, and on his Brooklyn birth certificate, Anthony Falco was listed as his father. His birth mother, Betty Broder Falco, later claimed that his real father was one Joseph Kleinman, her lover who refused to have a baby with her. They remained lovers until Kleinman died of cancer in 1965.

The baby's mother gave up the infant for adoption to Pearl and Nathan Berkowitz, a childless middle-aged couple living in the East Bronx. They switched the birth names around and called him David. Baby David was raised on Stratford Avenue in the Bronx. Nathan Berkowitz owned a hardware store and Pearl was a housewife. David was to be their only child.

In an attempt to interview David Berkowitz, I wrote him a letter and sent it to the prison where he is being housed. He answered.

> *Dear Mr. Sullivan,*
>
> *I received a letter from you informing me that you are planning on doing a story about my life. I was very saddened to learn this because, first of all, you do not know me at all. Second, so much has changed within the past years.*
>
> *I am unable to grant you an interview at this time. I cannot stop you from writing anything. However, if you would like to know my opinion about the case and*

*many things related to it I am enclosing some pamphlets
I wrote. Today, thanks to God, I am living with a lot of
hope.*

God bless you!

Sincerely,
David Berkowitz

David Berkowitz was, by all reports, a normal kid growing up in the Bronx. A number of his friends have stated that he was very good baseball player. His adoptive mother died in 1967 from breast cancer. In 1969, David moved with his father to Co-op City in the Bronx. They were a widowed father and son living together like in the TV show of that time *The Courtship of Eddie's Father*.

Berkowitz volunteered for the army in 1971 because he wanted to fight in the Vietnam War. He passed all his medical and psychiatric tests. In a typical illustration of government inefficiency, he was not sent to Vietnam, but to Korea. In June of 1974, he received an honorable discharge.

Berkowitz came back to the Bronx and got a job as a security guard, then left that position to become a cab driver. In 1975, after an armed robbery at his hardware store, Nathan Berkowitz left New York for Florida and gave the Co-Op City apartment to his son. Berkowitz soon lost that and then moved to New Rochelle and, finally, to Pine Street in Yonkers.

After moving to Yonkers he started working at a post office in the Bronx, pretty much finalizing the background requirements for a serial killer: got his army weapons training, did the rent-a-cop thing, a bid as a cabby, and now he was a full-fledged post office employee about to go postal.

* * *

One of the small pamphlets that Berkowitz wrote in prison and sent me was called: *SON OF SAMhain* [an ancient druid name for the highest-ranking demon] *The Incredible True Story of David Berkowitz*.

He explained that his cult members were "sons of sam . . . sons of satan!" He claimed that he became heavily involved with the occult and witchcraft in 1975.

> *I recall a force that would drive me into the darkened streets . . . I roamed the streets like an alley cat in the darkness . . . Thoughts of suicide plagued me continually . . . I was so depressed and haunted . . . I was so wild, mixed-up and crazy that I could barely hang on to my sanity . . . I was overwhelmed with thoughts about dying . . . Books about witchcraft seemed to pop up all around me. Everywhere I looked there appeared a sign . . . pointing me to Satan . . . To someone who has never been involved in the occult, this could be hard to understand . . . The power leading me could not be resisted . . . I had no defense against the devil.*

None of his victims had any defense against .44 caliber bullets.

After Berkowitz's July hit in the Bronx, he went out to Queens on October 23, 1976. There, he hunted down a man and a woman. The woman was the daughter of a New York detective. He found them in a red Volkswagen, on 160th Street in Flushing. Several rounds were fired into the car, shattering the windows. The woman was able to put the vehicle into gear and escape unharmed. The man suffered a head wound, but eventually recovered.

Berkowitz later said he went to a White Castle on Northern Boulevard to celebrate with a bunch of belly-bomber hamburgers. He claimed that shooting couples in cars was starting to be fun.

He certainly seemed to like Queens. On November 27, 1976, Berkowitz asked two girls on 262nd Street for directions to a nearby house. Before they could answer he opened fire, hitting both. They survived, although one remains paralyzed for life.

Neither of these attacks got much press. No one had made a connection between the three shootings in 1976.

That would change on the cold winter night of January 29, 1977—the day that TV actor Freddy Prinze of the hit series *Chico and the Man* committed suicide. A young Queens couple went out to Forest Hills on a date to see a movie called *Rocky*. Afterwards they stopped for a drink at a local pub and then walked quickly to their car, parked on Station Plaza.

They sat in a blue Pontiac Firebird, shivering in the bitter five-degree temperature, waiting for the car to warm up. As they started to snuggle, Berkowitz opened fire, killing the woman, Christine Freund.

February 1, 1977 marked the first story in the tabloids that alluded to the fact that the shootings might be connected. A sketch was shown of the gunman; it looked like the Berkowitz we later came to know. The police now suspected they had a serial killer on their hands.

But this was soon forgotten because on Valentine's Day 1977 a neo-Nazi nut stormed the Neptune Moving Company in New Rochelle, a town just north of the Bronx, killing five people and himself in an all-day siege.

The local news stations broadcasted live footage of this

and the next day's papers were filled with the horrific tales of Fred Cowan, a thirty-three-year-old man from New Rochelle. He was a bald, hulking six foot, 250-pound weight lifter. He was a self-described Nazi, and a hater of blacks and Jews. In a rage over being suspended from his job at the moving company, he decided to take out his Jewish boss and some of his black coworkers.

For days afterwards the papers and TV news were filled with stories on Cowan. What they all missed was his odd connection to Son of Sam.

On March 8, 1977, the now labeled .44 Caliber Killer took back the headlines by shooting a college student named Virginia Voskerichian as she walked home from the subway to her apartment in Forest Hills. As the gunman approached her, her only defense was her textbooks, with which she covered her face. The bullets tore through her books and found her head. The shooting was two blocks away from the January ambush.

This was a busy neighborhood, and eyewitnesses saw two completely different-looking people running from the scene. Two drawings were published; one looked like Berkowitz and the other showed a soft-featured person, maybe a woman, in a knit cap.

On March 10, 1977, New York's littlest mayor, Abe Beame, held a press conference at the 112th Precinct, just a few blocks away from the last shooting. He announced that a murderer with a .44 caliber weapon was stalking New Yorkers and that an NYPD command called the Omega task force, manned with more than three hundred cops, had been set up to apprehend the fiend.

Then came the aforementioned April shooting in the Bronx,

where Berkowitz dropped a letter giving himself the name *Son of Sam.* On May 30, 1977, he got the writing bug again.

David Berkowitz mailed a letter from New Jersey to the *Daily News* addressed to columnist Jimmy Breslin. I talked with Breslin about receiving Berkowitz's missive. He was home in Forest Hills when it reached the *News.*

"A secretary called and read some of this madness to me over the phone," Breslin said. "She really didn't even want to read it. Said she was scared of it. It was an eerie letter. Very eerie. I told her to get rid of it and give it to the cops. I've made a conscious effort to not remember what it said. It was a sick letter written by a sick, depraved mind. It was hurled out of the depths of insanity . . . but I will say he is probably the only serial killer in history that knew how to use a semicolon."

The letter started out: *Hello from the gutters of N.Y.C. which are filled with dog manure, vomit, stale wine, urine, and blood . . .*

This was reminiscent of Robert De Niro's character, Travis Bickle, in the 1976 film *Taxi Driver,* as the character let go with a tirade to a politician in his cab.

Berkowitz's letter went on:

> *JB . . . I also want to tell you that I read your column daily and find it quite informative . . . Sam's a thirsty lad and he won't let me stop killing until he gets his fill of blood . . . Here are some names to help you along: "The Duke of Death," "The Wicked King Wicker," "The Twenty Two Disciples of Hell," "John Wheaties—Rapist and Suffocater* [sic] *of Young Girls."*

It was signed *Son of Sam.* The return address was *Blood and Family, Darkness and Death, Absolute Depravity, .44.*

Breslin: "It has always fascinated me how they could make such a big deal over these serial killers. I mean, why study them? I find them depressing and dull. They're a depraved, hideous, and grizzly lot of men who are not even worth studying. Forget them."

After Berkowitz was arrested, Breslin felt spent.

"You were left with nothing after he was caught," he said. "Just this little bug with a mind full of oatmeal."

I asked him about people who deny that Berkowitz was the sole killer.

"They're crazy. He was the one who did it. The guy pleads guilty to all the shootings. They're a bunch of conspiracy nuts."

Breslin went on to tell me that after Berkowitz was in jail, he wrote him another letter.

"It went something like, *Dear Jimmy, How are you?* And it was full of clichés like, *The politicians are using me like a political football.*" Breslin laughed and said, "The letter was written in a scrawl like a twelve-year-old would write. Completely different from the first one. I guess they gave him his medication in prison and then he was all right."

The *Daily News* printed the first letter to Breslin and the Son of Sam was born.

Another one of Berkowitz's prison pamphlets read:

> The police and media used to call me "The Son of Sam," but God has given me a new name, "the son of Hope," because now, my life is about hope.

Like most convicted felons, Berkowitz had a very convenient memory. No one in the media or police force had named him: The Bogeyman had given himself his own moniker, Son of Sam.

I took a ride up to some of Berkowitz's old haunts in Yonkers. The years have changed the neighborhood as much as they have Berkowitz's appearance. He has gone from a stocky, wild-haired youth to a balding, middle-aged man who resembles the actor Richard Dreyfuss. His neighborhood in the north of Yonkers has slid from working class to ghetto poor.

It was a quiet Sunday in a desolate area that looked like a depressed small town in the rust belt. I sat in my car in front of the old Carr house on Warburton Avenue. This is where Berkowitz said a 6,000-year-old demon lived with his dog and commanded him to kill from his apartment up the hill on Pine Street.

The Carr house was a rambling three-story wood frame, with new aluminum siding and four cars parked in the front yard. Above the house, up on the crest of a hill, I could see Berkowitz's old seventh-floor studio apartment window, which had a curtain over it. I hoped it wouldn't move.

I made a left onto the hill of Wicker Street and passed the home where Berkowitz said the Wicked King Wicker lived. It didn't look he was home. Snaking up the steep drive, I came onto Pine Street and made a right. I started looking for Berkowitz's old address, number 35. I found his apartment building, but it's not 35 anymore. I guess they changed it to fool curious Berkowitz buffs. On a wall across the street was a sign: *Beware of Dog*.

I headed up North Broadway to Untermyer Park, where Berkowitz has claimed his Satanic cult held black masses. I made my way into a walled garden, and saw a sign that forbade photos being taken without a permit. I ambled around the gardens but stayed on the beaten paths. In a white stone gazebo there was a tiled floor with the face of a cherub in the middle. Someone had dug the tiles out of the angel's eyes, leaving him blind.

I slid over to a long trail of stairs that led down into the thick woods. An unleashed Labrador retriever ran by me, its owner nowhere in sight. A brisk river wind kicked up and the late winter sun was setting over the banks of the Hudson. I hurried back to my car.

For a time, Berkowitz laid low. Then around 3 o'clock in the morning of June 26, 1977, a kid named Sal Lupo left a Queens disco, Elephas, with a pretty girl named Judy Placido. As they got into a red Cadillac, Berkowitz sneaked up and shot Placido three times. The windows exploded and Lupo ran back to the disco to get help. Placido survived.

The only thing bigger than the Son of Sam story that July was the citywide blackout on the 13th. New York went dark and looters went wild. More than three thousand people were arrested. Sam was momentarily forgotten.

Berkowitz took out his pen again and promised New York he would strike on July 29, to mark the anniversary of his first killing. That night, most city streets were deserted. No one wanted to tempt the Bogeyman. Cops sat in cars with female mannequins hoping to lure him into an attack. The night passed without incident and that somehow made things worse. We all knew it was coming.

On July 31, Berkowitz returned to the borough of his birth, Brooklyn. He drove around the neighborhoods of Gravesend and Bensonhurst as Stacy Moskowitz and Bobby Violante had their first date. They had gone to see the Robert De Niro/ Liza Minnelli flick, *New York, New York*, before driving back to Bensonhurst and parking on a quiet street. As they kissed, Berkowitz opened fire, hitting Moskowitz once in the head and Violante twice in the face. The Violante boy survived, but Stacy Moskowitz died a day later.

The Son of Sam had now killed six people.

There has been a rumor circulating for years that the Moskowitz killing was filmed, and has been watched ritually by "snuff" fanatics. Snuff films constituted a 1970s urban legend, movies that supposedly caught actual killings on tape. No credible source for such films has ever stepped forward, nor have any ever been found. Law enforcement officials claim that snuff films do not exist. Still, in Bronx bars and in the blogosphere, some swear Berkowitz's crew of Satanists filmed the killing.

In a 1994 article on snuff films, Rider McDowell writes that journalist Maury Terry told him, "It is believed Berkowitz filmed his murders to circulate within the Church of Satan. On the night of the Stacy Moskowitz killing, there was a VW van parked across the street from the murder site under a bright sodium streetlamp."

Terry believed a crew was in that van making a snuff film of the death of the twenty-year-old Brooklyn woman.

What finally brought David Berkowitz down was the bane of the average Brooklynite: a parking ticket. He received one that night, two blocks from the shooting.

On August 10, 1977, four NYPD detectives nabbed him as he approached his 1970 Ford Galaxy in Yonkers. His .44 caliber gun was sitting on the front seat. Berkowitz allegedly told the cops, "You got me. What took you so long?"

* * *

Sid Horowitz, a former court officer captain in Queens Supreme Court, went to Kings County Hospital with a judge to arraign Berkowitz for his Queens shootings. He told me his impressions of the Son of Sam.

"I am standing there with the judge and Berkowitz comes out with his head down. I remember saying to myself, 'This is it? This is the Son of Sam?' I couldn't believe what a little twerp he was. He was a nothing. He just stared straight ahead with this blank look on his face. I left there shaking my head that this meek little nothing had killed six people."

I went to Brooklyn Supreme Court to talk with J.B. Fitzgerald, a retired court officer who had worked security for all of Berkowitz's Brooklyn court appearances.

Fitzgerald smiled at the memory. He and other Brooklyn court officers had been exuberant because they thought they were going to make a ton of money in overtime when the case went to trial. Also, since it was the biggest case to hit Kings County in decades, the courts were swarming with media and the officers were looking to become stars.

Fitzgerald was one of ten officers who escorted Berkowitz down a long hallway of 360 Adams Street on the seventh floor for a pretrial hearing. As they reached the back door to the courtroom, Berkowitz suddenly broke away from the officers and tried to throw himself out of a window. It didn't work. All the courthouse windows have strong steel mesh reinforcing the glass. Security wrestled the wild Berkowitz to the ground. He bit one of the officers, then started to foam at the mouth.

Fitzgerald: "So we bring him into the major's office to calm him down. I mean, ten guys are restraining him. One guy on one arm, one guy on the other arm, one guy on a leg—like that. After about fifteen minutes, he starts to calm down. We look around the room and it's just Berkowitz and us. Then one of the guys says, 'Maybe this flake really is a dog. After all, he bit Murphy.' One by one we start letting go of him, and just let him lay there on the couch. I remember one guy lit a cigarette, and another said to open the window because it's getting stuffy in here. I started to laugh, 'cause you gotta remember this nut just tried to throw himself out the window."

The next day Fitzgerald was assigned to watch the rail between Berkowitz and the victims' families.

"So Berkowitz walks up to the defendant's table and he's looking right at me," said Fitzgerald. "Then he starts yelling, 'Stacy's a whore! Stacy's a whore!' I'm thinking he's talking to me. Then I realize Stacy's mother, Mrs. Moskowitz, was right behind me. The crowd went wild and rushed the bench yelling they were going to kill him."

They hustled Berkowitz out of the courtroom and tried again the next day. Fitzgerald was assigned to watch the victims' families in plainclothes. As soon as Berkowitz came into the courtroom, someone from the Moskowitz family jumped up on a bench and made a dive for him. Fitzgerald caught the guy in midair and wrestled him to the ground.

While awaiting trial in Brooklyn, Berkowitz caught a brutal jailhouse beating from another inmate in the Brooklyn House of Detention, causing his eyes to hemorrhage. Brooklynite doctor David Klein worked on his injuries.

Previously, in July 1977, Dr. Klein had operated on Bobby Violante's eyes, saving his life, after Berkowitz had shot him in the head.

Klein told the *Sun-Herald* that he looked at Berkowitz and said, "I'm your doctor. I operated on one of your victims and now I am going to treat you." Klein recalled his mixed feelings: "In the back of your mind you want to strangle him. But you have to respect your oath."

Maybe the beating in Brooklyn did some good. On May 8, 1978, David Berkowitz pled guilty to all charges. In June he was sentenced to 365 years in prison. But his trouble in jail didn't end. In 1979, an inmate slashed his throat. It took fifty-six stitches to close his neck wound, but Berkowitz survived.

Berkowitz may have pled guilty to all charges, but he now claims that he only carried out two of the shootings and that members of a Satanic cult he was involved with committed the others. Did he commit all the crimes he was charged with? There are two prominent theories about the Son of Sam case. One is that Berkowitz was a type of Manchurian Candidate assassin who, on some unknown command, was sent out to randomly kill. For proof they offer that one of his letters reads, *I am programmed to kill.*

The other theory is the one that Berkowitz has been braying about for years. Son of Sam was not one person but an evil Satanic cult that wanted to bring mayhem upon the city of New York. The evidence for that, besides Berkowitz's words, are the police sketches of three distinctly different shooters. One of the closest eyewitnesses—Bobby Violante—said the shooter was a tall and thin blond man—very different from the chubby postman Berkowitz.

Maury Terry, in his book *The Ultimate Evil*, makes some good arguments for Berkowitz not acting alone. But Terry undermines his own perspective by connecting the Son of Sam shootings to the Mason family and every other murder with even the slightest whiff of Satanism that has hit the media from 1969 onward. Even so, there are some strange coincidences with David Berkowitz.

Berkowitz lived in New Rochelle in 1976 for a few months. His landlord worked at the Neptune Moving Company with Fred Cowan, the aforementioned Nazi, who went ballistic on Valentine's Day in 1977, killing five people and himself. Renting a room to the Son of Sam and working with another mass murderer is beyond weird.

In August of 1977, an NYPD detective called Yonkers PD on a routine matter, checking out one David Berkowitz, who had gotten a parking ticket in Brooklyn the night Stacy Moskowitz was shot. The daughter of Sam Carr, Wheat Carr, answered the phone. She told the detective that she lived behind Berkowitz and claimed he was a serious whacko. She also told them that he owned guns and she suspected him of being the Son of Sam. The Daughter of Sam was the best tip PD had.

A month after David Berkowitz was arrested, the postman who had delivered his mail to 35 Pine Street committed suicide.

In 1982, Leon Stern, one of Berkowitz's lawyers when he entered his guilty plea, was killed in his own house by an armed intruder. Stern was gunned down on May 8, four years to the day after Berkowitz gave his plea.

Both of the sons of Sam Carr—I guess that makes them the real Sons of Sam—were dead by 1980. John Carr committed suicide in North Dakota, putting a shotgun into his mouth and pulling the trigger. Berkowitz has suggested that John Carr (in his letter to Breslin he was identified as *John Wheaties—Rapist and Suffocater of Young Girls*) was a part of his cult.

The other son of Sam Carr, Mike Carr (*The Duke of Death* in the Breslin letter), died in a car crash on 70th Street and the West Side Highway.

* * *

I talked with former Brooklyn Supreme Court Justice Dominic J. Lodato, who handled the David Berkowitz case from the civil side, when the families of his victims were trying to prevent Berkowitz from profiting off of any publications or movies about his crimes. Lodato, along with former Queens D.A. John Santucci, had his doubts about whether Berkowitz acted alone.

Lodato told me, "I was very leery about the case. There was a suspicion that there might have been more than one gunman. The police sketches clearly showed two completely different people, and these were from eyewitness to the shootings. But it wasn't for me to decide that, and he did plead guilty, so that ended that."

During the civil case, Lodato got plenty of motions from Berkowitz's side. He remembered that one was for Berkowitz to change his name. Lodato couldn't remember what he wanted to change it to. Lodato also received strange and threatening letters from Berkowitz whenever he denied any motions made by him. I asked about the letters.

"I wasn't too scared," said Lodato. "He was in jail and I guess you just have to have faith in the system."

In 2003, I saw Berkowitz on television. He talked about being a born-again Christian and how he now sends Bibles to poor people.

A minister had sent him a letter in 1978. Berkowitz wrote back and said that when he got out of jail he would hunt down the preacher and kill him. Today, Berkowitz and the minister pray together and are, as the minister solemnly states, friends in Christ.

On the TV show, Berkowitz was shown a tape of Mrs.

Moskowitz saying that she now believes he didn't act alone and would he please just tell her who had murdered her daughter.

Berkowitz watched the tape and shook his head. "I can't, I'm sorry but I just can't do it," he said.

Berkowitz's Son of Samhain pamphlet ends with:

> *I believe we are now living in . . . the "last days" . . . Society is seeing an increase in demonic activity at this time. Tens of thousands of people are under intense pressure. Life in America has never been harder . . . We are a nation in chaos and crisis.*

Berkowitz first came up for parole in 2002. He refused to attend the hearing, admitting he deserved to be in jail until his death. In 2004, he was denied parole and this year will be the same. Berkowitz will only leave prison in a coffin.

In 2005, Berkowitz wrote a book titled, *Son of Hope*. It is all about his conversion to Christianity and how Jesus is now his savior. Christian organizations push the book and the proceeds go to the needy. It seems that David just can't quit writing.

When Berkowitz was arrested on August 10, 1977, the *Post* ran his picture with the headline: CAUGHT. Berkowitz's eyes are unnaturally bright and he has the smallest smile on his face. Like he knows something that he's never going to tell.

Son of Sam was bumped from the headlines that August thirty years ago after one week. The reason: the death of Elvis Presley.

He's never gone away, either.

SLAVES IN BROOKLYN

BY KIM SYKES

Weeksville

W ith land you have food, drink, and shelter," Olga said in a lilting Caribbean accent. Her rusty eyes peeked over her mirrored sunglasses to register my reaction. "They created eminent domain while we were sleeping, you see. And all those shops over on Fulton Street are there to distract us."

We were a few blocks from the Fulton Street Mall, standing in front of a row of Civil War–era buildings on Duffield Street that had been declared "blighted" by the city, in order to build a parking lot for a new hotel. The owners fought back, claiming the nineteenth-century buildings were part of the Underground Railroad, that they were the homes of abolitionists who harbored fugitive slaves on their way to freedom.

Signs that read *Eminent Domain Abuse*, the words circled and crossed out in red, were plastered on the windows and doors. Remnants of their historic past were still visible in the architecture of the small brick buildings, but over the years burglar bars and shoddy repairs had scarred what was left of any beauty. It would take millions of dollars to restore them to what they once were, but that was not going to happen. Using outside consultants, the city commissioned a study and found no conclusive evidence of Underground Railroad activity. The construction of the hotel had begun. Directly across the street from the homes, a bulldozer emitted a loud beeping sound as if it were counting the days until their destruction.

Olga had seen me taking pictures and came over to check me out. I could tell she wasn't sure whose side I was on. I introduced myself but she would only give me her first name. "They make us slaves by taking away our land. You know, all these people going off to get their master's degrees. I call them Master's Degree. Because that's who it is for. They get *Master's* Degree to become highly qualified slaves." Olga walked with me toward the Fulton Street Mall. She wanted to know what I was doing on Duffield Street. I told her that I was research-ing the city's connections to the Underground Railroad for a play I was going to be reading in the fall. I'm not sure if she believed me.

The play is about Elizabeth Keckly, a seamstress who bought herself out of slavery and became the dressmaker to Abraham Lincoln's wife, Mary Todd. After writing her auto-biography, Keckly moved to 14 Carroll Place in New York and I wanted to see it, but first I had to find it. Originally I as-sumed Carroll Place was in Carroll Gardens, Brooklyn, but there was no such street on the local map. I decided to go anyway, and after several hours of walking the neighborhood and asking around, I gave up. At home on the computer I dis-covered a Carroll Place on Staten Island, but I told myself Ke-ckly was sophisticated, and a seamstress to the elite. It didn't seem possible that she would live all the way out on Staten Island. There had to be another Carroll Place that Google Maps hadn't heard of. One that had been lost or renamed in subsequent years. But the old maps in Manhattan's Midtown library pointed to the New Brighton district on Staten Island, which in the 1860s was a fashionable summer resort. A place where the rich would bring their seamstresses and hairdressers to have on hand. It had been staring me in the face, I just didn't like what I saw.

The librarian scolded me. "See, this is why we have to be wary when reading history. We have to ask who wrote it and what their motives were. You can't change history because you don't like what you find."

Of course he was right, but I was not going to Staten Island. The building where Keckly lived had been torn down, and it wasn't going to help me to look at what I was sure by now was an office building or a parking lot.

Researching the everyday lives of African Americans in the nineteenth century and earlier is like putting together a puzzle with almost all of the pieces missing. You get accustomed to seeing words and phrases such as, "most likely happened," "probably," and "no conclusive evidence." Keckly's memoir made it a bit easier. As a slave, she had learned how to read and write, and she freed herself and her son by paying off her owners. She achieved some fame as a seamstress and a companion to Mary Todd Lincoln. Even then, what was written in her book, *Behind the Scenes: Thirty Years a Slave and Four Years in the White House*, seemed to me to have been composed mostly for white consumption during a time when few African Americans could read, or even purchase a book. I wanted to know about the daily life of a black woman in the 1860s, which was how I ended up at the library going through government and police records and reading old newspapers. But whenever I do something like this, I inevitably find myself taken in a completely different direction than where I started. That's what happened when I began with 14 Carroll Place and ended up at the Underground Railroad homes on Duffield Street.

Olga was carrying heavy bags, so we walked slowly past

the wig and pawn shops and the Rastafarians selling incense on rickety card tables. Without any regard to aesthetics, storefronts selling everything from french fries to sneakers were jammed next to each other. As we walked, a young woman raced by us talking on her cell phone. She was beautiful and she knew it. Her tight pants showed off her perfect figure and I marveled at her ability to walk in such pointy-toed, high-heeled shoes. Everyone within twenty feet of her could hear her conversation. "Yo, meet me on Fulton by the Duane Reade! . . . Fulton Street!" It is hard to imagine that this Fulton Street was once a dirt road on which Harriet Tubman led escaped slaves to safe houses. The crowd around us was dense. Olga stopped to make sure I took it all in. Once again, she peeked at me over her shades. Downtown Brooklyn was undergoing major reconstruction. It was only a matter of time before even this stretch of consumer distraction became gentrified. I was going to ask what she thought about that, but we had arrived at the corner of Fulton and Flatbush.

In 2005, the city conamed this section of Fulton Street Harriet Ross Tubman Avenue in honor of the African American abolitionist who ferried slaves from the South to freedom in the North. Olga followed my gaze up at the signage. I was sure she was going to comment on the fact that Ms. Tubman had to share billing. I wondered about that myself since Robert Fulton, the steamboat inventor, also had streets named for him in Manhattan and elsewhere. She set her bags on the sidewalk without taking her eyes off the signs. Her red-and-white striped hat covered all of her hair except for fuzzy gray and black curls poking out at the sides.

"Look at the sign," Olga said. "What do you see?" Fulton's green metal sign hung above the one for Harriet Ross Tubman. Her lips curled into a half smile. I was missing her point.

"But what else do you see? Look closer." Fulton Street had been written in all caps and Harriet Ross Tubman's wasn't. If her full name had been in all caps, I thought, the sign would probably be too long and snap off in a stiff wind. But I said nothing. I played dumb.

"His name is capitalized!" she said, her finger pointing to the sign like a first grade teacher. "Except for the first letters, her name is in lower case! And you see, she is at the bottom. He is at the top. They call us minority. What does minority mean? It means less than, not as good as. That's what they want us to believe. Minority. It's in the dictionary. Look it up."

On the corner of Atlantic Avenue and Fulton/Tubman, I listened to Olga's tutorials on racism and capitalism. She told me about her family, how she is the only one to live and work in the states. How her children are back on the island of St. Vincent protecting the family land. I asked her where she worked, but she was vague, still unsure if she could trust me. I looked down at her bags and saw that they were filled with books. Occasionally, someone passed by and called out a greeting to her and she would respond, but she never lost her train of thought, moving from African land grabs to the bio-genetic seeds that corporations are sending to the Caribbean and South America.

"They send us seeds that grow the vegetables for one sea-son and then we have to buy the seeds again for the next year! Non-fertile seeds! These men are smart but evil. They are enemies of nature."

All was going well until she moved on to religion, starting with Abraham and the Egyptian slaves and what was left out of the Old and New Testaments. It had nothing to do with Olga. It was me. When anyone starts talking religion, my eyes begin to glaze over and I want to run away screaming. It's the fault of my Baptist upbringing in Louisiana that promised rewards only after you were dead. I politely interrupted Olga, thanked her for her insight, and told her that I had to get to the library before it closed, which was true. She gave me one of those half smiles again, this one with all sorts of meaning behind it. The one I went away with was, *Can you handle what I've just told you?*

At the Brooklyn Public Library, I was given a file labeled *Plymouth Church.* Inside of it I discovered a newspaper drawing of Henry Ward Beecher, the famous abolitionist minister standing before his congregation with a young girl at his side. The description under it read, *Reverend Henry Ward Beecher auctioning "Pinky" slave girl.* I had heard of Beecher, mostly because of his sister, Harriet Beecher Stowe, who wrote *Uncle Tom's Cabin,* but who was Pinky? What happened to her? In the drawing her long hair fell below her waist. Her features were Caucasian, except for a small rounded nose that hinted at Africa. Elizabeth Keckly would have to wait, I thought. I left the library and headed back to Brooklyn Heights.

Like most Americans, when I think of slavery I think of the South, which is why I was shocked to discover that in 1790, according to the first U.S. Census, Brooklyn was the second largest slave-holding city after Charleston, South Carolina, the center of the slave trade. In 1860, Abraham Lincoln came to Plymouth Church in Brooklyn to hear Henry Ward Beecher preach against the evils of slavery, which had been abolished for more than three decades in the state.

Lois Rosebrooks led myself, a young man, and his uncle to pew 89 where Abraham Lincoln sat in 1860, the day before he gave his antislavery speech at Cooper Union; the speech that would help win him the Republican nomination and set the stage for the Civil War. The young man sat in the pew while his uncle snapped a picture of his beaming face. Lois gave a brief talk about the day Lincoln visited Plymouth and then they left. The young man was on his way to college and had to catch a plane. Once they were gone, Lois and I settled in. This time, I took the seat were Lincoln had sat and imagined his long legs, his knees knocking against the pew in front of me.

Lois didn't look anything like what her card said she was: Director of History Ministry Services. She was wearing a short-sleeved blue housedress with colorful flowers embroidered around the neck. Her reddish-brown hair was styled nicely, just below her ears. It was as if she were in her own home and any minute would offer me cookies and a cup of tea. I glanced down at her feet, half expecting slippers, but saw instead sensible black shoes. Her eyes sparkled when I told her I wanted to know about the mock slave auctions. It was obvious that she loved her job.

"Plymouth Church was called, by some, the *Grand Central Depot*" she began, with a strong, pleasant-sounding voice. "Beecher encouraged his congregation to purchase the freedom of actual slaves in order to draw attention to it. We've found evidence of at least eleven mock slave auctions in our files. We can tell by the financial records of the church. Pinky was the most famous. She was nine years old, and auctioned here just before the war. The church returned her to her grandmother."

I looked around the large room. It reminded me of an Elizabethan theater with its crescent-shaped seating and no center aisle. Stained-glass windows flanked the second-floor balcony depicting famous leaders of the time, including Beecher, his sister, and Abraham Lincoln. A pleasant change I thought from the bloody crucifixion scenes found in most churches. When I asked how she came to be the historian for Plymouth, which was renamed Plymouth Church of the Pilgrims after a merger in 1934, she said, "I realized one day that something had to be done about the history of our church." Her voice resonated off the high ceiling. "There was too much of it here."

Lois had a presence and ease about her delivery that made me ask if she was a performer. "I used to sing professionally." She tilted her head modestly to one side. The light caught a small flame of gray hair above her forehead. "I was a soprano. I would sing all over the city. I sang at Mother Zion up in Harlem for fourteen years. I started in 1967, or was it '66? I'd have to check to be sure.

"At the time, Adam Clayton Powell, who preached at Abyssinian Baptist Church, didn't like the idea of me singing in Harlem. In one of his sermons, he complained about me: *Those black churches that hire white sopranos . . .*" The memory amused her and me. "But soon after, Mother Zion's choir went to sing at Abyssinian. Reverend Powell walked up to me and shook my hand and he said, 'Welcome to Harlem.'"

All this time I had been talking to Lois about history and not realizing that she was a part of it herself.

I asked her if I could stand on the platform where Pinky stood. To my surprise, she said yes. I climbed the few steps up to the small stage, which was about four feet wide and eight feet long and covered in red carpet. Lois stood off to the side and told me about the baptismal recently discovered under the pulpit there, but the pounding in my chest rose to my ears and drummed out her words. The church was empty except for Lois and me; I crossed my arms protectively in front of myself. I couldn't help but cast my eyes down, like Pinky's were in the drawing. I felt exposed, vulnerable, and frightened. Mock or real, it must have been awful having your life in the hands of complete strangers, even well-meaning ones. I wanted to get down off the stage.

Lois completed the tour by showing me the basement under the church. A flight of stairs took us down to it. I ran my hand along the brick walls, piecing together yet another part of the puzzle. There were no records of who was hidden here, of course. Thanks to the Fugitive Slave Act of 1850, the federal government could be called in to aid in the arrest and return of slaves to their masters. Runaways and those who assisted them were careful not to leave tracks—yet still I wanted to discover some mark, anything left behind; though I was sure that if such evidence existed, Lois would have found it long ago, as would the rats. "I have to stomp my feet on occasion before coming down here. That usually scares them off," she said.

The basement was neat and clean considering we were under the church. There were three openings that led underneath separate parts of the building. The entrance to one of them was covered with an iron fire door that led beneath an addition that was built after a fire in the 1920s. Another was blocked by fallen debris and construction material, making it impossible to go inside; but the third opening was unobstructed. Lois switched on a light and I could see the brick pillars that held up the foundation. The dirt floor was strewn with rocks but there was plenty of room to hide.

"One day, the workmen for Con Edison discovered a tunnel under the street next to the church, but they filled it in before we were called." Lois's stricken face mirrored my own. "It was unfortunate. It could have given us valuable information."

Knowing history, and having a physical place to connect it

to, is a magical combination. It binds you to that place in time in a way books and films on their own can never do. To be where a momentous event happened, to sit were Lincoln sat, to walk were Harriet Tubman walked, brings the past present, so that for a moment their pain and sacrifice, victories and losses, are yours. Their mistakes are ours not to repeat, and their triumphs to advance upon. It's why the Holocaust Memorial Museum keeps the shoes from the concentration camps, why we mark where George Washington slept, and why I asked to stand where a slave girl named Pinky once stood. Keeping these artifacts and preserving these places honors our past and is essential to our future.

After I left Plymouth Church, I walked through Brooklyn Heights on streets named after some of the earliest Dutch and English settlers—Hicks, Remsen, Boerum—landowners who made their fortunes in no small part from the efforts of slave labor. The homes are beautiful, pristine, like the homes on Duffield Street once were. Brooklyn Heights is a historic district, with well-documented evidence of its past. It is where, during the revolutionary war, George Washington and his men fought the British and where homes stood through which Harriet Tubman scuttled fugitive slaves to safety during the Civil War. Washington and Tubman couldn't be more different, and yet their defiant spirit, their determination to do what needed to be done against a formidable enemy, is a large part of what Brooklyn is made of.

"May I have your attention, please?" said a young man who looked like he had just begun shaving that morning. I was on the train headed for Bedford-Stuyvesant. "I don't mean to disturb you, but I'm selling candy this morning." I buried my face in my newspaper. Others busied themselves with electronic devices or fiddled inside their purses. "And I'm not selling them for a basketball team or for a school. I'm selling them for myself. *Me*," he said tenaciously. I looked up from my paper. I hadn't heard this one before. "And I plan on spending my money wisely and in a responsible manner. Thank you."

As our train pulled into the Utica Avenue station, an older gentleman, a black Muslim dressed in a long white tunic, called the kid over. "I don't want the candy," he said. "Take the dollar." He shoved the money into the kid's hand with as much cockiness as the kid had shown delivering his speech. Such a display of industriousness and pluck was a perfect introduction to my next destination.

African American historical landmarks are disappearing at an alarming rate. Too often what is left can only be imagined, but sometimes we get lucky. Weeksville was one of the earliest free African American communities, the center of intellectual, cultural, and economic life in Brooklyn. At its peak during the 1860s and '70s, five hundred to seven hundred prosperous African American families lived there. Susan Smith McKinney-Steward, the first female African American doctor in New York State, and Moses P. Cobb, Brooklyn's first black policeman, were among them. Some of the homes and churches were key stops on the Underground Railroad, undocumented of course; and there were at least two forgotten newspapers, the *Freedman's Torchlight* and the *People's Journal*. But despite that history, the four remaining structures of Weeksville had been scheduled to be torn down in 1968 in order to build more housing projects. Thankfully, they were saved by the efforts of James Hurley and Joseph Haynes, an historian and an amateur pilot, armed with an old map and a plane. They flew over the area and spotted an unfamiliar lane and several dilapidated homes partially hidden by overgrown weeds.

Hunterfly Road, which looks like a wide dirt path, runs diagonal to one of the modern streets. I entered the gate and found four perfectly restored pre–Civil War wood frames that look as if they were out of Colonial Williamsburg. The Hunterfly Road Houses, as they are now called, are surrounded by the Kingsborough projects, condos, and single-family homes built later in the twentieth century. They tower over the Weeksville Heritage Center like invading alien ships.

Like most eighteenth- and nineteenth-century homes, these houses have small rooms, box-shaped, with low ceilings and narrow staircases that can only accommodate one person going up or down at a time. Architects working for the Center have discovered that two of the homes were built in the same style as Southern slave quarters. Inside, the rooms are sparsely furnished; the Heritage Center needs more funds.

I came armed with a list of questions, the answers to most of which could only be speculated upon. The town of Weeksville is where victims of the Draft Riots escaped to in 1863. Hundreds of blacks from Manhattan and other parts of Brooklyn took refuge here from white mobs who lynched, burned, and beat them because they were angry about being drafted into the Civil War.

"We don't know if anyone came to these particular homes," Lauren Rhodes, the educational coordinator and guide, told me, "but there's a good chance that they did." The local celebrities back then, Dr. Susan Smith McKinney-Steward, Moses P. Cobb, and Junius C. Morel, a journalist and principal of Colored School No. 2, lived in Weeksville, but their homes as well as the school are now gone. The African Civilization Society met somewhere in Weeksville, and the Garnet Field

Club practiced baseball in a field, somewhere. The Brooklyn Howard Colored Orphan Asylum, which took in homeless children and those fresh from slavery, now belongs to a repair shop for the New York City Transit Authority.

Thanks to the *Brooklyn Daily Eagle*'s online archives, I know that Harriet Tubman spoke in Weeksville, as did Fredrick Douglass and Booker T. Washington. Elizabeth Keckly had a correspondence with Fredrick Douglass, and when she retired she taught at Wilberforce University in Ohio, the same place that Susan Smith McKinney-Steward worked after her retirement. At some time during her stay in New York, Keckly probably visited Weeksville, but I can only guess, since all that remains of the place is four little houses and a few churches scattered inside of what used to be its boundaries.

I was ready to work on the play, and though I didn't find a lot of what I was looking for, I had a sense of what a woman like Keckly experienced in 1860 New York. Hope and fear is what African Americans were living with back then. Hope for a better life, and fear that the outcome of the Civil War would throw them back into slavery. On that the evidence is pretty clear. How wonderful it would be to see more of the places in which their dreams and struggles took place. Back at Plymouth Church, I had asked Lois Rosebrooks why white people tend not to think of black history as their own history. The minute the question came out of my mouth, I wanted to take it back. It seemed a rude thing to ask of a woman who has devoted much of her life to preserving African American history. I could tell she was taken aback by my question but thankfully not offended. "People are bored by history," she said. "They don't want to know it, black or white. I don't know," she continued, "I'd have to think more on that."

Clearly, I had to as well.

I can't stop thinking about what that librarian said to me: "You can't change history because you don't like what you find." So much of American history lifts up our triumphs, while ignoring our infamy. And though black history is white history, much of it is a painful place to revisit, and so preserving it is not a priority. Changing it—or worse, destroying it—is like saying it never happened. The crimes are perpetrated once again.

In her retirement, Keckly taught at Wilberforce College before returning to Washington, D.C., where she died. The Harmony Cemetery, where she was buried, was paved over in the 1960s and her remains, unclaimed, were placed in an unmarked grave. Unfortunately, I won't be going to Washington, D.C.

PART IV

SKELSIES

In which two to six players assemble around a crooked course of obstacle lines and periodic stopping points chalked on the street or sidewalk pavement. Each player uses fingers to shoot a bottlecap (the "skelly") step by step through the obstacle course, halting just before the stopping points. Succeeding players may elect to "kill" opponents by knocking into their skelsies en route to the finish.

THE CREAMFLAKE KID

BY JESS KORMAN

Crown Heights

I t was to have been a productive workday. He would grind out six more pages. In the television industry swamp, in that summer of 1985, "pages" meant scripted scenes that a producer deemed worth a camera's time and trouble. This was how the Burbank geniuses measured their employee's worth: How many shootable pages could the hack du jour grind out?

According to Larry Sloan, né Scharfsky, you could substitute the word pounds for pages. That's what they wanted. Pounds of shootable crap for a low-budget series set in Brooklyn. They wanted to film "real people" and let them act out the stories, a terrible idea in which a bunch of nobodies carried on like somebodies. It was also wonderfully cheap to produce.

Manufacturing the six pages of this proposed disaster in his eight-by-ten rental office in the Artists and Writers Building on Little Santa Monica Boulevard in Beverly Hills was no easy feat. The director Billy Wilder rented the office across the hall. The aging and iconic Kirk Douglas, carrying a container of English Breakfast tea, sometimes shuffled through one of the smoked-glass doors three down. Larry's fellow tenants, highly worshiped avatars of the craft, were a stinging reminder of how low he had sunk in the scheme of things.

Larry Sloan was taking the buck and running. A shameful crime, he felt, but he was getting away with it. After all, nobody got hurt but Larry.

The walls of his office were painted in a particularly tired-out shade of gray. The cool of the Mexican stone floors seeped through his thin-soled Rockports. A dusty window looked out upon an alley, offering a glimpse of bougainvillea and the back wall of a garage. The stunning California sun, as reliable as it was relentless day after day, redeemed an otherwise grim view. As it is said in L.A., another goddamn beautiful day.

The pages were not coming today because Larry Sloan was somewhere else in his head, lost in his own Brooklyn, a long time ago, where his crime wave began.

The Creamflake Bakery, on Utica Avenue between Carroll and President, was a popular establishment in Crown Heights, catering not only to the Jews, but the Irish too, as well as some Italians—and, lately, newly arrived Caribbeans, whatever they were.

You could get challah at the Creamflake and Irish soda breads. Green cookies were sold on St. Patrick's Day, of course, and elaborate confections were available for Christmas, Hanukkah, Easter, and other religious events, such as when the Brooklyn Dodgers won the National League pennant the year before, which was 1952.

They called him Loo-Loo. The nickname had stuck since his baby days. He was ten now, and Al and Dotty still called him that. This was before being sensitive to your kid's feelings was called "good parenting." At P.S. 189 on East New York Avenue, the kids ragged on him about the girly-sounding moniker.

"It's not Lulu," he would snarl, spelling it out. "It's Loo-Loo, you stupid moron." This was the big put-down of 1953, the gilded age of "moron" jokes on the tube.

Anyhow, Loo-Loo's skin was thick. He had tons of friends.

He was a first-class punch-ball player. He could fire a pink Spalding—duly pronounced spal*deen*—the whole length between a pair of sewer covers in a neat trajectory. Automatic homer. On President Street, this was status.

The other thing about Loo-Loo's popularity was that Al Scharfsky owned the Creamflake. When your father sells chocolate cookies, jelly doughnuts, and charlotte russe, there is no shortage of kids who will gladly accompany you to the bakery for the sweet possibility of a handout.

Jack Horn was Al's partner. Jack was in charge of cakes. Al himself took care of the breads and rolls. Everything was baked in old stone ovens with piles of coal that glowed eternally in the corners.

Loo-Loo hung around sometimes. Jack and his father would let him squeeze jelly into the doughnuts, using a metal contraption with a lever and a long spout. Sometimes, the Russian help baked alligator-shaped bread with raisin eyes, especially for Loo-Loo. Ten o'clock at night or so, the cops drove by to collect bags of "stale," leftover breads and rolls which they took back to the 71st Precinct station house on Empire Boulevard.

Along Loo-Loo's stretch of Utica was the usual constellation of neighborhood shops—fruits and vegetables, butcher, freshly slaughtered chickens, fish, dresses, radio repair, barbers, and a candy store with a soda fountain. Two blocks further up, the retail pattern repeated, including a bakery just like the Creamflake, only it was called the Union because it was near Union Street.

Although people preferred shopping as few steps as possible from where they lived, they would sometimes cross the continent into the next block. Which is why Al Scharfsky considered the Union Bakery his arch competitor, especially in the summer of '53 with the place under mysterious new management.

Trolley cars once clanged their way up and down Utica, their motormen wearing neckties. Kids put pennies on the tracks and they got flattened out when the cars rattled past. Now there were buses, though the old tracks remained on the cobblestones as parallel reminders of the past, beyond Eastern Parkway into the unknown and ominous infinity of Bedford-Stuyvesant.

This was Loo-Loo's universe. President Street terminated at the enormous Lincoln Terrace Park, which separated the Andy Hardy tranquility of Crown Heights from the mean and dangerous Brownsville, birthplace of Murder Incorporated. While the park had plenty of green spaces for a game, the kids preferred the "gutter," a.k.a. the street. Two grand maple trees on either side were markers for first and third. The sewer cover in the middle was second.

Crown Heights was not at all like the fabled and dangerous Brooklyn of Cagney movies. It was more like some small town in middle America, at least the small-town America image perpetrated by Hollywood's immigrant studio heads.

Very innocent. Very tranquil. There were rows of one- and two-family houses, some of them in the Renaissance Revival, Georgian, and Romanesque styles, sometimes bookended by five-story apartment houses on each corner. Looming shade trees, elms and sycamores, lined the sidewalks like protective uncles.

But for some, danger seemed near at all times. Something in the air, obviously lurking yet inexplicable; a conventional notion that someone was coming to get you if you didn't watch your ass. One minute, everything seemed safe in the neighborhood. Then a cop car would come tearing down Utica on the way to a murder or a holdup someplace, its siren splitting the June air like heat lightning.

At the supper table, to make matters even more unsettling, Loo-Loo would sit staring into the dry chicken on his plate—chicken cooked to within an inch of its taste—exchanging looks with Rita, his little sister, while Al Scharfsky sang disturbing arias.

"It's changing, you know. The whole neighborhood. They're coming in."

"Who's coming, Pop?" Loo-Loo asked.

"People. The Immigrants. Coloreds. Spanish. People from Aruba."

"Where's Aruba, Pop?"

"It's down there. The rich people go there for gambling and ha-cha-cha and the criminals from there come to Crown Heights."

"What's wrong if they want to come here, Pop? Maybe you'll sell more rye bread."

"They don't eat rye bread, Loo-Loo. They eat their own food. Things with fish in it."

"Maybe they'll like your rye bread."

"Maybe," Al said, then changed the subject. "No sooner we got rid of Murder Incorporated, we got to deal with this element."

"What's an element?" Rita asked.

"A criminal element. Criminals are attracted to this neighborhood, honey."

"Uh-huh," said Rita, nodding her head, dimly satisfied.

Loo-Loo's mother raised her hand to say, "They're just poor people, Al. Besides, Murder Inc. around here, that was ten, twenty years ago."

"Oh, they're still around," said Al. "Believe me, Dotty. And nearby—just over into Brownsville." He lowered his voice, so as not to scare the kids, which scared the kids. "You saw on the Senator Kefauver hearings a couple years ago—those mobsters. Albert Anastasia. Frank Erickson. Frank Costello. They're still around assassinating each other left and right. Some of them live right around here, probably."

"I never saw Frank Costello on President Street," said Dotty.

Al leaned closer to his wife.

"You know those people who just bought the Union Bakery?" Al paused. "They could be connected to the mob."

Dotty snickered, which did nothing to soothe the frightened kids. "You're crazy, Al. What would the mob want with a bakery? And why are you whispering?"

"I'm just saying, the criminal element's all around and we have to be careful. Furthermore, look what happened to that shoe salesman last year—what's-his-name, Arnold Schuster. A Brooklyn guy. One of us. An innocent citizen."

Loo-Loo, an inveterate reader of the tabloids his father brought home every day and likewise an ardent viewer of the Kefauver hearings, enlightened his mother: "Anastasia had him bumped off. Schuster snitched to the cops about Willie Sutton the bank robber."

"Where'd you get that?" Al asked his boy.

"From Kefauver. Remember, Pop?"

Al, grumpily attempting to keep control of the conversation, replied quickly. "Arnold Schuster had nothing to do with Murder Inc., which was before you were born, Loo-Loo. What you say we change the subject?"

"Murder Incorporated were the ones who threw Abe Reles out the window," Loo-Loo now informed his goggle-eyed sister.

"Where'd you hear that?" Al barked.

"I dunno," said Loo-Loo. Not wishing to be forbidden access to tabs, he lied, "The schoolyard."

"Ah-hah! Schoolyard University," Al said with disgust.

"They said this guy Abe Reles gave names of gangsters to the G-men," continued Loo-Loo in a rush, "and the detectives were supposed to be guarding him, but then he fell out of the window at the Half Moon Hotel on Coney Island and it's a big mystery because they don't know if he was pushed out of the window of room 623 or if he was trying to escape."

Al eyed his son despairingly. "You know the room number, I see?"

The boy was on a roll. "They called Abe Reles 'the canary who sang but couldn't fly.'"

Al pushed away his plate. "Who's feeding you this trash?"

"I'm interested in crime. Just like you, Pop."

I'd prefer you to be interested in long division," Al said, after which he grumped into the living room where he could read the *Post* and maybe the *Brooklyn Eagle*—and certainly the *Journal-American* and the *World* and the *Daily Mirror*, these three being the reading mainstays of the bathroom—after which he would probably doze off, having begun his day at the bakery at the usual starting time of 5 o'clock in the a.m.

Gangsters were just the half of it. Spies also fascinated Loo-Loo, especially the Rosenbergs.

Convicted of being in league with the Reds a couple of years back, Julius and Ethel Rosenberg were sent up the river. Loo-Loo hadn't thought much about it at the time; he was only eight, after all. But he knew Mr. and Mrs. Rosenberg were parents, like his own, and that they had two sons about Loo-

Loo's own age. This made the case seem closer to home than the business about the racket guys Senator Kefauver talked about, guys like Joe Adonis and Frank Erickson.

But the thing that kept the spy case hot for Loo-Loo was Al Scharfsky's supper-table lament that it was an awful shame that Mr. and Mrs. Rosenberg were Jewish.

Weren't they guilty?

Al summarized the case. "Guilty? They're Jewish. We got enough troubles."

One warm night in that June of '53, Loo-Loo went out to Utica Avenue after supper for an ice-cream cone. Then he strolled to Chudow's radio repair store, across the street from the Creamflake, to watch television. Very few people owned TV sets, and a small crowd had gathered, as usual, to watch a flickering black-and-white DuMont screen in the store window. This was evening recreation in Crown Heights.

The news was on. Julius and Ethel Rosenberg had been executed in the electric chair at Sing Sing at sundown.

Loo-Loo worked his way through the onlookers, his cone dripping. There was no sound from the TV set, just the ghostly screen, with mugshots of the recently departed spies. A man in an Adam Hat and a business suit stood watching.

"What's goin' on?" Loo-Loo asked the man.

"They stole atomic bomb secrets, Sonny. Gave 'em to the Russians."

Loo-Loo was silent. He already knew that.

"Yep. Espionage. They fried 'em both for espionage."

"Jeez," was all Loo-Loo could say, wondering what espionage was.

"Yeah, and they said that Julius went just like *that* after the juice was turned on," said the man, snapping his fingers. "But they had trouble with the missus. Electrodes weren't working right. A witness said he saw smoke coming out of her head."

"Thanks, mister," Loo-Loo said to the man in the Adam Hat.

Then his knees went soft, and Loo-Loo felt as if he'd be reviewing his supper in about a minute. Still, he managed to finish the cone. When he got home, he consulted his dictionary:

es•pi•o•nage /n [F espionage.] the act of obtaining information clandestinely. Applies to act of collecting military and industrial data about one nation or business for the benefit of another.

Loo-Loo also looked up *clandestinely*. Which made his heart thump even faster.

The phone rang. Stunned out of Crown Heights, Larry Sloan picked up. It was the producer demanding to know: "How many pages?"

"I haven't counted. Leave me alone, Roger. I'm trying to work."

"Well, work fast. We've got another project coming up. You could be right for it, Larry. No promises."

"Want to tell me now?" Larry asked.

"We'll talk about it," Roger said, dangling the invisible carrot with which Larry was so familiar.

"Goodbye," Larry said.

"Don't go anywhere. Pages, okay? Later."

* * *

Even before school let out for the summer, some June days of 1953 could be stifling at P.S. 189, this being the era before everything in the city was routinely air-conditioned.

On such blazing days, school ended early, releasing to the damp heat Loo-Loo and a couple of his inner-circle pals, Teddy Newman and Lester Dank. They hightailed it across Lincoln Terrace Park to the Creamflake, in the cause of a guaranteed gratis charlotte russe for each.

The coveted charlotte russe consisted of a slab of sponge cake set in a little white cardboard cup, topped with whipped cream and a ceremonious glazed cherry—a particular favorite of the chunkier Lester. As the boys entered, Al Scharfsky sized up the troop and ordered Manya, the Czech refugee beauty with the visible gold tooth who worked behind the counter, to give the boys what they wanted. Manya did.

Manya always wore a tight sweater, making it hard for Loo-Loo and his friends to keep their eyes off the cushiony outlines. Whenever Manya saw the boys staring, she smiled, and her gold incisor would catch the light in Slavic appreciation.

As instructed, she now gave Loo-Loo and Lester and Teddy a charlotte russe. Then Al asked his son's two pals to take a hike because he needed to talk to Loo-Loo privately. This was unusual, but the boys left, their faces smeared with whipped cream as they stole a last look at Manya's majestic sweater.

"What'd I do, Pop?"

"Nothing. Come in the back, we got a job for you."

"We" meant Pop and Mr. Horn, who never talked much. The two men moved to the end of a long butcher-block work-table, motioning for Loo-Loo to come close. Back by the ovens, the Russians turned to watch.

Al Scharfsky lit up a Chesterfield and took a deep drag.

He spoke in a muted tone, with exhaled smoke punctuating his words. "You know the Union Bakery?"

"Yeah."

Al reached into the secret petty cash drawer under the butcher block and extracted a five-dollar bill. Loo-Loo knew about the drawer because it was where his father and Mr. Horn kept a gun in case of a robbery.

"Take this and go to the Union Bakery," said Al, handing over the fiver to Loo-Loo. "Buy a chocolate layer cake. Don't tell them who you are or where you're from. Just give them the money and bring back a chocolate layer cake."

"The Union is our competitor, right? Can I go in there?"

"Sure you can. Just don't say nothing."

"But why, Pop?"

Mr. Horn—in charge of cakes, after all—chimed in. "Because we need to know what they're putting into the layer cakes," said the man who didn't say much. "Understand? It's business."

"But what if they find out that you sent me?"

Al placed a fatherly hand on his boy's shoulder. "They're not gonna find out, bright boy, because you're not gonna say nothing. Just buy the cake. Is that so hard?"

"No," said Loo-Loo. He liked being called *bright boy*. "I thought you said the Union is owned by the mob."

"I didn't say. I only heard."

"They're gonna know where I'm from."

"No. They don't know who the hell you are," said Al. "You're some kid buying a layer cake. Now hurry, before they sell out."

All eyes were on Loo-Loo. Al, Mr. Horn, and the Russians were studying him, assessing his bravery. Especially the Russians, immigrants being naturally curious about matters of risk.

Al said, "You can keep the change, Loo-Loo. After you do it, that is."

Mr. Horn inquired, "You ain't a sissy, are you?"

With the fiver deep in his pants pocket, Loo-Loo proceeded up Utica toward Eastern Parkway—past Chudow's radio repair shop, past the chicken store, past the fruit market.

At Union Street, a hotness crawled across his chest. It felt like the prickly heat rash he sometimes got in August, but this was only June.

Espionage! They were asking him to commit espionage. Loo-Loo, a bright boy, was about to procure secrets from the competitor and deliver said intelligence to the Creamflake.

Wasn't this kind of thing against the law? Wasn't it punishable by J. Edgar Hoover and his federal authorities, who had sent Mr. and Mrs. Rosenberg to the electric chair? And what about that higher court in the sky that Al and Dotty had talked about when Loo-Loo was little?

At that moment, he caught sight of McEntee, the huge cop of the neighborhood. He was ambling down Utica with a bunch of grapes in one hand and a peach in the other. He was always eating something he got from the storekeepers for free. Loo-Loo jaywalked to the other side, trying not to look suspicious.

What if McEntee asked him where he was going? Would Loo-Loo confess? Kids could go to jail. The city was getting tough on juvenile delinquents. Loo-Loo had seen plenty of reform schools in the movies. Full of delinquents, mostly Irish kids who would beat the crap out of you if you looked at them funny. Especially if your name was something like Loo-Loo.

Loo-Loo passed Union Street now, and found himself in the repeat line of little shops. Then the big sign over the street like a movie marquee: *Union Bakery*. Loo-Loo dragged his heels over the pavement, shuffling forward. He didn't want to move, but he was somehow moving anyhow.

What if it was true that gangsters had taken over the Union? Gangsters would know the minute Loo-Loo walked in that he was up to no good, that he was a spy for the Creamflake.

They'd grab him right there, take him in the back of the bakery, and tie him up, make him talk. *So you won't talk, huh? Hey, Tony, get a hot coal out of the oven and let's burn a hole in his freakin' head.* Or else they'd stick the spout of the doughnut machine in his ear and press the lever, filling his skull with strawberry jelly. They did things like that, these gangsters. Loo-Loo had heard the stories, he'd watched the Kefauver hearings. And didn't he faithfully study the crime blotter in the *Daily Mirror*, just the same as Al himself did during his long stays in the can?

But even if the Union guys weren't gangsters, Loo-Loo reasoned, he was still doing something really wrong in buying their cake—*clandestinely*!

So when J. Edgar Hoover sat Loo-Loo Scharfsky down on Old Sparky, would the electrodes function properly? Or would smoke come billowing out of his head? Say—how about if Loo-Loo managed to escape to Coney Island and hide out in room 623 at the Half Moon Hotel? Would somebody toss him out the window, making it look like he did the old brain-dive?

Funny how the Union Bakery smelled just like the Cream-flake. This was comforting for about five seconds. Things even looked alike.

Tall glass showcases displayed cakes and cookies, breads and rolls. Loo-Loo had never gone into this shop, of course—ever. It was off limits. Yet the merchandise looked so familiar, and the girls behind the counter looked so much like Manya.

A few customers were ahead of him, so Loo-Loo lingered at the counter, waiting his turn. *What's that? You say you can hear my heart beating, mister? That's not my heart, it's coming from the subway tracks. Get outta my way. I got business.*

"What would you like, dear?" asked a cushiony Manya look-alike.

"A chocolate layer cake, please."

"What size, honey?"

"Size?"

"Seven-inch or nine-inch?" The woman gave a nod of her head toward the showcase with the fancy cakes.

This was a monkey-wrench question, thought Loo-Loo, who felt as if he was suddenly coming down with a fever. If he hesitated, the woman would suspect. She'd send some kind of signal, and a couple of thugs would come bursting out from the back of the shop.

Loo-Loo studied the cakes. *Don't try anything, sister. My father owns a gun.*

"Well, dear?"

"The nine-inch," said Loo-Loo, figuring Mr. Horn would want as much as he could get.

Sister took the chocolate cake out from the showcase, slid it into a half-opened cake box, closed the sides, and deftly tied and bowed it with a curly red-and-white string that spooled down from the ceiling—just like the spool at the Creamflake.

"Two dollars," she said. Loo-Loo dug in for the bill, passed it up to her, took the change, and ran like hell.

He shouldn't have bolted out of the Union like that. He should have left slowly. But he couldn't take it. They could probably hear his heart pounding in Brownsville, clear across the park.

Obviously, the woman suspected something fishy was going on. She'd be in the back by now, telling the hard guys. And then they'd come tearing out of the store after him.

If not the hard guys, then somebody. Cops maybe, or the FBI. Or even the dreaded "element." It could be anybody, but one thing was for sure: *Somebody* was going to get Loo-Loo today.

It didn't matter who. Loo-Loo was in too deep. He'd crossed the mob. He'd committed a federal crime. He was tangled in a clandestine web of lies. At least that's how they talked when he listened to *The Shadow* on the radio. A *web of lies*.

But this was the real thing, not some stupid mystery show. Loo-Loo ran for his life, and the faster he ran, the faster the tears washed down his face. *You big sissy! What are you crying about, you moron?* The tears burned, and blurred.

The big hand seemed to come out from the sky.

It gripped his arm. It seized him powerfully and held fast, bringing the bawling Loo-Loo to a dead halt.

It was all over. The end of the line, and inspiration for the big block letters in tomorrow's *Daily Mirror*: BLOODY DEAD KID SPLATTERED ALL OVER UTICA AVENUE.

Not quite.

McEntee's shiny badge was slowly becoming visible through the big puddle of Loo-Loo's eyeballs.

"Now where's the fire, boyo? You looking for trouble?"

"No."

"You know you almost ran into that bus? You trying to wreck a bus or something?" McEntee laughed. "You want to be more careful. You could hurt people, feller."

"Sorry."

"Watcha got in the box? Looks like a cake."

Loo-Loo now sized up McEntee, noting with disgust how the big cop was smacking his lips. "Yeah," he said, "it's a cake."

"How's about donating a big piece to the Patrolmen's Benevolent Association?"

"It's for my father," said Loo-Loo, prepared to run like hell again. "Gotta go!"

McEntee laughed.

They were waiting for him at the Creamflake. Al and Mr. Horn and the Russians and Manya in her sweater.

Wordlessly, Loo-Loo's father took the Union box and had the boy follow him to the back, where he plunked the parcel down on the baking table.

Mr. Horn picked up a huge knife. He cut the string and opened the box and slid the chocolate layer cake onto the surface, positioning it under a glaring overhead light, and there it sat: pristine, a work of the baker's art and toil, a prize.

Then—*whack!*—in a sudden motion, Mr. Horn brought down the knife, like it was a six-pound meat cleaver, slashing the chocolate cake in two. Everybody watched as Mr. Horn surgically slit the layers.

There were three layers of dark chocolate, with viscous spaces defining them: one space filled with raspberry jam, chocolate buttercream in the other. Again like the careful surgeon, Mr. Horn scraped at the fillings, determining their thickness, their richness. He handed a layer to Al, who tasted it.

Then the Russian bakers closed in for a taste. All the men

made knowledgeable comments as they probed and dissected and sampled the enemy booty. Mr. Horn took notes, writing on a brown paper bag, which he would later hang over the worktable.

"You did a good job," Al said to Loo-Loo. "Just don't mention it to your friends."

"Why not?"

"On account of it's nobody's business. Understand?"

"Yeah."

"How much change did you keep, Loo-Loo?"

"Three dollars."

Al reached into the petty cash drawer.

"Here's two dollars extra," he said. "Go buy yourself a present at the Woolworth's. Good job, kiddo."

Loo-Loo heard the bleating siren of a cop car as it sped past the Creamflake, heading for Brownsville, no doubt, where somebody was holding up a liquor store or maybe a Plymouth exploded with somebody inside of it.

Loo-Loo studied the dollar bills, saying nothing. Five bucks in all. Pretty good. He stared at the engraving on the bills, particularly the triangle atop the pyramid with the one eye on it—staring back at Loo-Loo Scharfsky, as if it knew all about him.

"When we finish this project—remember, we got something more for you, Larry"

"What? A game show?"

"No. It's a movie script we picked up. White Heat meets Diff'rent Strokes. A gritty urban story, only there's no grit yet. We need you to—you know—Brooklyn it up."

"Brooklyn it up?"

"Yeah. Think you can handle it?"

"Piece of cake."

"Money's good too."

"I'm all over it."

EDITORS' NOTE: *The author of this report, Jess Korman, is a shy person. He is of the same quirky generation of television writers as Neil "Doc" Simon, with whom he shares two impulses: recounting life experience comedically, as a means of relieving pain through laughter; and hiding behind alter egos. In writing his memoir, Jess Korman employs assorted aliases. In the case of "The Creamflake Kid," a true tale (though some names have been changed), the character Larry Sloan, né Scharfsky, a.k.a. Loo-Loo, is indeed the alter ego of a shy person.*

MOMMY WEARS A WIRE

BY DENISE BUFFA

Borough Park

Judge Gerald Garson, a cigar-smoking, suntanning Brooklyn jurist, was known to hold court in chambers. After sliding off his heavy overcoat, he would strut around in his crisp, dark suit and talk nonstop at whoever would listen. Those who needed favors from the foul-mouthed seventy-year-old would give him their full attention. They'd laugh on cue.

Attorney Paul Siminovsky—young enough to be Garson's son—was a sorry excuse for a lawyer, but a professional ass-kisser. When he wasn't wining and dining Garson at the Brooklyn Marriott hotel's bar/restaurant—feeding an estimated $10,000 worth of food and drink to the judge's belly over the years—Siminovsky was hanging out with the jurist in chambers, right off the courtroom Garson controlled at 210 Joralemon Street in Brooklyn Heights. The two men—Garson, the product of a well-connected Democratic family, and Siminovsky, who hoped to be adopted—shared the same sense of humor. For a while, they acted like a couple of frat boys.

The senior Garson sat behind his big desk one day in March 2003, making lewd and demeaning remarks about women, some of whom he was railroading in his courtroom. The sophomoric Siminovsky, then forty-six, popped candy into his mouth, indulging himself from the bowl on the judge's desk.

"Rose Ann C. Branda. What's the C. for?" Garson mused.

"I don't want to say what comes to mind," Siminovsky retorted.

"Cuchita," the judge said.

"Cuchita?" Siminovsky asked.

"*Cuchita banana . . .*" the judge sang, as he waved his hands in the air from his chair.

Siminovsky laughed on cue.

Siminovsky was at home inside the judge's private parlor, plopping himself into a black leather chair, crossing his legs, throwing back his big curly head, and laughing all the way to the bank.

Siminovsky garnered more jobs from Garson than any other lawyer. When kids needed to be represented in contentious custody battles, which paid tens of thousands of dollars in legal fees, he was Garson's first pick.

The powerful matrimonial judge—who decided the financial and familial fates of desperate men and women in highly disputed divorce cases—had a reputation of favoring those with brawn over those with breasts.

Anyone familiar with Garson's courtroom knew Siminovsky was on a winning streak there. No wonder. Judge and jester hammered out cases behind closed doors—without opposing counsel, blatantly violating rules of fairness.

Siminovsky once told Garson to give a house to his client, Avraham Levi, who was getting divorced. And the judge guaranteed him a win.

"The house. Oh, you gotta order custody. His father owns half of it and he owns a quarter of it," Siminovsky urged the judge at one point.

"Oh, you mean *your* guy," Garson said.

"Yeah," Siminovsky said.

"I'll order, I'll award, I'll award him exclusive use on [the house]," Garson assured Siminovsky. "She's fucked . . ."

Frieda Hanimov, a mother of three, feared she too would get screwed by Garson. Hanimov, a nurse who had reared three well-mannered children with her diamond-dealer husband, noted that Garson was so abrasive to her in the courtroom one might think she was a crack-addled streetwalker.

"I'm a mother, three kids, married to a multimillionaire, and I lose everything. How could a mother lose?" she said. "I'm not a drug addict. I'm not a prostitute. How could you not be suspicious? I knew this judge was not normal."

The feisty Israeli émigré was convinced her ex-husband had fixed the outcome of their custody case. And she was determined to keep her kids at any cost.

Hanimov, a sociable woman who made friends easily, had already been warned by Levi's wife, Sigal Levi—who was fighting for her own children before Garson—that rumor had it wealthy men were able to fix their cases before the judgmental jurist. All they had to do was pay off the judge through a middleman, Nissim Elmann—a close associate of Siminovsky, who not so coincidentally had been appointed guardian for at least one of Hanimov's children.

Elmann, a disheveled businessman who wore a yarmulke and an unbuttoned shirt under his tie, sold wholesale electronics just a few short miles from the courthouse. He worked out of a graffiti-emblazoned warehouse, which served as a front for a second lucrative business: brokering divorces and custody battles in Brooklyn's Orthodox Jewish communities.

A desperate but daring Hanimov—with more verve than

the Energizer bunny—walked into the warehouse to see Elmann. At risk were her three priceless jewels: fourteen-year-
old Yaniv, ten-year-old Sharon, and five-year-old Natti. She
had given up everything in her divorce for them.

"They are my soul," said Hanimov, who feared she
would lose all three to her husband. He had already accused her of beating their eldest son with a belt—an accu-
sation she tearfully denied, and of which she was ultimately
cleared.

Elmann was a smooth-talking salesman, and used his
shtick to convince men and women that they needed his
services to get the upper hand on their soon-to-be exes in
Garson's courtroom.

"He said, 'This guy is in my pocket,' and I was like . . . I
was in shock," Hanimov said.

When Hanimov left Elmann's electronics business, DVD
Trading on Brooklyn Avenue, the not-so-dumb blonde—who
had spoken to the shady businessman in Hebrew—knew
that the rumors were true: Elmann was selling far more than
DVDs and electronic equipment from his warehouse; he was
peddling justice in Garson's courtroom.

After that first visit, a frantic Hanimov called the Brooklyn district attorney's office. Within days, intrigued investigators had the nurse—very pregnant with her fourth child,
the first by her second husband—going undercover, wired for
sound.

"I was putting one [electronic bug] in my bag, the other
one in my pocket, and the other one in my breast, in my bra,"
she said.

This amateur sleuth—whom one movie studio has dubbed
the Erin Brockovich of Brooklyn—has now been credited with
cracking the biggest corruption case to ever rock the Brooklyn

courts. The pregnant mother of three wore wires and captured conversations behind closed doors that would shock the public conscience.

Her heart raced as she made her way back into the salesman's office, the metal gate of the desolate warehouse closing her off to the outside world, including the investigators sitting outside in an unmarked car.

"If he knew I had that device on me, he would shoot me on the spot. I was nine months pregnant," Hanimov said.

She captured Elmann's claims on audiotape in October 2002.

"Your husband paid money, a lot of money. And he has the upper hand," Elmann told her.

"What is the upper hand?" Hanimov asked.

"Like whatever he says, he'll get, okay? He also doesn't care about wasting money because he knows that you don't have money," Elmann said.

Hanimov knew it was true. Cold hard cash—not motherly love—would win her three kids. She left Elmann's warehouse crying.

About two weeks later, she met with Elmann and told him she would come up with her own money to win the bidding war for her children.

But, she asked, could he speak to those in control in the meantime?

"There's no way. It doesn't work like that," Elmann told her in no uncertain terms. "Bring them something so that they will start to work. You'll see something substantive, and you'll bring the rest." He added that otherwise, "Garson will destroy you . . . That's business."

They agreed on a $5,000 to $10,000 price tag.

Ever the salesman, Elmann then offered Hanimov a TV on the cheap. "A television like this, that I give you now for one hundred and fifty, costs three hundred in a store," he said.

But Hanimov remained focused on the far greater commodity. Could Elmann really deliver?

He showed her Garson's telephone number in his cell phone, and files of others he claimed to have helped. And the businessman reassured her in broken English, "He [Garson] will do everything for me. The problem is here, how much you can to sacrifice."

Two weeks later, the investigation intensified, and a frightened Hanimov returned to the warehouse.

"If I scream, 'Help,' please help," she told investigators who were listening to her over the wire from outside.

"Okay," Detective Investigator George Terra reassured her.

Waddling with the weight of the baby she was carrying, she knew that once that metal gate closed behind her, she could be a goner.

"Even if they [the investigators] wanted to get to me, they couldn't," Hanimov said. "It's [a] huge warehouse where they gotta find me."

She made her way to Elmann's office—with a $500 down payment.

Elmann told her that Siminovsky was in the warehouse. The lawyer's Volvo was in open view outside. But the boorish barrister, who wouldn't give her the time of day in court, was nowhere to be found.

"Why doesn't he want to see me?" Hanimov asked Elmann.

"It's dangerous, you know. It's really dangerous," he replied.

A week later, Hanimov arrived with more cash. And the electronics salesman gave her a lesson in law.

"What is 'chamber'?" she asked.

"Chamber [is] where they talk, they arrange things before they come to court," Elmann said. "And afterwards, they put on a show for you."

Hanimov gave Elmann $3,000 in marked $100 bills, provided by the Brooklyn D.A.'s office, to get Garson to perform for her.

Although pleased with her progress, Hanimov left the warehouse angry. As the metal gate lifted to let her out, she uttered a single word caught on her body wire: "Bastard!"

She gave Elmann $9,000 in total during the course of the five-month investigation, and noted that Garson and Siminovsky immediately began treating her with civility.

Throughout her visits with Elmann, Hanimov repeatedly insisted on listening in on a conversation between the businessman and the judge. "I am begging," she said.

But the fast-talking fixer who boasted that he called the shots in Garson's courtroom (although evidence shows the only one he had a direct link to was Siminovsky) wormed his way out of it.

"There is no reason for you to, I cannot let you hear such words," he told Hanimov. "What do you want, that he [Garson] go to jail?"

By late November 2002, Hanimov had gathered enough evidence to give prosecutors probable cause to tap both Elmann and Siminovsky's phone lines, and to plant a bug in the ceiling of Garson's chambers.

Evidence tapes show that the two tangential targets were tight. They embraced when they bid each other goodbye one cold dark night outside the warehouse. Like close friends, they also reassured one another when things weren't going well. When Elmann was uneasy about which way his client

Levi's case was going to go, Siminovsky, who was representing Levi, assured him of a win.

"I was getting Garson, I was getting Garson drunk for two hours. He'll do what I want . . ." a cocky and confident Siminovsky said.

In January 2003, prosecutors decided to "tweak the wire"—to create an incident that would cause their suspects to engage in a flurry of phone calls. They sent their secret weapon, Hanimov, to bribe Siminovsky directly with $1,000.

"Siminovsky freaks out and goes crazy," Assistant D.A. Noel Downey recalled.

Griping to Elmann the next day, Siminovsky said, "I thought she just flipped out and I thought she knew something . . ."

But Elmann reassured him, "No, she don't know shit."

Siminovsky, sounding a bit like his mentor Garson, boasted that he could have demanded sexual favors from Hanimov in exchange for helping her get her kids back. "You know what I could have told her? . . . I could have said to her, 'You want your kids? Get on all fours and suck my dick,'" Siminovsky said. "You know what she would have done? She would have done it."

Mother Nature was as cold as those words on the clear February morning when Siminovsky spied flashing lights in the rearview mirror of his Volvo—and pulled over not far from his house in Whitestone, Queens.

The probers worked quickly. They wanted to flip Siminovsky into cooperating with them against Garson before anyone noticed they had picked him up.

They took a scared Siminovsky to the austere Fort Hamilton army base in Bay Ridge for questioning. Once inside the prison-like complex, enclosed by barbed wire, they entered a cold room in a bare brick building and read Siminovsky his rights—but he didn't want a lawyer. Confronted with the evidence against him, the father of two, wringing his hands and rubbing his head, asked to call his wife. Then, with the promise of a misdemeanor conviction and no time behind bars, the big-bellied barrister agreed to help investigators nail Garson.

"He flips in like fifteen or twenty minutes," Downey said. "He folded like a house of cards."

During the interrogation, Siminovsky's cell phone kept ringing. It was none other than the judge himself.

"He wanted to go to lunch," Assistant D.A. Michael Vecchione, head of the Brooklyn D.A.'s Rackets Division, said, laughing.

A week later, Siminovsky was in Garson's chambers and gave the judge a box of cigars. "I feel like Groucho," Garson said as he chomped on a stogie.

The turncoat lawyer put the carton in the top drawer of the judge's desk. Siminovsky said he got the cigars from a client, but in actuality investigators bought the box, spending upwards of $200.

The action was captured in grainy black-and-white images by the eye of the camera above.

"Romeo y Julieta. *Warning: Cigars are not a safe alternative to cigarettes . . .*" the judge read from the carton, commenting, "They are not a safe alternative to sex neither . . . but what are we going to do about it?"

He then took the box from his top drawer and put it in the lower one as if to hide it in a safer place. Minutes later, the plotting protégé Siminovsky thanked Garson for all his help, and asked for more guidance regarding the Levi divorce.

"Because you have my head together. You know, you gave

me little pointers. Now you just have to tell me what to write in the memo and then we'll be okay," Siminovsky said.

The judge helped Siminovsky draft the memo, seeming disinterested as he gave dictation.

"The only evidence in the case is . . . whatever the hell it was by stipulation or blah, blah . . ." he said. Then he gave a bit of unsolicited advice to Siminovsky. He wanted his boy to cash in on the extra work they were doing. "I am telling you, charge for it . . . This is extra . . . this was not contemplated . . . The judge made me do it . . . Fucking squeeze the guy . . ." Garson said.

Less than a week later, Siminovsky slipped an envelope containing ten marked $100 bills to the judge, as thanks for referring a client to him. The judge stuffed the envelope into his pants pocket, even though he was prohibited from taking referral fees. It was only after Siminovsky left that the judge, alone in chambers, opened the envelope and counted the cash. He panicked, and summoned Siminovsky back.

"Yeah, ah, Paul, this is, ah, Garson, do me a favor, ah, why don . . . ah, if you can get back here I'd appreciate it," he told the lawyer by phone.

When Siminovsky returned, the judge said, "This is a lot of money for whatever you call it . . ."

He gave back the bills, but Siminovsky told him, "Don't worry about it," and threw the envelope on the judge's desk.

Garson picked it up and half-heartedly tried to hand it to Siminovsky again—there was at least three feet between the far edge of the envelope and the tips of the lawyer's fingers—and then put it in his desk drawer.

After a little more back and forth between the two, Garson finally said, "I appreciate it."

Earlier that same day the judge had made a remark to

Siminovsky about his work that would prove prophetic: "One of the greatest things about this job is I don't know what the fuck I have tomorrow until I get here. I don't give a shit either, you know."

Two days later, the judge got the shock of his life, before he got to work. Investigators picked him up outside his Upper East Side apartment and took him to the same army barracks in the shadow of the Verrazano Bridge where they'd brought Siminovsky.

Garson was carrying the marked $100 bills—and insisted on a lawyer (not Siminovsky).

Once the attorney arrived, the judge refused to cooperate. That was when investigators asked if they could speak to him alone.

They fed Garson a little detail: The candy dish Siminovsky regularly reached into on the judge's desk had broken recently—and had to be replaced.

That seemingly harmless anecdote got the judge's attention. How could anyone know it unless the place was bugged? Then a peek at the cigar video had the judge singing a tune far different than his raunchy renditions in chambers.

A fidgety Garson—who took long pauses between sentences as if to catch his breath—offered to help prosecutors nail Brooklyn Democratic Party bigwig Clarence Norman. And as if getting pledged into Siminovsky's new fraternity, Garson agreed to wear a wire. He maintained he could prove that on sale in Kings County was far more than the justice that prosecutors suspected, but whole judgeships.

Despite the try, Garson turned up nothing. However, prosecutors have credited the judge with providing information that led to Norman's subsequent indictment on unrelated corruption charges.

On April 23, 2003, Garson traded his robes for handcuffs. He turned himself in—a stogie in his mouth, curl of smoke swirling upward—under the lights of TV and newspaper cameras, so his fingerprints and mug shot could be taken.

"When I asked him, 'Why did you do this with Siminovsky? Why did you take care of him? Why did you accept that?' he said, 'I like him and he kind of reminded me of myself,'" Vecchione said.

Siminovsky has pleaded guilty to a misdemeanor charge of giving unlawful gratuities for wining and dining the judge in exchange for receiving lucrative guardianship jobs. Prosecutors have asked that he be spared jail time, but he could be sentenced to up to one year behind bars.

Having resigned from the bar and having promised never to practice law again in New York State, Siminovsky is doing manual labor in a warehouse to help support his wife and two kids. He's a key witness in Garson's upcoming trial.

Also busted were Elmann, Levi, and others, including a court clerk and court officer accused of steering cases to Garson's courtroom for cash and cameras—bypassing the computerized random-selection process aimed at stemming corruption.

Among the others were a rabbi and his daughter, who greased Elmann's palms in an attempt to get Garson to rule in their favor.

While most wore frowns as they looked forward and then to the side for the mug shots, Garson sported a smirk across his lips and a steely glint in his eyes.

Suspended without pay from his $136,700-a-year job and later retired, Garson maintains his innocence. He is awaiting trial on charges of receiving bribes in the form of drinks and dinners from Siminovsky. He is not charged with fixing cases for cash.

Garson claimed he was on his way to report Siminovsky to authorities when he was intercepted by investigators.

"I regret very much not turning in Mr. Siminovsky immediately," he told CBS News as the media storm continued.

His lawyer, Ron Fischetti, has maintained the judge was set up. He has convinced a judge to throw out many of the charges. While Brooklyn D.A. Charles Hynes is appealing, left are one felony and two misdemeanors.

"It's an extremely weak case and I think he'll be acquitted," Fischetti said.

Elmann—the mysterious electronics salesman—has pleaded guilty to thirteen counts, including seven felonies of bribery, bribe-receiving, and conspiracy. He's throwing himself on the mercy of the court at sentencing and could get anywhere from probation to twenty-eight years. There is no evidence he knew Garson personally.

"You see, I bullshit these people left and right just for [them] to come up with money," he once told Siminovsky. ". . . I don't give a shit about them."

Levi, fifty-one, has pleaded guilty to giving Elmann $10,000 to fix his case. There is no direct evidence that Garson ever received a dime.

Rabbi Ezra Zifrani, sixty-seven, and his daughter, Esther Weitzner, thirty-seven, each pleaded guilty to one misdemeanor conspiracy charge in exchange for 210 hours of community service and three years of probation. They made it clear in court the only person they knew was Elmann.

Court Officer Louis Salerno—caught on videotape taking from Siminovsky a bag prosecutors say contained a VCR and DVD player outside the courthouse for steering cases to

Garson—was convicted at trial of two felonies: taking a bribe and receiving a reward for official misconduct. Salerno, fifty-two, faces up to seven years behind bars.

Retired Court Clerk Paul Sarnell, fifty-eight, has been acquitted of bribe-receiving.

Hanimov's husband was never charged with any wrongdoing. There was no evidence to support Elmann's claim that he had tried to buy the custody of his children.

Hanimov has landed herself a $200,000 movie contract with Warner Brothers for the rights to her story, heads a support group for women, and is looking forward to the final real-life scene of the saga, testifying against Garson.

"One of the happiest days in my life was when Judge Garson got arrested," she said. "He destroyed many, many, many lives."

Her best reward of all, of course, has been gaining custody of all three children. She is enjoying them now, along with the baby she gave birth to before Garson's bust.

"If a mother loses her kids, she lost one of the parts of her body. When you take her kids away from her, her life is over," she said. "Thank God, I have my kids back."

_____

POSTSCRIPT: *Since this piece was written, more of the Gerald Garson saga has played itself out.*

Nissim Elmann was sentenced to 1 1/4 to 5 1/2 years in prison.

Court Officer Louis Salerno was sentenced to 1 to 4 1/2 years.

Judge Jeffrey Berry, disregarding prosecutors' recommendations for leniency, sentenced Paul Siminovsky to one year in jail.

Garson was convicted of bribe-receiving and receiving rewards for official misconduct after trial. He wept when he was sentenced to 3 to 10 years in prison.

In sentencing Elmann and Salerno, Berry declared, "Justice is not for sale."

BEEF KILLS

BY ROSEMARIE YU
East New York

> *Let reverence for the law become the political religion of the*
> *nation.*
> —Abraham Lincoln (as seen on the entrance to Thomas
> Jefferson High School, East New York, Brooklyn)

N o one much cares what happens in East New York.
Most folks outside of Brooklyn likely don't know
where the neighborhood is, much less how to get
there. And for the most part you can't blame them. In a city
of eight million, where homeless people are scattered across
city streets and at least a handful of violent crimes are regular
occurrences in said streets, caring is a luxury you can't afford.
This was especially true in 1991.

East New York in '91 was a neighborhood where abandoned cars littered the curbs because no one cared enough
to tow them away. Children would be kept up at night by the
sounds of semi-automatic weapons fired off in abandoned lots,
which continued because they were rarely hushed by the subsequent wail of police sirens. It was a neighborhood where a
small, narrow, darkly lit bar could house fully naked prostitutes dancing salsa in a corner and pass itself off as a "strip
bar" rather than a whorehouse.

In one residential block, a marijuana dealer peddled his

wares through a small hole, just large enough for a hand, cut into a small square steel plate installed on the wall of the house. The buyer would knock and state his order, then money and pot would change hands through that hole—with neither buyer nor seller ever seeing one another's faces. It was well understood that in a place where the police don't respond to the sound of machine guns, the DEA wouldn't be busting marijuana dealers over nickel bags.

East New York in the early '90s was a dumping ground for the city's marginalized, each immigrant group that moved up and out replaced by the next off the boat. The population was primarily black and Latino and, for the most part, freshly arrived to these shores. It had, as yet, failed to enjoy the gentrification brought to other parts of Brooklyn by young families seeking spare bedrooms and middle-class professional singles pushed out of the Manhattan housing market. Crime, isolation, poor schools, and drugs would keep such potential gentrification groups uninterested for quite some time.

East New York was a strange island of impoverished, neglected housing projects amidst a sea of burned-out homes and commercial buildings that were never restored to use—by people with rent money, anyway. It was a long subway ride from the business centers of Brooklyn and Manhattan, and, lacking shopping centers, museums, decent housing, or any type of job prospects, the neighborhood offered the outside world little reason to ever stop by. It was a place where the isolation of its residents made them distrustful of outsiders, especially the law, meaning the police. And like any group of people left to their own devices, the rules of the outside world ceased to matter.

Handguns were plentiful and cheap, but were not regarded as flashy ornaments. Many residents, including teenagers, carried concealed guns and knives because they genuinely feared for their own safety. But though the 75th Precinct reportedly confiscated numerous unregistered weapons on a daily basis, countless more went unnoticed.

In '91, the story of a skinny twitch named Bernhard Goetz was still fresh in everyone's minds. Several years earlier, Goetz, who had taken to carrying an unlicensed handgun after his second mugging, encountered four black teenagers on the subway. The boys were carrying blunt screwdrivers they planned to use to break into video arcade games. When the boys approached him and asked for money, Goetz—in a fit of rage, fear, desperation, prejudice, or hatred, depending on the account you believe—fired his gun repeatedly into each of them at close range. The boys survived, with one left a paraplegic. Goetz, ultimately convicted only of illegal weapons possession, went on to run for mayor, then public advocate—both futile campaigns.

After the shooting, the "subway vigilante," as Goetz was tagged by the tabloids, became the embodiment of either the proposition that a middle-class white male can shoot black kids with impunity, or of the desperation of law-abiding citizens fed up with crime run amok. Either way you looked at it, it was a sign of the racial polarization of the time.

In August 1991, this point was driven home even harder in Crown Heights, when a young Guyanese boy was hit and killed by a rabbi's motorcade. Within hours, an angry mob looking to kill a Jew—any Jew—wreaked vengeance upon Yankel Rosenbaum, a bystander with the poor luck to be in the wrong place at the wrong time. For the following four days, a torrent of unchecked, pent-up outrage from the neighborhood's black Caribbean community poured onto the streets.

"The racial divide then was palpable and high," recalled

Michael Shapiro, a lawyer who defended one of the Jewish motorcade drivers whose out-of-control limousine caused another vehicle to collide, fatally, with the Guyanese boy.

The ensuing political fallout would shed light on a police department that hung back without getting involved, a conspicuously absent police commissioner, and Mayor David N. Dinkins—who appeared to lack any ability to manage the racial polarization.

The rest of the city stopped for a while and stared, jaws agape, then went about business as usual. This was, after all, blasé New York.

In the early 1990s, after years of steady escalation, the crime rate in New York City had hit its peak. In 1990, the city suffered 2,262 murders, 109 of them in the Brooklyn neighborhood of East New York, just a year before three teenage boys met their end in the halls of their own high school.

Jason Bentley was a fourteen-year-old boy who was smart but underachieving, typical of a kid trying to fit in at Thomas Jefferson High School. He also adored his older brother Jermaine, whom he had followed to "Jeff." Jason, like so many others teens, owned a handgun for what he believed to be personal protection.

Jermaine, unfortunately, had "beef" with another boy, Jesse, over an issue most adults would consider minor—an inaccurate rumor that Jermaine "disrespected" Jesse's sister. But in the culture of adolescent boys in East New York, things escalated and, predictably, turned deadly.

So it was that on November 25, 1991, in the hallway of Thomas Jefferson High School, Jermaine and Jesse began a fight over a book bag that quickly heated up. And when Jason thought he saw his brother in danger, he pulled the gun to defend him and fired twice, missing Jesse, but unintentionally hitting sixteen-year-old Darryl Sharpe and a teacher.

The teacher was wounded and eventually recovered. Darryl Sharpe died.

"I did what I had to do," Jason stated ten years later to researchers from the National Academy of Sciences, who came seeking answers about why kids shoot kids. To the boys themselves, it was simple. It was a matter of survival.

"A lot of the kids felt like they had to arm themselves," recalled Maria Newman, who wrote extensively about the shooting and the kids at Jeff for the *New York Times*. "It makes me sad that it was so commonplace."

To the *Times* and its readers, the shooting was news. To the teens at Jeff, the only thing new about it was the attention it garnered.

For some time, Thomas Jefferson High School had maintained a student burial fund because so many poor families wound up needing the service. The school had also set aside special grieving rooms where students who had lost friends or relatives could discuss their feelings and receive counseling. According to varying reports, somewhere between thirty and seventy-five Jefferson students had been killed over a five-year period, and a good fifty percent of the surviving students had been wounded in some way.

As more of the story revealed itself through media coverage, the city had to hear what most people probably didn't care to know: For so many of New York's children, violence was a part of everyday life, something to be endured with little hope of escaping.

The mayor had responded to previous calls for tighter security with the rotating use of handheld metal detectors; in practice, the detectors traveled to Jefferson once a week.

Like many administrators and teachers, the principal, Carol Beck, had mixed feelings about the message metal detectors sent to the students. But in three months' time, both she and the mayor would come to rue the rotating detector policy when two more Jefferson students were shot and killed at school.

This time, the killing was intentional, a grudge that one youth, fifteen-year-old Khalil Sumpter, held against two others—Tyrone Sinkler, sixteen, and Ian Moore, seventeen. The grudge resulted in Khalil gunning down Tyrone and Ian at point-blank range.

To the boys' classmates, the shooting didn't come as much of a surprise. Everyone who knew the boys knew trouble had been brewing among them. And although all three had had skirmishes with the law, no one really thought of them as "bad" kids, just regular guys with a beef.

Only in East New York, beef kills.

In East New York, a kid with a beef acted on it or faced the humiliation of his peers, which could mean he, himself, could be made a victim. Minor disputes, in that way, became matters of life and death.

Thomas Jefferson High School, though a beacon of hope early in the twentieth century for ambitious neighborhood immigrants, was clearly on the skids in the 1990s.

Early in 1992, on the very day of the murders of Ian Moore and Tyrone Sinkler, Mayor Dinkins came to Thomas Jefferson High to speak to the students, urging them to resist drugs and violence.

The mayor's testimony addressed the day's tragedy and touched upon his own personal history. David Norman Dinkins, the city's first African American mayor, was raised by a mother separated from her husband, along with his grandmother. Both women were domestic workers. Young David refused to allow poverty and disadvantage to curb his determination to succeed.

The mayor's visit and poignant memoir were meant to inspire hope in the desolate little strip of Brooklyn called East New York.

At least he tried.

Darryl Sharpe's funeral was notable for who did not attend—neither the mayor nor anyone from his office; likewise, nobody from the police department or any other department of the city. During the service, the reverend called out for representatives of these institutions. He was answered each time with silence.

But Ian Moore's funeral made up for the neglect. More than a thousand mourners, including Mayor Dinkins and a flock of other city officials, attended. The service was as much about mourning Ian Moore as it was a community that allowed such tragedy to occur.

When the mayor rose to say that Ian had "gone home to God," the Reverend Johnny Ray Youngblood angrily responded, "What's he going to tell God about us when he gets there?"

It was a service of soul-searching, anger, and sadness over the resigned acceptance of tragedy by the people of East New York.

The ensuing months saw antiviolence campaigns that included the mayor, the Reverend Jesse Jackson, and even Bill Cosby—all of them invoking Martin Luther King, Jr.'s message of nonviolence. At great expense, permanent metal detectors were installed by a side entrance of Jeff, complementing the one by the main lobby where stood the polished statue of the third president of the United States.

A number of students responded with something rare in East New York, something approaching optimism. But in the habit of people who have been ignored too long, most shook their heads and said, *Nothin's really gonna change.* It was too much to believe that a few marches and visits from celebrities could alter poverty, drugs, and violence.

Maria Newman's career as a journalist had taken her to several landmarks of poverty and violence—Los Angeles, Nicaragua, Cuba. But what she encountered in New York was more chilling, for the indifference with which it was met.

"Where was the outrage? That's what I wondered over and over again when stories took me to places like Thomas Jefferson High School, where kids were killing other kids," she said. "Where was the outrage?"

In 1993, Newman became a mother, at which point, she said, "I couldn't look at stories like this."

That was the year that the crime rate in New York hit an all-time high, with East New York at the top of the chart.

Then, suddenly and inexplicably, crime fell. The number of homicides in East New York dropped from 126 in '93 to 44 by '95. In an article for the *New Yorker*, Malcolm Gladwell, author of *The Tipping Point*, identified an "epidemic theory" behind the statistical turnabout.

Criminal justice players, including the lawyer Michael Shapiro, credited Mayor Rudolph Guiliani's crackdown on quality-of-life crimes and, in particular, "community policing," in which police officers go out of their way to learn the particular needs of civilians on their beats.

Perhaps it had simply happened because the shootings were able to shine a spotlight on the culture of violence among the teens in East New York. Reverend Youngblood told researchers, "Maybe God allowed the violence to get out of hand so that we would finally pay attention to violence and young people."

In the immediate aftermath of the shootings, attention was indeed paid. In addition to metal detectors, the school established student retreats and antiviolence programs, which included posters that carried the images of a gun next to a coffin. But the change that would have the most widespread, lasting impact would be the decision by the schools chancellor to cut up large, impersonal high schools into smaller mini-schools focused on a theme, such as legal studies, civil rights, or fire safety.

And so it came to pass that in 2004, Thomas Jefferson High School, which had been placed on a list of seven low-performing schools in Brooklyn, announced that it would accept no more freshmen, and instead opened its doors to four new schools that would be housed within its campus. The last of the "Jeffheads" graduated in June 2007, after a school year marked by little fanfare and no incident.

The public attention on Jeff died down along with the plunging neighborhood crime rate, and the area has shown some signs of revitalization, such as new apartment complexes and a shopping center. But a reduction in crime statistics doesn't necessarily change the reality of poverty for those who continue to live it. For the kids who are too young to remember Jason Bentley, Khalil Sumpter, and the day the mayor came to speak, hope still seems illusive.

There are stories, less dramatic but nonetheless poignant, that don't make the news.

Theresa Reel, a high school teacher who'd moved up to the city from Mississippi, recalled how one of her students, a quiet sixteen-year-old boy who'd never caused trouble, stood up one morning and began a noisy tirade on the hopelessness of school and life. After the boy was removed from her classroom, she learned that he was upset because his baby cousin had died only the night before of SIDS—Sudden Infant Death Syndrome. When the new teacher expressed her shock and sorrow at what had happened to the boy, the other kids in the class shrugged and told her, *This is East New York, didn't you know?*

If anybody anywhere else in New York City noticed, they might surely have stopped for a moment and shaken their heads. Then, just as surely, they would have gone about their day.

SESAME STREET FOR GROWN-UPS

BY AILEEN GALLAGHER

Cobble Hill

S o, where else would Peter Braunstein head for cover but Brooklyn? He was a writer, after all.

According to his indictment, freelance journalist Peter Braunstein entered the Chelsea apartment building of a former co-worker on Halloween evening, 2005, wearing a New York City Fire Department uniform purchased on eBay.

He thereupon set two small fires in the hallway, then knocked on the young woman's door. When she answered, Braunstein chloroformed her, bound her, and sexually assaulted her for some twelve hours. For good measure, he videotaped the ordeal.

Soon after, on November 9, the police named Braunstein the prime suspect in the crimes and released photographs of him, taken on November 1 at a Super 8 Motel on West 46th Street in Midtown Manhattan.

The day after his Super 8 stay, Braunstein slid a personal credit card into a subway station vending machine and bought himself a MetroCard. Then he vanished. He could have been anywhere. He seemed to be everywhere.

The media website Gawker chided, "A CITY OF 8 MILLION PEOPLE, ALL WITH THEIR EYES CLOSED."

As the New York City police department searched frantically for Braunstein, the tabloids delighted in flaying one of their own. The *New York Post* called Braunstein a "convicted creep" who was serving three years' probation for menacing another woman. The *Daily News* went with the "kinky journalist" angle, noting that Braunstein's victim worked at a high-end fashion magazine. And he had taunted her with designer shoes.

Until 2002, Braunstein was the media reporter for *Women's Wear Daily*, the fashion trade publication that shared offices with *W*, the magazine at which his victim worked.

Braunstein's desk at *WWD* had sight lines to the fashion closet, where young, pretty women flitted about with shoes and accessories for shoots and stories. Thirty-year-old Greg Lindsay, now a freelance writer and resident of Brooklyn's Cobble Hill, inherited Braunstein's gig at *WWD* and was assigned his desk.

"You feel creepy in the sense that you're inadvertently scoping out these women," Lindsay recalled. "That part in *Silence of the Lambs* where Hannibal Lecter asks, 'And how do we begin to covet, Clarice? We begin by coveting what we see every day.' It was totally that." Ten months after Lindsay characterized Braunstein with that line, the man himself agreed with the armchair analysis. In a jailhouse interview with the *New York Post* published on December 16, 2007, Braunstein quoted the same *Silence of the Lambs* bit "to explain his 'theory' of why he chose his victim."

The journalists who populate this city as freelancers and staffers—the writers and editors who pump out the words and ideas that make this place the media capital of the world—began to question each other. There was concern for the victim and horror at the nature of the crime, of course. And not a little bit of fear.

All that along with the impulse to conclude, *What a story!*

Sex! Depravity! A police manhunt!

But this was no Dominick Dunne society murder. This crime involved two of their own. The alleged perpetrator had worked at enough editorial shops, and long enough, to know a lot of people in this smaller-than-we'd-all-like-to-think world. And so the writers turned to each other, with questions and motives and what-ifs and what-have-yous.

Writing in the online magazine *The Black Table* on November 16, Greg Lindsay tried to answer the questions: "No, I never met the guy . . . [A]nd the more I learn now about how much fear and terror and misery he has inflicted upon my former colleagues, the more relieved I am that I never met him, and therefore never gave him the benefit of any doubts."

The next day, Braunstein was spotted in Brooklyn.

Walt Whitman made Brooklyn the writer's borough. His own Brooklyn Heights neighborhood was home to the likes of W.H. Auden, Carson McCullers, Benjamin Britten, Richard Wright—and is where Norman Mailer hung his hat, and boxing gloves, until his death in late 2007. Nearby Park Slope is home to contemporary novelists Paul Auster, Jonathan Safran Foer, and husband-wife authors Kathryn and Colin Harrison, among many others. (Brooklyn's 11215 is rumored to be the American zip code with the highest concentration of published writers.)

Though the twentieth century was the age of Manhattan newspapermen—Jimmy Breslin, Pete Hamill, Murray Kempton—many of today's journalists are Brooklyn-based, and not necessarily bound by employment to a single periodical. The northwest neighborhoods of Boerum Hill, Cobble Hill, and Carroll Gardens belong nowadays to the freelance writers and magazine editors who attempt to interpret New York to the outside world.

These three neighborhoods, formerly distinct one from the other, have melded to the point where most residents who have established themselves during the past five or so years don't actually know the lines of demarcation. Real estate agents, attempting to broker rentals surpassing prices even in Manhattan, sometimes call it one area: BoCoCa. And though the name is unpleasant to those people who label everything but themselves, it successfully blends the area into a mass of comfortable familiarity that attracts BoCoCa's newest tenants.

Roughly speaking—some might say generously—the three neighborhoods run from Atlantic Avenue in the north to 9th Street in the south. West to east, BoCoCa extends from Hicks Street to Hoyt. From Manhattan, you take the F train to Bergen Street, Carroll Street, or Smith and 9th Streets.

Where mom-and-pop corner stores and butcher shops and bakeries once lined Court and Smith, the neighborhoods' right and left ventricles now pump bars and boutiques. The restaurants have gained new respect among food critics; you are not necessarily eating Brooklyn food at Manhattan prices anymore.

Apartments are often entire floors of brownstones, large and sunny with the kind of amenities people leave Manhattan for—washers, dryers, dishwashers, backyards!—and include smallish rooms perfect for a desk and filing cabinet. BoCoCa is, accordingly, well-suited to those who write from home all day.

In the fall, when the treelined streets turn red and gold, and in the spring, when the canopy above you is green, it is enough to forget that you are even in Brooklyn—anyhow, the Brooklyn you thought you knew a decade ago. The Italian immigrants who settled there have given way to yuppies who fled the suburbs for the city.

While the old Brooklyn was made up of ethnic enclaves, immigrant warrens, and strivers' rows of the middle class, Bo-

CoCa has transcended traditional insularity. For some, this is all so different as to suggest that Boerum Hill, Cobble Hill, and Carroll Gardens—and most certainly the Valhalla of Park Slope—are not truly a part of Brooklyn anymore. For others, it is all some sort of über-Brooklyn, a Sesame Street for grownups where the neighborhood cinema shows foreign films and friends gather at readings rather than potluck suppers.

In warm months, the Gowanus Yacht Club on Smith and Warren serves beer outside on rickety picnic tables, sating its customers with a side of irony: The establishment is not at waterside. Laptops abound in cafés and bars, leaving a weekday visitor with the impression that no one here actually works. On Fridays, friends meet for drinks at Abilene and potential lovers set dinner dates at Grocery, the restaurant. Sunday mornings are reserved for brunch at places like Bar Tabac, or Bloody Marys at the Brooklyn Inn.

Where is Manhattan in all of this? Nowhere. Unless you have a staff job, Manhattan exists only as a place for meetings. The Gotham skyline is moot; the city that everyone thought they came for has been abandoned by many.

It was here, in this demimonde of BoCoCa, where Peter Braunstein was sighted on November 17, some two weeks after the Halloween attack, buying a cup of coffee—in a place named after the real estate brokers' made-up moniker, the Bococa Café. (The café opened in 2005. It's cheering and bright, and stocked with dozens of coffees you've never heard of. Go in the morning. The place shuts down early in the evening.)

John Arena, proprietor of the Bococa Café, was at work on the morning he thought he saw Braunstein.

A man in an overcoat bought a large coffee—"regular," which in Brooklyn means with milk and sugar—and paid with two singles. Just as Arena was checking his face against a photograph in the *New York Post*, Mr. Large-Coffee-Regular took off without collecting his sixty cents in change. The customer was heavier and had longer hair than the photos circulating of Braunstein, but Arena did not doubt his identity.

"I looked at him like I saw a ghost," Arena told the daily papers. "He caught on right away. In other words, he knew that I knew who he was."

Large-Coffee-Regular left the café and walked north at about half past 7. Arena notified police.

By 9 o'clock, reporters and cops in riot gear were sharing the sidewalks with moms and strollers. Other officers perched on rooftops. The press trolled for a scoop and a team of dogs sniffed for Braunstein. "I was working from home all day," Greg Lindsay remembered. "I heard the helicopters circling overhead for hours."

A reader wrote in to Gawker to describe a "gaggle of reporters . . . standing across the street from the stupidly named Bococa Café." Cops mingled with the press on the street while helicopters looked down from above. "On a side note," the reader added, "a beat cop walked up to one of the cameramen and asked what was going on. The cameraman gave him the 411. I love when the media fill in the fuzz."

Patrick Cadigan, who lived on Smith Street between Dean and Pacific at the time, was following the story in the papers and found the café owner's account at least somewhat credible.

"He saw him, thought he recognized the customer, and the guy took off. That sealed it. It must have been him," Cadigan said. "Or," he considered, "it was a guy who got his coffee and wanted to leave."

Braunstein's mother spoke exclusively to the *New York Sun*, telling the conservative broadsheet that her son regularly drank coffee with milk and was likely at least somewhat familiar with Cobble Hill, as his ex-wife lived near the Bococa Café.

Sophie Donelson, then an editor at *City* magazine, believed Braunstein was around somewhere nearby, but doubted that he got his coffee at Bococa Café.

"No one really goes to that café. If he was at Bar Tabac or Patois, I'd believe it," she said. "But there were moms and nannies everywhere and a rapist on the loose. It was such a weird juxtaposition."

Gawker was quick to blast Bococa Café owner John Arena on November 18:

> *Oh, you saw the fiend, did you? Peter Braunstein came into your Cobble Hill coffee shop and bought a $2 cuppa joe? You even looked him in the eye? You were sure it was him, yeah? He knew that you knew, oh yes!*
>
> *So, uh, why the hell did you just watch him walk away? Here's a suggestion: follow him out the door, shout and point, and CHASE THE MOTHERFUCKER DOWN! He's a journalist, for chrissakes, just some wussy writer!*

Clearly, this was a matter best left to police dogs.

With a pillow from Braunstein's mother's house in Kew Gardens as a reference, the NYPD's canine members picked up the fugitive's scent. A bloodhound named Chase tracked Braunstein two blocks and then lost him again, the *Sun* reported. A few blocks on, Chase showed signs of a trail. He took his handlers to an abandoned brownstone on Henry and Congress, but Braunstein wasn't there. Police found no evidence that anyone had been there at all. But still, it was possible.

Possible enough for the *Post*'s Andrea Peyser, who gave

Braunstein a shrill, staccato scolding for showing up in Brooklyn, headlined, *BRAZEN BRAUNSTEIN'S GOT A LATTE NERVE*. Whereupon the column tore into neighborhood residents for failing to lead the manhunt.

"As he walked through a neighborhood where his former colleagues live, no one recognized Peter Braunstein," Peyser wrote. "That's because no one was looking."

But Cobble Hill is not the type of place for neighborhood watch groups. That's more Park Slope. The mob did not light torches, grab pitchforks, and go from brownstone to brownstone. Instead, neighbors stayed home. Children disappeared from the streets. Police distributed *Wanted* leaflets with an unflattering drawing of a Jheri-curled Braunstein and the promise of a $12,000 reward for information leading to his capture.

"Every single door on our street had that blue flier attached with that awful, awful sketch," Lindsay remembered with disgust. "For days you would see them up and down the street. Peter Braunstein had come to my block, my entire universe as a freelancer. He was there for at least a week, quasi-haunting us."

Lindsay tore the flier down—"I couldn't bear to have it there," he said—but Braunstein's face lined Smith, Court, and countless cross streets for days. Patrick Cadigan saw the posters littering the train station for at least a week, but noticed that the fear died down after a day or two.

"I wondered why he would still be here unless he had a network of people hiding him, which didn't seem very likely," Cadigan said. He walked his girlfriend to the train station as usual, but tried to be more alert. Otherwise, what else was to be done?

Andrea Peyser's urgings to the contrary, the people of Boerum Hill, Carroll Gardens, and Cobble Hill got self-cautious. It is a similar mind-set to the one adopted after September 11:

Protect yourself as best you can and be mindful that there is little you personally can do about terrorists flying into buildings or depraved sex offenders on the lam in your neighborhood. Detached thrills are perhaps, in part, why people live here.

Laura Davis was working at HarperCollins in November 2005 and sharing a Cobble Hill apartment with two room-mates. One of them joked about seeing a man on the roof who may have been Braunstein. But in a serious conversation concerning personal safety, Davis said, "We talked about making sure we pushed the door to our apartment shut as we were coming and going, instead of trusting it to swing shut on its own. It had been left open many times before and I remember Peter Braunstein's name being invoked as to why we needed to make a greater effort to close the door."

Braunstein was spotted again on November 18, this time at a business on Henry Street. At M&N Cleaners, a man who the *Post* said was "looking rushed, and possibly covered in stage makeup," asked for a coat hanger because he had locked himself out of his car. An employee told the tabloid that the customer was rude and demanding and then took off. "It is not known if Braunstein really had a car, or what he wanted with the hanger," the *Post* reported dryly.

Then again, just past midnight on November 21, a resident swore he passed Braunstein walking east on Degraw between Hicks and Cheever.

So—memorize the face, lock the door, walk the ladies to the train. Be mindful to whom you sell coffee. Report all agitated people who lock their keys in the car to the police. Be vigilant during your late-night walks home. Because you never know who you might see.

"I have never known my son to even go to Brooklyn," Peter Braunstein's estranged father told the *Daily News*. The article—published on November 19 and smugly titled, *CAFÉ SEARCH GROUNDLESS?*—was the first whiff of doubt about Braunstein hiding out in BoCoCa.

The *New York Observer*, a contrarian weekly, pooh-poohed the bulk of daily tabloid reportage by suggesting in a December 5 article that maybe—just maybe—Braunstein had never been on the unglamourous side of the river.

"Forget the massive manhunt," wrote the *Observer's* Mark Lotto. "Is Peter Braunstein the last freelancer in New York who thinks he's too good for Brooklyn?"

Well into December, more than two weeks after the last Braunstein sighting, there was no hint of him in Brooklyn. The *Wanted* posters got weirdly more detailed—*Braunstein drinks Guinness and vodka! He likes beef curry with extra mustard!*—but BoCoCa's watchful citizens saw nothing.

Which makes sense, really, because when the city thought Braunstein was buying coffee and borrowing coat hangers in Brooklyn, the closest he got to the County of Kings was at a storage facility on 36th Street and Northern Boulevard in Queens, which is home to so few media folk that it took newspapers at least three days to report the extent of a 2006 blackout affecting more than 125,000 residents.

By half past 11 o'clock on the night of November 2, Peter Braunstein was in Cleveland. Not Brooklyn. He never came back to the city after that. He spent a few nights chewing a bartender's ear about working on the plastic surgery TV drama *Nip/Tuck*. He said he was researching striptease joints for his next writing project—and isn't that what they all say?

"He didn't strike me as creepy," the Moriarty's bartender told the *Daily News*.

At the University of Cincinnati on November 17, Braunstein robbed a psychologist's office at gunpoint for sixteen bucks in cash, plus a Visa card. He made his way south, first to Nashville and then to Memphis, where on November 28 he sold his blood for twenty dollars.

At the University of Memphis, better than a thousand miles from the Bococa Café, Peter Braunstein collapsed in a pool of his own blood on December 16. A campus police officer found Braunstein after a woman named Annette Brown, who'd seen him on the TV show *America's Most Wanted*, spotted him walking around with a backpack and sleeping bag.

"I looked into his eyes and he looked into mine," Brown told the *Daily News*. "They were very dark, empty, unfeeling, and cold. I felt like I was looking at a dead person, just evil. He was so close to me, I could have hugged him."

Brown flagged a campus patrol car from a safe distance away. The car trailed Braunstein for a while, until an officer ordered him to stop in his tracks. Braunstein pulled a knife and began to stab himself in the neck. The officer sprayed Braunstein with half a can of pepper spray, but the knife went in and out thirteen times.

"I give up," Braunstein said, dropping the knife. He fell and the officer took away the gun he was packing. Cuffing him, the officer asked his name.

"Peter Braunstein," he said, after which he passed out. Alternate versions of the capture had Braunstein declaring, "I'm the guy the world is looking for." But such are mostly television accounts and not to be trusted.

In his backpack, police found a video camera, two digital video tapes, and a diary. The tapes were blank. But in the diary, police read Braunstein's commentary on his own press coverage.

"He was very interested in what was being written about him, and how he was portrayed," a cop told the *Daily News*.

Under court order, New York police on January 23 released notes of a conversation detectives had with Braunstein shortly after his capture in Memphis. Braunstein laughed off media reports. "[He] stated that he thought the Cobble Hill thing was funny because he does not even know where Cobble Hill is located," police told the papers.

On his return to New York, Braunstein repeated his Manhattan-to-Queens trip of the previous November.

First housed in Bellevue, he was then moved to Rikers Island to await trial. Braunstein's defense team released a psychiatric report on June 1, 2006, indicating a likely diagnosis of schizophrenia. In her report, Braunstein's psychologist said it was the gig at *Women's Wear Daily* that made him snap.

"Working in the highly competitive, glitzy, and sexually charged atmosphere of a celebrity-driven fashion periodical was an extremely toxic and unsuitable environment," according to the doctor.

Was it a life that he missed? When the *Daily News* published an interview with Braunstein at Rikers on October 8, 2006, it appeared that he was happy to chat. "Look, I used to do this," Braunstein told the journalist. "I used to be you."

Hear that, Brooklyn?

POSTSCRIPT: *Peter Braunstein was convicted of kidnapping and sexual assault in a trial ending on May 23, 2007. The jury deliberated for only a few hours. In a letter to the judge pleading for leniency, Braunstein railed against the tabloid coverage of his case, singling out New York Post columnist Andrea Peyser. She "declared that I was not sick; I was evil," Braunstein wrote. "This kind of tabloid rhetoric is essentially a mandate for harsh sentencing." Braunstein is now in prison, serving an eighteen-years-to-life term.*

ABOUT THE CONTRIBUTORS

Kim Sykes

THOMAS ADCOCK is a veteran New York City journalist and an Edgar Award–winning novelist. He has contributed stories to *New Orleans Noir* and *Bronx Noir*. A longtime Manhattan resident, he is nevertheless often seen in the company of his granddaughter, Gianna Maria, who lives in Windsor Terrace, Brooklyn.

Matthew McDermott

DENISE BUFFA is a native of Brooklyn. A *New York Post* reporter for more than a decade, she has covered numerous beats, including Brooklyn courts. She is currently penning *Mushy & Mama,* a book about the life and times of her mastiff, Mushy. A former Bay Ridge babe, she currently resides with her new dog, Baci, in Harlem. She has a not-so-secret weapon when chasing down stories on New York City streets: her accent!

Christopher Varmus

CONSTANCE CASEY, who was a New York City Parks Department gardener for five years, is a member of the Brooklyn Botanic Garden board of trustees, and a judge in The Greenest Block in Brooklyn contest. She writes about gardening and natural history for the online magazine *Slate.* In a former, more indoor life she was an editor at the *San Jose Mercury News* and the *Washington Post*, then a national correspondent for Newhouse News Service.

Renaissance Studios

REED FARREL COLEMAN was born and raised in Sheepshead Bay, Brooklyn. *The James Deans*, the third installment of his Brooklyn-based Moe Prager mystery series, won the Shamus, Barry, and Anthony awards. The novel was also nominated for the Edgar, Macavity, and Gumshoe awards. He is the editor of *Hardboiled Brooklyn* and his short stories have also appeared in *Wall Street Noir* and *Dublin Noir.*

Steve Sneddon

AILEEN GALLAGHER is an editor at *New York* magazine's website, nymag.com. She was a founding editor of the online magazine *The Black Table* and has written for the *New York Law Journal, New York Post, New York Press, Bust, Maxim,* and *New York* magazine. A native of suburban Philadelphia, she resides joyously in Carroll Gardens, Brooklyn.

Denise Kronstadt

DENNIS HAWKINS, formerly Chief of Rackets, retired from the Brooklyn district attorney's office on April 1, 2001. Since then he has taught, written, and circumnavigated the globe as an anticorruption advisor. He is currently working on a novel about the down and dirty office politics of a large, urban prosecutor's office.

Rose Knightly

ROBERT KNIGHTLY spent his youth in Greenpoint, Brooklyn, leaving for Manhattan at the tender age of forty-four. During his Brooklyn years, he was an NYPD patrol officer and sergeant in the Brooklyn North neighborhoods of Bushwick, Bedford-Stuyvesant, Fort Greene–Clinton Hill, and Williamsburg. He has published three stories in the Akashic Noir Series, one of which was selected for *Best American Mystery Stories 2007*.

JESS KORMAN grew up in Brooklyn and left at age twelve. He later wrote plays for off-Broadway and regional theater, comedy for TV shows, and he did time as a creative director on Madison Avenue. His pieces have appeared in *National Lampoon* and other publications. His one-man shows as a satirical singer-songwriter-pianist are often performed in Greenwich Village.

Tony Chiminiello

ROBERT LEUCI worked for twenty years as an NYPD detective assigned to narcotics and organized crime. Many of those years were spent working the streets of Brooklyn. Since retirement, he has published six novels and one memoir, as well as various TV scripts, book reviews, and magazine pieces. Leuci is currently an adjunct professor in the English department of the University of Rhode Island.

ERROL LOUIS has been a columnist for the *New York Daily News* since June 2004. He lives in Crown Heights, Brooklyn with his wife, Juanita Scarlett, and their son, Noah Louis. His father, Edward Louis, is a retired NYPD inspector whose assignments included a stint as commanding officer of the 73rd Precinct in Brownsville.

Renette Zimmerly

TIM MCLOUGHLIN is the editor of the multiple–award winning anthology *Brooklyn Noir* and its companion volume, *Brooklyn Noir 2: The Classics*. His novel, *Heart of the Old Country*, won Italy's Premio Penne award and is the basis for the Serenade Films motion picture *The Narrows*. His short fiction and essays have appeared in *Confrontation*, *A Public Space*, and the *Brooklyn Rail*, as well as the anthologies *The Subway Chronicles*, *New Orleans Noir*, and *Best American Mystery Stories 2005*.

Laurie Sermos

PATRICIA MULCAHY has lived in Clinton Hill, Brooklyn, for almost twenty years, and has owned the coffee bar and arts space Tillie's of Brooklyn in Fort Greene since 1997. A former book publisher, she edited crime writers such as Michael Connelly and James Lee Burke. She now operates an editorial consulting company called Brooklyn Books, and is at work on a novel.

Anne Musella

CHRISTOPHER MUSELLA has been living and writing in Brooklyn with his wife Anne (and now their daughter Gianna) for more than twelve years.

Passport Agency

C.J.SULLIVAN has worked as an associate court clerk in the Brooklyn Supreme Court since 1994. He is also a crime reporter for the *New York Post* and the author of *Wild Tales from the Police Blotter*.

Ron Rinaldi

KIM SYKES is an actress and writer who regrets not living in Brooklyn. She is also a contributor to *Queens Noir* and is at work on her first novel.

Kenneth Kencaid

ROSEMARIE YU is a New York–based writer. She is a former legal journalist and a graduate of the New York University School of Law.

Also available from the Akashic Books Noir Series

BROOKLYN NOIR
edited by Tim McLoughlin
350 pages, trade paperback original, $15.95
*Winner of Shamus Award, Anthony Award, Robert L. Fish Memorial Award; finalist for Edgar Award and Pushcart Prize

Brand new stories by: Pete Hamill, Robert Knightly, Arthur Nersesian, Maggie Estep, Nelson George, Sidney Offit, Ken Bruen, and others.

"*Brooklyn Noir* is such a stunningly perfect combination that you can't believe you haven't read an anthology like this before. But trust me— you haven't. Story after story is a revelation, filled with the requisite sense of place, but also the perfect twists that crime stories demand. The writing is flat-out superb, filled with lines that will sing in your head for a long time to come."
—Laura Lippman, winner of the Edgar, Agatha, and Shamus awards

BROOKLYN NOIR 2: THE CLASSICS
edited by Tim McLoughlin
316 pages, trade paperback, $15.95

Stories by: H.P. Lovecraft, Lawrence Block, Donald E. Westlake, Pete Hamill, Jonathan Lethem, Colson Whitehead, Carolyn Wheat, Thomas Wolfe, Hubert Selby, Jr., Stanley Ellin, Gilbert Sorrentino, Maggie Estep, Irwin Shaw, and Salvatore La Puma.

"An assortment of the borough's crime-fiction masterminds get down to the gritty details in this entertaining collection of chilling stories."
—*BKLYN* magazine

"This collection of reprints is packed full of literary treats."
—*Mystery Scene* magazine

MANHATTAN NOIR
edited by Lawrence Block
260 pages, trade paperback original, $14.95

Brand new stories by: Jeffery Deaver, Robert Knightly, Lawrence Block, Liz Martínez, Thomas H. Cook, S.J. Rozan, Justin Scott, and others.

"A pleasing variety of Manhattan neighborhoods come to life in Block's solid anthology . . . the writing is of a high order and a nice mix of styles."
—*Publishers Weekly*

BRONX NOIR
edited by S.J. Rozan
368 pages, trade paperback original, $15.95

Brand new stories by: Jerome Charyn, Lawrence Block, Suzanne Chazin, Terrence Cheng, Kevin Baker, Abraham Rodriguez, and others.

"Akashic's latest city-themed crime anthology successfully captures the immense diversity of the Bronx, from the mean streets of the South Bronx to affluent Riverdale . . . Rozan, herself a contributor, has put together one of the series' better entries."
—*Publishers Weekly*

QUEENS NOIR
edited by Robert Knightly
342 pages, trade paperback original, $15.95

Brand new stories by: Denis Hamill, Alan Gordon, Maggie Estep, Tori Carrington, Joseph Guglielmelli, Kim Sykes, Jillian Abbott, and others.

"Keen Queensian eyes will find that no mistakes were made in capturing the borough, form its subway lines to its edgy sensibility."
—*Queens Times Ledger*

WALL STREET NOIR
edited by Peter Spiegelman
382 pages, trade paperback original, $15.95

Brand new stories by: John Burdett, Henry Blodget, Peter Blauner, Megan Abbott, Jason Starr, Lauren Sanders, Reed Farrel Coleman, and others.

"Spiegelman, the ideal editor for the Wall Street entry in Akashic's noir anthology series, assembles a stellar cast of seventeen crime genre luminaries, many with financial backgrounds."
—*Publishers Weekly* (starred review)